Crouchback

The Welsh Guard Mysteries

CROUCHBACK

by

SARAH WOODBURY

Crouchback
Copyright © 2019 by Sarah Woodbury

This is a work of fiction.

www.sarahwoodbury.com

To my mom
I think you really would have liked this one.

A Brief Guide to Welsh Pronunciation

Names derived from languages other than English aren't always easy to pronounce for English speakers, and Welsh is no exception. As far as I am concerned, please feel free to pronounce the names and places in this book however you like. I want you to be happy!

That said, some people really want to know the 'right' way to pronounce a word, and for them, I have included the pronunciation guide for Welsh sounds below.

Enjoy!

a an 'ah' sound, as in 'car' (Catrin)

ae an 'eye' sound (Caernarfon)

ai an 'eye' sound (Dai)

c a hard 'c' sound (Catrin)

ch a non-English sound as in Scottish 'ch' in 'loch' (Fychan)

d as in 'David' (Dafydd)

dd a buzzy 'th' sound, as in 'there' (Dafydd; Gwynedd)

e an 'eh' sound as in 'bet' (Medwyn)

f a 'v' sound as in 'of' (Caernarfon)

ff as in 'off' (Gruffydd)

g a hard 'g' sound, as in 'gas' (Gruffydd)

i an 'ee' sound (Catrin)

l as in 'lamp' (Hywel)

ll a breathy /sh/ sound that does not occur in English (Llywelyn)

o a short 'o' sound as in 'cot' (Conwy)

rh a breathy mix between 'r' and 'rh' that does not occur in English (Rhys)

th a softer sound than for 'dd,' as in 'thick' (Arthur)

u a short 'ih' sound (Gruffydd) or (Tudur), or a long 'ee' sound if at the end of the word (Cymru—pronounced 'kumree')

w as a consonant, it's an English 'w' (Llywelyn); or as an 'oo' sound as in 'book' (Bwlch)

y when it is located in any syllable before the last one, it is an 'uh' sound (Hywel). At the end of a word it can be 'ih' as in 'Llywelyn' or 'Gruffydd', or 'ee' as in 'Rhys' or 'Cymry'.

Cast of Characters

<u>The Normans</u>
Edward – King of England
Eleanor– Queen of England
Edmund – Prince of England, Edward's younger brother
Henry de Lacy – Earl of Lincoln, Lord of Denbigh
Guy fitz Lacy – Coroner, illegitimate half-brother of Henry
de Lacy
Oliver de Poitiers – Undercoroner
Rolf le Strange – son of Roger le Strange
John le Strange – Rolf's twin brother
Simon Boydell – captain of the King's Guard
Margaret – lady-in-waiting
Adeline – lady-in-waiting

<u>The Welsh</u>
Catrin – lady-in-waiting
Rhys – quaestor; knight
Gruffydd – village headman
Sian – Gruffydd's wife
Dai – assistant to the undercoroner
Father Medwyn – priest of St. Peblig's Church
Tudur – Welsh nobleman, Catrin's brother, Rhys's liege lord
Hywel – Welsh nobleman, Catrin's brother

About Crouchback

The word *crouchback* might conjure an image of some kind of deformity, and indeed for many years scholars believed King Edward's brother, Edmund, to have been hunchbacked because he was referred to by contemporary chroniclers as *Edmund Crouchback*.

Rather than being a reference to Prince Edmund's physical appearance, however, *crouchback* was actually an accolade and referred to his participation in the Ninth Crusade. During the medieval period, by going on crusade, a man was not only cleansed of his sins for a lifetime but from then on was accorded the honor of being allowed to have a cross embroidered onto the back of his clothing. The word *crouchback* derives from the French word for cross, *croix*, which became 'crouch' in English. Thus, *crouchback* is another word for crusader—and the title of this book.

1

Caernarfon Castle

April 1284

Day One (late evening)

Catrin

"I want the truth, Catrin." Queen Eleanor of England, being one of the most perceptive and intelligent people Catrin had ever met, was aware of her roiling emotions, even as she tried to mask them in polite smiles. "Don't pretend with me."

"Yes, my lady. It is true. They do not reverence you."

Eleanor eased into the cushions at her back, a pleased smile on her lips. The heavy curtains around the bed were drawn back, and the window was open, letting in the fresh evening air, scented strongly with salt, since Caernarfon Castle was located on the edge of the Irish Sea. Eleanor liked a cool room to sleep in, and she had little patience for anyone who told her it was bad for the baby she was carrying. "They hate us, you mean. I knew I was right about that. But even better, they fear us."

"Yes, my lady."

The previous evening, the queen's party had arrived later than intended, having made the grueling twenty-mile journey from Conwy in a carriage. Eleanor was past eight months pregnant but nonetheless supported her husband's agenda. What better way to convey the king's might than to have his latest child born in Wales, in his magnificent stone castle of Caernarfon? The walls were going up at an astounding rate, already rising forty feet above the Gwynedd countryside.

Eleanor wasn't finished. "You hate me too, of course."

"My queen—"

"Don't lie to me, child. Never lie to me."

At thirty-six years old, Catrin was hardly a child, but Eleanor saw all the Welsh as children in need of instruction. On the whole, that might be better than viewing them as criminals or slaves. If the Welsh were children, their need for rebellion wasn't their fault and could be forgiven. Eleanor herself was forty-three, about to give birth to her sixteenth child. Having endured the deaths of nine of them, she'd earned the right to call Catrin, who had one grown son, *child*.

"No, my lady. I won't, my lady." But, of course, that too was a lie, if only of omission. Though Catrin could not be openly hostile to the queen and serve her, she never hid the fact that she was Welsh and would do what she could for her people.

Even Catrin didn't know the lengths she would go to if pressed. She hoped Eleanor didn't, either.

The queen maintained that slight, enigmatic smile she often wore to hide what was in her mind. "That will do for now. You're dismissed."

Catrin curtseyed and backed out of the room.

For the whole of the trip across Gwynedd, the queen and her other ladies had looked out the window of the carriage at the ruggedness of the mountains of Snowdonia and voiced dismay at the coarseness of the country. Nowhere to be seen were the orderly fields and gentle rolling hills of England. The majority of smallholders in Wales weren't farmers like the English, but herders, driving sheep and cattle up the valleys to mountain pastures and back according to the season. Except for a few instances, they rarely congregated into villages.

And while the carriage had been surrounded by a company of a hundred men, and patrols had swept through the entire area to ensure its safety, the women had still feared that, at any moment, a band of rebels might descend out of the mountains and murder them.

Catrin shared none of that fear because she knew what they didn't: her people were pragmatists. With their own prince dead, they had no leader, no goals, and no hope. Even for the chance to kill King Edward, they wouldn't be sacrificing their lives for nothing.

For her part, Catrin had spent the journey basking in the beauty and glory of the scene before her. In the heart of spring, the hills were green and blooming with wildflowers, and the highest peaks still showed a last residue of snow. It was as if she'd been holding her breath for twenty years and hadn't known it. She was home, and she could breathe again. She felt the joy of it to her very bones.

Not that she could show that either, of course, not really, given the company in which she traveled. Part of her would have preferred not to come home at all if it meant riding through the countryside like a triumphant conqueror. Even though Catrin had known when Prince Llywelyn died at a place called Cilmeri that it was the end of her world as she knew it, she hadn't truly understood what that meant until yesterday.

King Edward was everyone's liege lord now. Aided by his brother, Edmund Crouchback, a nickname the prince had earned by participating in the Ninth Crusade, Edward had conquered Wales from stem to stern and everywhere in between, just as he'd sworn to do thirty years earlier after Prince Llywelyn had swept across the Conwy River into eastern Gwynedd and conquered domains Edward believed rightfully belonged to him. At the time a prince of seventeen, Edward had felt derided and humiliated, and neither emotion was one he could or would ever forgive or forget.

As she looked into the eyes of the people they passed on the brand new road leading up to the entrance to the half-finished castle of Caernarfon, Catrin had seen humiliation in their eyes, along with raw hatred, even as their mouths said something different.

Just like hers.

Now in the corridor outside Queen Eleanor's room, Catrin eyed a servant coming towards her. With every step, he slopped water from the bucket he carried, intended for the maid, who was scrubbing the stone floor of the corridor. Both servants were English, brought to Caernarfon from England because no Welsh people were allowed to serve the king and queen within their private quarters. None except Catrin, that is.

Only a few with special skills were even allowed inside the castle walls. In the last year, the steward had learned the hard way that when Welsh people were conscripted to work, the running of the castle went less smoothly. These particular servants were working so late in the evening because the queen didn't like to see them cleaning during the day. Only now that she'd retired for the night could the corridor be scrubbed, and the stones would be dry by the time Eleanor rose in the morning.

Catrin's own conscription into the queen's retinue had come nearly simultaneously with her son's eighteenth birthday. As the only native Welsh person in Eleanor's company, she'd been called upon time and again over the course of the last few weeks to explain what her people were thinking as well as translate their words.

That was the reason she'd been asked to join Eleanor's retinue in the first place. Catrin's husband, Robert, had died not quite two years earlier in a battle against the Welsh, led by Gilbert de Clare, the Earl of Gloucester and one of King Edward's most trusted companions—as well as Robert's liege lord. The English army had just sacked one castle and were returning to another when they were set upon by a Welsh army and destroyed. Catrin had mourned appropriately, for her son's sake more than for her husband's or her own, and she'd continued to manage his estate near Bristol as she'd done for the whole of her marriage.

Once the war was over, Gilbert de Clare had not only con-firmed Justin in his inheritance and knighted him, but arranged for his marriage to the daughter of another local baron. There had been no place for Catrin in the household, not with a new bride who would want to do things her way. Besides which, the queen's summons had been impossible to turn down.

None could go against the King and Queen of England, least of all Catrin.

Not overtly, anyway.

2

Day One (late evening)

Rhys

"*C*ombrogi."

Rhys didn't glance in acknowledgment of the person who'd spoken, one of a dozen locals who'd gathered in the darkness of late evening to stand vigil over the dead body they'd found at the abandoned barn set on rising ground amidst a wood above Caernarfon Castle. The accolade had been said in an undertone, for Rhys's ears alone, and it told him someone he'd passed knew who he was and respected him for it.

Countryman, the speaker had said.

It was a cry in the dark and a thumbing of the nose against the winds of fate. For the truth was stark: they didn't have a country anymore. Combined as they now were into one country, serving one king, the Welsh and their Norman masters had never been further apart than they were today.

Guy fitz Lacy, an illegitimate son of the deceased Earl of Lincoln and the county coroner, was walking beside Rhys, but he gave no sign he'd heard. Of course, as a Norman, he spoke no Welsh, so even if he had heard, he wouldn't have understood either the obvious meaning or the more subtle one.

A coroner was a most trusted servant of the king, responsible for collecting taxes and payments owed to the king upon the death of one of the county's residents. King Edward had created coroners and sheriffs as part of the statute that annexed Wales to England. To the king's mind, *Divine Providence* had *wholly and entirely transferred under our proper dominion, the land of Wales, with its inhabitants, heretofore subject unto us, in feudal right ...*

Gone was the Kingdom of Gwynedd, replaced by English counties. Except for a few remnants, gone also were the ancient Laws of Hywel Dda, which had governed Wales for hundreds of years, replaced by English common law.

Oliver de Poitiers, the coroner's underling, was waiting for them at the entrance to the barn. "It isn't pretty." He spoke in French and also had a Welshman at his side to translate commands and questions to the Welsh peasants who surrounded them. "And it smells worse."

"*Pretty* covers a great deal of ground," Rhys said to Dai, Oliver's Welsh companion, whom he knew well. Every Welshman in Caernarfon knew every other one well, by virtue of their joint survival.

Dai grimaced. "The *mochyn* is right. It's worse than I've ever seen. And odd. Oliver almost vomited on his boots." *Mochyn* was the Welsh word for *pig* and the standard epithet everyone had taken to using when referring to any Norman. Dai had spoken, however, in an utterly calm tone and with an expressionless face. "You're going to be sorry you came."

Rhys shook his head. "The summons saved me from having to stay a moment longer at the feast."

"Lord Tudur had to bend the knee again?"

"All of us did. No knight could refuse. I managed not to throw up on my own boots. Truly, I'll take a dead body any day over having to grit my teeth and smile for one more hour."

The Normans he served knew Rhys was a knight, but since he didn't dress like one, nor attempt to garner privileges to himself, more often than not they dismissed him as irrelevant. As a rule, it was how he preferred it, the better to go about his business without interference. That wasn't to say he didn't miss the comforting weight of his sword at his hip.

"You have many more hours of that ahead of you, *combrogi*. Know that we thank you for it." Dai paused. "And so you don't have to lie about what we've been discussing, my mother is well, thank you very much."

In another life, any conversation about submitting to some Norman overlord, if necessary at all, would have been accompanied by rolled eyes and smirks. The two of them managed it tonight with hardly a twitch of an eyebrow. It was a matter of personal pride.

Guy glared at the two Welshmen. "What are you saying? We haven't even seen the body yet!"

Rhys smoothly switched to French. "I apologize, but it is our way to speak of our families when we encounter one another before discussing murder."

"Save it for your own time. I want to get this over with. I have a great deal to do, as you well know. I'll be leaving in a few days, and I don't want some local murder keeping me here overlong."

Rhys bowed. "Of course, my lord."

In recent days, Guy had spoken of little else beyond his promotion. For the last year, he'd acted as coroner for this region of Gwynedd, but last month he'd been promoted to Sheriff of Denbigh. Denbigh castle and town were similar in every way to Caernarfon except, rather than being ruled directly by the king, they were controlled by Guy's half-brother, Henry, who'd inherited the title Earl of Lincoln. Earl Henry also managed all of Gwynedd east of the River Conwy, making him the second most hated man in Wales, after King Edward. Rhys was just as happy to see Guy gone as Guy was to leave—except for the fear that his replacement would be smarter and more cruel.

Guy also avoided saying Rhys's name because he could never manage the breathy sound and the trill of the *r*. And since a Welsh surname wasn't a place name like Poitiers or a family name like Lacy, but rather the name of a man's father, Guy couldn't call Rhys by that either, as it was Iorwerth, which Guy couldn't pronounce—or spell had he been able to write in Welsh. To Rhys, in public, Guy was *Coroner Lacy* or *my lord*, and when Guy referred to Rhys as anything at all, he called him *Reese*.

They followed the undercoroner and Dai into the barn—and almost found their way back out again immediately, driven off by the promised foul smell. Rhys had the foresight to bring a sachet of herbs, which he held to his nose. He tossed another to Dai and then, with a bow, handed two more to Guy and Oliver, who accepted them without thanks.

The scene was as difficult and odd as Dai had indicated. A larger-than-average man, broad-shouldered and tall, with hair long enough to curl around his ears, much like King Edward himself wore, and clothed only in a knight's surcoat, lay in the center of an incomplete hexfoil or daisy wheel—a six-pointed petaled flower inscribed inside a circle. Except, in this instance, the circle was incomplete and the sixth petal missing. Rhys had a momentary flashing memory of heat and dust and sunbaked bricks, before coming back to the coolness of the Welsh April night.

By the narrowness of the line and its depth, the curse had been drawn with the point of a knife—maybe the same knife used to kill the man—rather than a stick or, God forbid, the dead man's blood.

Every woman in Britain, whether Welsh or English, had at one time or another carved a hexfoil, either in the dirt, on a door frame, or in a whitewashed church wall. Hexfoils were a request to God and the saints for protection—to *foil a hex*, in other words. The miracle of the symbol was in its endless loop. A demon would follow the circle or along the edges of the petals perpetually, never getting out again to do harm.

No housewife would ever leave the circle open. It was possible the dead man had carved this particular hexfoil as a last request for protection as he was dying, but when making the symbol, generally a person made the full circle first and then etched the flower within it. It would have been far too much to ask of the man who lay within the circle, dead from what appeared to be, after a quick check under the surcoat, three stab wounds to the right side of his belly.

The circle had been drawn in the center of the barn, which, for all that it was abandoned, remained in relatively good repair. The roof was solid, and wisps of hay trailed down from the loft. The floor was hard-packed earth, still dry and swept clean by wind blown through the open doors, one of which was half-off its hinges.

"Madness!" Guy stared at the body with a mix of horror and revulsion, standing well back to prevent blood from marring his boots and where the smell was slightly better.

A decade younger than Rhys, Guy wasn't even thirty, and while he'd participated in the war that had destroyed Rhys's prince, he hadn't led forces of his own. It was Rhys's thought that Guy had never actually killed another man himself, and thus his familiarity with violent death was limited. He hadn't been acting as the coroner for Caernarfon because of his experience, but because of his name.

Thus, when Guy's revulsion turned to anger, his face flushing, and he asked, "Do we know the man?" Rhys was hesitant to say anything at all. Guy was right to wonder, since the dead man was cleanshaven like a Norman rather than sporting a mustache like most Welshmen or a full beard like an Englishman.

Oliver cleared his throat. "I don't recognize him myself, my lord."

Guy was forced to move closer and stare into the dead man's face. Though Guy hated showing uncertainty at the best of times, he forgot himself long enough to scratch the back of his head. "Nor I.

There's something familiar about him, however." He gestured to the incomplete hexfoil. "And about this."

Rhys himself had seen an incomplete hexfoil many times before. He very much wanted to know where Guy had seen it, but before he could figure out the most diplomatic way to ask, Dai said with total innocence, "You have come upon such a symbol before, my lord?"

Guy shot him a look that said he was irritated at being questioned, but he still answered. "Not I myself, but I have heard tales of others seeing it."

"Where would that have been?"

"The Holy Land."

Rhys had mouthed the words even as Guy spoke them out loud. In the Holy Land, it had been a symbol of a renegade group of Templars who were trying to bring down their order. Since then, others had adopted it for their own nefarious purposes.

Oliver's focus was elsewhere, and he spoke tentatively. "Note the crest on his surcoat, my lord."

"She couldn't have had anything to do with this." Guy glared at his underling, as if the sight of him was a personal affront.

Oliver put up both hands. "I would never think it, my lord!"

The *she* in question was Catrin, a widow in the royal court and one of the queen's ladies. Just this evening, before he and Rhys had been called to the scene of the death, Guy had made a foray in her direction—and been roundly rejected. It seemed the pair had encountered each other before, not surprising since Catrin had spent the last twenty years living in England, and Guy was the brother of the Earl of Lincoln, even if he had no title himself.

Guy carried the Lacy name, since his father had acknowledged him, but in the Norman system, he would inherit nothing and had to fight for everything he had. Until the conquest, the law in Wales had said that all of a man's sons, including the illegitimate ones their father had acknowledged, inherited equally. Now under English law, illegitimate sons had no standing anywhere. At the same time, given the Norman penchant for bestowing all of a dead man's wealth on the eldest son, Guy wasn't much worse off than if he'd been legitimate but simply born second or third.

Such was the case with Rhys's childhood friend, Hywel, whose family had owned extensive estates in Gwynedd and Anglesey and been second in status only to Prince Llywelyn himself. With the abrogation of Welsh law, his elder brother Tudur inherited everything—land the family had been able to hold onto only by bowing to Edward and begging forgiveness for supporting Llywelyn. Suddenly deprived of lands he'd held for half his life and having survived the war and the purge afterwards, Hywel was making his way in the world the best he could. At this point, his station was hardly higher than that of Rhys himself, whose family had been noble but far more minor.

Catrin was Hywel and Tudur's sister.

Rhys could conjure dozens of images of Catrin, growing from a ragamuffin with unruly red hair and mischievous hazel eyes to the smooth perfection she'd developed as a young woman before her marriage. The way her eyes had snapped at Guy in the exact same way they had at Rhys himself a thousand times as a youth had made Rhys smile, even as he worried that she shouldn't antagonize Caernarfon's coroner any more than Rhys should.

Given that rejection, and that it was Catrin's dead Norman husband's crest on the victim's chest, Rhys had to give Guy credit for not holding her treatment of him against her. So far, all Rhys had done was lift the surcoat, but now he bent to touch the body, putting his fingers gently around a wrist. The skin was cool to the touch, and the arm came up, though not flaccidly, indicating rigor was passing but had not entirely passed. In truth, the smell had told Rhys the timing before he'd lifted the arm.

Rhys set the dead man's wrist down again.

"We *will* have to address the issue, my lord," Oliver said, still talking about the surcoat.

Rhys wet his lips, considering the wisdom of offering an opinion and deciding it was worth the possibility of censure. "My lord, you have so many duties, it would be a shame to trouble yourself with something so slight. If you were to delegate me to confer with the lady, you needn't concern yourself with the matter again." Though still crouched by the body, he gave another partial bow. If courtesy were butter, it wasn't possible to lay it on too thick. "I'm sure you're correct that she is blameless. The man has been dead longer than the royal party has been in Caernarfon."

"Why do you say that?" Guy narrowed his eyes, looking for ridicule or worse, pity, in Rhys's eyes or voice.

"I'd say he was killed roughly two nights ago and not in this barn."

"Explain," he said, snapping his fingers with impatience.

"The body is cool and still has a touch of rigor, so he has been dead in the vicinity of two days. He was stabbed in the belly, but I see no blood on the floor of the barn, indicating he was killed elsewhere and placed here after."

Guy grunted, finding nothing to dispute in what Rhys had concluded. "I will leave Lady Catrin to you, then. But first, determine which of these *villeins* found the body so we can bring him to the castle for questioning. Clearly one of *your* people did this. If the dead man *is* Norman, an example will have to be made." He turned on his heel and made for the door.

Rhys simply rose to his feet, smiled politely, and said to Guy's retreating back. "Of course, my lord."

Dai understood French as well as Rhys, which was the reason he'd been assigned to the undercoroner in the first place. For once, he was unable to maintain his impassive façade. In urgent tones he said to Rhys in Welsh, "No, *combrogi*! You cannot do as he asks! We know what will happen to anyone you take."

Rhys did know. He scrubbed at his hair, though he kept it too short these days to truly muss, a legacy from when the monks, in the aftermath of the disaster at Cilmeri, had shaved his head in order to bandage his wounds. Before, he'd kept it longer and tied back from his face with a leather string. With his trimmed beard, which he'd started growing only in the last year, his current presentation was a disguise of a sort, for those who might remember him in his youth.

"Who found him?"

"Iago, the butcher's son."

"What possessed him to come here?" Before Dai could answer, Rhys put up a hand. "Never mind. I know why. Who was he with?"

"Mari, one of headman Gruffydd's girls."

Rhys growled his acknowledgement and understanding. Since the fall of Gwynedd to the Normans, the barn had become derelict and thus an ideal meeting place for young couples. It was located on the edge of a property that, until a year ago, had been a royal *llys*—a palace—of Gwynedd's princes and kings for generations if not centuries. King Edward had ordered the palace dismantled and pieces used to build Caernarfon Castle itself.

Of the palaces in the region, only the one at Aberffraw on Anglesey remained intact. One of Edward's many vassals lived there now, despite its overall lack of grandeur and eight-foot-high walls, designed more to keep out marauding cattle than men.

After Prince Llywelyn's death, Rhys had contemplated leaving Wales entirely, taking the cross again perhaps, or selling himself as a mercenary in someone else's war. In the end, he'd come to the decision that to do so would be the coward's way out. His people were indentured to Edward, *villeins* as Coroner Lacy had said. Rhys had returned to help them if he could. These days, the Welsh had very little left to them except their lives. King Edward had defeated them utterly, and now he was solidifying his control by building castles and taxing the people into impoverishment.

For Rhys, there could be no nobler place to stand than alongside them.

3

Day One

Rhys

Rhys turned to the crowd gathered outside the barn. "The coroner wants me to take the man who found the body to the castle for questioning."

Instantly, a murmur of fear spread amongst them. Iago stood with his arm around his girl and was about to step forward when Dai blocked his attempt. The addition of Rhys's stern look had him staying where he was.

"I am sorry to have to ask this of you. I will try to protect whoever comes forward, but you know as well as I that I cannot guarantee his safety. It appears we have a dead Norman in the barn, and there is a very real chance the coroner will want to find someone to blame as quickly as possible so as to put this behind him, especially with his own departure imminent and the king in residence. He will view a quick arrest as a way to impress the king. You have my word that I will work to find the real killer equally quickly." Then Rhys smiled. "Provided Iago didn't do it, of course."

That prompted a general laughter and a momentary easing of the tension, as Rhys hoped it would. Iago was eighteen years old, large and awkward as boys sometimes were before they grew into their bodies. He was also lovable, quite handsome, and wouldn't hurt a fly. His father despaired of ever properly teaching him his trade, but there was merit in the attempt. Iago also really liked girls, and Mari was hardly the first one who'd fallen for his sweet smile.

"I'll do it."

Rhys let out a sigh to see Aron stepping forward. He was in his mid-fifties, lean to the point of thinness and short of stature. He had lost his wife the year before, and he had a hollowness to his cheeks that meant he wasn't as healthy as he liked to pretend. He was also one of the people in the village whom, from long experience, Rhys respected and trusted. He didn't want to see him imprisoned, but he wasn't surprised either that he'd been the one to come forward.

The people around Aron eased away from him as a sign of respect for his sacrifice.

"What were you doing when you found the dead man?"

"Looking for a lost lamb," Aron said promptly. "My dog sniffed out the body in the barn."

"Good." Rhys bobbed his head. "Where were you before that?"

"He was with me." Aron's son-in-law piped up. "We shared a cup of mead."

"And with me." This came from Iago's granny.

"Did you find the sheep?"

One of Mari's older brothers put up a hand. "I did. He was caught in a bramble."

Rhys looked at Aron again. "Where were you two nights ago when the man was killed?"

The timing was news to them, and they murmured amongst themselves. While in a normal investigation Rhys might have held that information back, and he *was* concerned about finding the real killer, in this moment, he most cared about protecting his people. That meant giving them as much information as he had himself.

Then an older woman, a widow, blushed to the very roots of her hair. Her red face was visible even in the light of the torches and lanterns they carried. "He was with me."

Aron swung around, eyes wide, but at her sharp nod, he bent his head respectfully and turned back to Rhys. "Bronwen speaks the truth. I was with her all night."

"Excellent." Rhys's gaze traveled among them, unconcerned that nothing they'd concluded was true—except for maybe the liaison between Aron and Bronwen. "We'll start with that and see how it goes. Thank you."

Rhys walked Aron to where Guy waited. The coroner's face held a look of extreme disgruntlement. Mostly, Guy viewed the Welsh language, like everything else in Wales, as beneath his dignity. At the same time, it irked him to know it was up to Rhys to explain: "Aron says he found the body while looking for a lost lamb, and a woman in the village claims he was with her all night two nights ago."

"Can he prove any of that?"

"Several other villagers will attest to his whereabouts this evening."

"We'll see." Guy jerked his chin towards Oliver. "Take him to the castle. We'll hold him until we know more, and we have enough evidence to question him further."

"Yes, my lord."

Dai met Rhys's eyes for a moment. The two of them would do their best for Aron, as Rhys had promised, even as they both knew their deception was extraordinarily dangerous to continue. Rhys didn't see any suspected traitors amongst the people before him, but the harder Edward squeezed, the more of Rhys's people would defect. Selling out a neighbor—selling out *him*—might put food on an otherwise empty table.

But in deciding to return to Gwynedd, Rhys had also resolved not to let fear of the future stop him. Ever since Cilmeri, he'd been living on borrowed time anyway. If he had to live as a lackey and cooperator in order to protect his people, he would do it.

In this moment, that meant going back into the barn to inspect it for any evidence the killer had left behind. Someone also had to deal with the body itself. Rhys could see in Guy's eyes that he had no stomach for it.

So he ventured another suggestion. "My lord, if all that remains here is the matter of the body, perhaps I could be of service and see to it before I visit Lady Catrin. You could return to the castle and the feast. The longer you remain outside the walls, the more likely it is that the king and his officers will notice your absence and remark upon it. Given the distastefulness of the scene, perhaps you don't want to trouble the king with the details unless and until it's absolutely necessary?"

It was a convoluted way to tell Guy what to do, and for a moment Rhys feared he'd bungled it, but then Guy's expression cleared. "Fine. See to it. I suppose Dai can return to the castle with me and manage any necessary translations with this villager—though once you return, I will dismiss him. His French isn't as good as yours."

Rhys bowed to cover his surprise. "Thank you, my lord. I am happy to be of service."

The sneer returned. "I'm sure you are."

Sometimes Rhys feared his sycophancy was excessive, but Guy appeared to wallow in it, viewing it as his due while at the same time despising him for exhibiting it. In truth, Rhys despised himself for it too.

"To where shall I have the body brought, my lord?"

Guy hemmed and hawed for a moment, legitimately debating. St. Peblig's was the church nearest to the barn, a matter of a few hundred yards away, and had been the local place of worship for as long as there had been churches in Wales. And maybe longer, if some of the oldest burials in the associated cemetery were any indication. Those stones were engraved with Latin names, from that long-ago time when a Roman legion had ruled the land.

These days, the little church was overseen by a Welsh priest, and thus out of favor, as one might expect, with the newcomers. The church building wasn't grand enough for the royal court anyway, though it was built in stone, whitewashed inside and out, with a stone wall that went all the way around it to keep out roaming sheep and to demarcate sacred ground.

King Edward and his court worshipped within the castle itself, but the garrison, the English workers, and the imported English settlers in the newly established town of Caernarfon had only a wooden church tucked into the corner of the town wall to worship in, if they didn't want to make the trek to the Welsh church on the hill above them.

Most didn't—and anyway, St. Peblig's could hardly accommodate the spiritual needs of all those people. Certainly the nave couldn't handle the nearly one thousand laborers on the castle, plus the garrison and servants. Thus, on Sundays, the English priest had taken to holding an open-air mass in the bailey of the castle for everyone who wanted to attend. The king liked this because it, in effect, made the entire castle sacred ground.

Much of what Rhys himself had been thinking was visible on Guy's face, which is why in the end he made a genuinely sensible decision. "Bring him to St. Mary's within Carnarvontown. If he turns out to be Welsh, at this point highly unlikely, we'll send him out again."

Rhys bowed his head, trying not to bristle at the harsh way Guy pronounced Caernarfon. Instead, Rhys spoke words that yet again were what his response had to be: "Yes, my lord."

Their departure did leave Rhys alone with the body and without a living Norman in sight, which was just the way he liked it. He could feel the relief in the villagers too, who began to disperse, though Rhys asked Iago and Mari to remain behind, and that meant Iago's father, Bron, and Mari's father, Gruffydd, stayed too.

In addition to being Mari's father, Gruffydd was the community's headman, and he and his wife, Sian, had become Rhys's landlord—in that Rhys had been given a bed in their homestead.

Hospitality was a fundamental principle of Welsh society, though Rhys had since found ways to supplement their food supply and their livelihood, suggesting that the cook at the castle take advantage of Sian's exceptional baking skills. Sian had no small children underfoot anymore and (so she said) enjoyed the change of pace. She'd promised Rhys not to spit in the king's food before serving it to him.

In addition to being the headman, Gruffydd was an accomplished fletcher. Since the English didn't know how to fletch arrows properly, he'd been conscripted to work at the castle too, and it was his job to train several apprentices. Meanwhile, Rhys, though hardly the best archer he knew, had been called in to teach everyone to shoot.

Thirty years ago, after losing badly to the Welsh in a battle, King Henry, Edward's father, had decreed that all men between the ages of fifteen and sixty *must equip themselves with bow and arrow.* The law had never been routinely enforced in England and anyway missed the mark in not recognizing that in order for a man to become accomplished with a bow, he not only had to practice (something the statute failed to mention) but ideally should train from the age of seven, as the Welsh had done for centuries.

Surprisingly, after the war ended, Edward hadn't confiscated the Welsh bows that had wreaked so much havoc on his army. Instead, every Sunday after mass, he required every man to practice his archery on the green outside the castle. They were Englishmen now, subject to English law, even here in Gwynedd.

To Rhys's mind, the ulterior motive was clear: by making the populace practice in public, the king's officers were able to document who could shoot well and who couldn't—and record the owner and location of every bow. So far, none of his countrymen had betrayed the large stash of bows and arrows, many of which Gruffydd had also fletched, hidden in caves scattered throughout the mountains of Snowdonia.

"Now," Rhys said to Mari and Iago. Standing as they were in front of not only him but their respective fathers, Rhys imagined a wedding might be in the offing sooner rather than later. "Tell me what really happened."

When neither made to answer and Mari blushed to the roots of her hair, Rhys made a dismissive motion with his hand. "I'm not talking about what happened between the two of you."

"Nothing happened between us! We were out walking, that's all," Iago said.

Mari nodded vigorously. "We looked in the barn, and there he was!"

Having been young once himself, Rhys guessed that at first they'd been too involved with each other to notice the dead man. Likely, they hadn't had a light. But as he'd said, he didn't care what they'd been doing. "And then what?"

"We ran for help, of course." Iago spoke without hesitation.

"They came to find me first," Bron said, "and then together we went to Gruffydd."

As had been the case every time Rhys had glanced at Gruffydd up until now, the fletcher was glowering at his daughter, who was refusing to meet his eyes. Rhys managed to attract his attention. "There really is nothing more?"

His reply was four head shakes.

"Did any of you see any activity up here in the last few days?" While the coroner had been present, Rhys had deliberately avoided touching the body more than was absolutely essential, but now he walked all around it to study it before finally bending to it again.

Rhys tried not to read too much into the presence of the tunic with Catrin's dead husband's crest but, like Guy, it made him uneasy to see the connection to her. After a twenty-year absence, she'd returned to Wales yesterday with the queen. She and Rhys had been amiable as children, since he was a companion to her brothers, but so far she'd refused to speak to him beyond what was required to be civil.

His only consolation—if one could call it that—was that she'd barely spoken more than three words to any of her brothers either. As a girl, she'd been smart and capable, so he didn't see how she could have changed so profoundly, even in twenty years married to a Norman. That just wasn't the girl Rhys had thought he'd known. But even if she might bear Rhys ill will for some reason, he didn't want to see her involved in a murder any more than Guy did.

"You haven't said you know him. Am I to understand that none of you have ever seen this man before?"

Again, to a person, they shook their heads.

Rhys sighed. "Any doubt he's Norman?"

"He could be a Welshman attempting to pass as a *mochyn*," Gruffydd suggested, "like you can."

"Believe me, no Norman has ever mistaken me for one of them."

"Dai says you speak French better than they do," Bron said.

"I think that might be the problem." Rhys laughed ruefully. "I need you to stay away from here, all of you, until this is resolved."

They nodded somberly, and Gruffydd added, "Yes, my lord."

"Find me some strong boys to carry him back to town, will you?"

Gruffydd hesitated. "They won't be let in the gate."

"They will on my say-so. And if the guards at the gate don't like it, they themselves can carry the body the rest of the way to the laying out room by the church."

Rhys swung his arm in a *get out of here* motion, and they departed, leaving Rhys alone in the barn with his lantern, his doubts and fears, and the murdered man.

4

Day One

Catrin

As Catrin headed down the corridor, making for the kitchen, she could hear the laughter still arising from the hall. The queen had dismissed Catrin from her presence, but she required a morsel of food beside her bed in case she woke in the night. Thus, her highest-ranking lady-in-waiting, Eleanor's cousin, Margaret, had set Catrin the task of retrieving it.

The kitchen was located on the northern wall in the western half of the castle. At the moment, it was hardly more than a makeshift shack, though the bread oven had been built in stone, as it had to have been, and even at this late hour was wafting the delicious smell of baking bread across the bailey. The cooks and their assistants slept in shifts because food had to be produced day and night for the residents of the castle until the king and queen and all their people—including Catrin—left.

All of the castle workers had to be fed too, but those that couldn't afford a place in the town ate and slept outside the castle walls within an encompassing wooden palisade. It had been thrown up as a temporary measure, creating what amounted to an additional bailey outside the castle walls on the southeastern side along the River Seiont. Tents and makeshift huts lined the road leading east from the Queen's Gate, keeping the residents close enough to the castle to retreat inside its stone walls if the Welsh attacked in the night and overcame the outer defenses. Ultimately, water would be diverted from the river, and the castle would be surrounded by a moat, but it would be dug only towards the end of construction, once the castle and town walls had been fully raised.

Caernarfon castle was being constructed over the top of the old motte built on the edge of the Irish Sea by a Norman who'd conquered Gwynedd, for a time, two hundred years earlier. He eventually lost his life, so the tales said, when the Welsh fought back. The story of Robert of Rhuddlan and his ill-fated castle was one Catrin had known from birth, used as an object lesson as to what happened to foreigners who had the audacity to attempt to conquer so far west. Catrin also knew, sadly, that the comparisons to Edward were misguided. Caernarfon was no wooden keep on a hastily raised motte, and Edward was no Robert, dozing away a lazy Sunday afternoon to be awoken by the battle cries of the Welsh and tricked into a hasty counter-attack.

He was the King of England and the conqueror of all Wales. There was no coming back from that.

A dark shape separated itself from the wall near the King's Gate and came towards her. Though the torchlight wasn't bright enough to make out the man's face, she knew by his walk—even after all these years—that it was her brother Hywel. Only two years older than she, it was he, of all her siblings, whom she'd missed the most when she'd married at sixteen and been sent to live in England. They'd been natural allies growing up in a large family.

As when she'd ridden through Gwynedd on her way to Caernarfon, a joy she couldn't suppress rose within her. It must have showed on her face, because, once Hywel came close enough to be seen properly within the torchlight under which she stood, he scooped her up into a hug, even going so far as to lift her off her feet. She wrapped her arms around his neck, finding tears pricking at the corners of her eyes, and she pressed her face into the soft wool of his cloak. It was a real greeting, and a far cry from the stone-faced nods they'd given each other earlier in the hall.

After a moment, he set her gently down again. "I missed you."

"And I you."

"When you were so cold to me, I thought you had grown to hate me."

Catrin shook her head vehemently. "I would never hate you. How could I?"

"Because you had to leave, and I didn't. And look what's become of us now." He bent forward and spoke in a low voice that was no more than a whisper, and in Welsh. It was a sensible precaution, though nobody else was about, even in a castle as busy and crowded as this one. Everyone had work to do tomorrow and needed sleep.

Her expression softened. "The marriage was hardly your fault. Everyone thought it made sense at the time, which it did. I was sixteen and believed myself to be in love. What did I know? How many girls have felt and done the same?"

"But while you were gone, we lost our country. Twice our brother forsook Llywelyn's cause and bowed to Edward. This last time, after Llywelyn's death, he didn't delay for even a day."

"I already know from Tudur that he did what Llywelyn and he had agreed he would do."

Hywel practically sagged against the wall behind them. "You believed him? I feared you wouldn't."

"Seven years ago, after Llywelyn lost the first war and had to submit to Edward at Rhuddlan, Tudur wrote to me and told me he'd pledged himself to the king and asked me not to hate him. I did hate him for a time." She canted her head. "I never hated *you*."

Hywel's jaw was tight. "I did as I was told. As always."

She looked at him a bit harder. "As did Tudur. He obeyed his prince. He *survived*. Our family survived. I do believe that's what Llywelyn intended." But then her jaw clenched. "I just wish I had that kind of consolation for myself."

Now it was Hywel's turn to shake his head. "We all understand why you are here serving the queen, Catrin. We know the position you're in because we're in it too. Even Tudur." He grimaced. "Especially Tudur."

Catrin bent her head, nodding as she did so, but then it came up again as Hywel added, "So if that's true, you don't actually hate Rhys either? He tried to speak to you tonight, and you rebuffed him. He was hurt, I think."

"*He* was hurt?" Catrin laughed mockingly. "He is serving as a quaestor again—and assisting Guy fitz Lacy of all people!"

"He does so at Tudur's bidding."

"If Rhys were still the same person I knew him once to be, they would never allow him in the castle, much less to serve as an officer of the king. He was in Llywelyn's *teulu,* his personal guard! The only way they could know that and still trust him was if he was working for them the whole time!"

Her voice had risen in her agitation, prompting Hywel to put his finger to her lips. "Shush, Catrin. We don't speak of such things here."

But Catrin was too angry to be silent. "You are blind to the truth because he was your friend, but you must see he isn't that man anymore. He was at Cilmeri, and he lived. Surely you realize the only way he could have survived the attack was if he was the one who ensured Llywelyn was found in the open in the first place!"

Surprise filled Hywel's face, and he opened his mouth to reply, but at that moment a host of guardsmen came out of the barracks, passing within a few feet of them. The men nodded their respect to Hywel and then passed on.

Catrin watched them disappear into the great hall before returning to a fierce whisper. "On top of which, Rhys let me think he was dead for the last year and a half. Why would he do that if he wasn't guilty?"

"For Rhys's safety, Tudur agreed it was best—as you correctly pointed out—if nobody from the old days knew he was alive and in Caernarfon."

"You knew. I imagine his sister knows."

"By necessity."

She laughed scornfully.

Hywel pressed his lips together, studying her face. She glared back until, after a moment, he shook his head. "It is not my place to convince you, and I really must go. Tudur has me overseeing the estate at Penrhyn, and I have things to attend to on the morrow. Take care of yourself. Hopefully I will see you again before you leave Gwynedd." He hugged her to him, but before he released her, he whispered in her ear. "You *know* Rhys. He has suffered, as we all have. Hear his story before you condemn the man."

Catrin had carried the pain of Rhys's death in her heart every day for the last year and a half, ever since she'd heard about the circumstances of Llywelyn's death. When she'd seen Rhys in the hall tonight, she'd initially been overjoyed to learn he was alive, but by the time he'd bowed to the king with the rest of the nobles and then threaded his way through them to her, that pain had turned to anger.

If Rhys was working for the coroner only because Tudur had made him, why hadn't he been able to look into her eyes at first? And then, when their eyes did meet, why did she not see joy or love in them, but shame?

5

Day One

Rhys

"What is a Welshman doing inside the city walls at this time of night?" John le Strange, Prince Edmund's sigil emblazoned on his chest, accosted Rhys in the street as he reached the last house before the castle gate—a matter of a dozen yards at most.

Rhys was coming from the makeshift chapel, having installed the body in the even more makeshift laying out room next door. While he knew he needed to examine the body as soon as possible, it was late enough by now that first he needed to speak to Catrin—or at least make the effort to try.

He was both looking forward to seeing her again, because he'd always liked her, and dreading it, since it appeared she no longer liked him. He didn't know much about her life in England, but he couldn't help feeling that, in marrying a Norman, it had taken a turn for the worse.

Other than his origins, Rhys had never had anything against the man Catrin had married, but the Norman who stared down at him from his horse now was another matter entirely. John le Strange was the son of Roger, one of the masterminds—if not *the* mastermind—behind Edward's conquest of Wales. His family had acquired the name *le Strange* when they'd come to England from France, and it was no less appropriate today than it had been a hundred years ago: *John the foreigner.*

Should the son bear the sins of the father? That was a matter for priests to debate, but John le Strange and his twin brother Rolf, who was older than John by an hour, had never had a civil word to speak to Rhys in the times they'd encountered each other since Rhys had returned to Gwynedd. The two men were identical to look at in every way, not even having a difference in hair to distinguish themselves, since both were prematurely bald and had forgone any attempt to grow their hair long, instead clipping what was left close to their heads.

Thus, to aid in identification, John wore a blue chevron on the shoulder of his surcoat, and Rolf wore green. This was John tonight, and he appeared to have just arrived at Caernarfon after a lengthy absence—one in which he had not been missed, at least not by Rhys.

"I am on business for the coroner," Rhys said, choosing to answer civilly instead of turning John's question back at him. If he was in such a hurry to get to the castle, he should have entered it directly through the Queen's Gate rather than riding first through the town.

"See that you take care of it quickly, rather than cluttering up the streets of our fair city. You aren't allowed within the town walls after dark, you know."

Rhys bowed his head. "Thank you for the reminder, my lord."

John scoffed, possibly detecting a degree of insincerity in Rhys's tone, and pointed his horse's nose towards the King's Gate, riding a little too close to Rhys as he spurred the horse away. If it had rained recently, John would have spattered Rhys with mud. As it was, Rhys's already dusty boots grew only more dusty. As he let John get ahead of him, Rhys pulled a cloth from inside his coat and wiped down the leather. It wouldn't do to enter the castle looking disheveled. He would have done the same two years ago when entering any of Prince Llywelyn's palaces.

Even without the delay, it would have been later than polite when Rhys finally stood on the western end of the castle outside the doorway of the suite in the newly constructed Eagle Tower that had been given over to the queen and her ladies. The stones of the walls were not yet whitewashed and showed the masons' marks of those who'd carved them. A few tapestries had been hastily mounted in order to add warmth and color to the otherwise gray corridor. It seemed the floor had been recently scrubbed, as the edges were still wet. Rhys could be glad for the servants' sake he'd chosen to clean his boots. Everything in the castle smelled of stone and fresh mortar, for Caernarfon was to be the greatest castle ever built. That meant the corridors that led between the towers were *inside* the walls. It was like nothing he had ever seen before.

In his passage across the bailey, Rhys had inquired as to the whereabouts of the queen and her ladies and learned that the queen had retired from the hall some time ago—though well after Rhys himself had left. Eight months pregnant she might be, but her loyalty to her husband was absolute, and they'd wanted to put on a good performance tonight as they welcomed the obeisance, yet again, of many lords of Wales—Rhys among them, of course.

"Is the Lady Catrin within?" Rhys asked the guard who stood to one side of the door.

"She is."

Rhys went straight for a figure of authority as justification for his presence. "I realize it is late, but Coroner Lacy tasked me with speaking to her. It really is a matter of great urgency."

Rhys could see the reluctance in the guard's face, but the man didn't want to go against Guy any more than Rhys did.

"Yes, sir."

That very night in the hall, when he'd raised up all the men who'd pledged to serve him, King Edward had decreed that any Welsh knight who submitted was to be treated with the same deference as a Norman knight. Present at the time had been Hywel, his brothers, and a dozen other noblemen from all over Wales. The king had waved a hand over them and, between one heartbeat and the next, they'd become citizens of the realm. Some among the Norman nobles felt the inclusion of formerly rebellious Welshmen corrupted their ranks. But King Edward had declared the Welsh to be returned to the fold, and he would have no distinctions amongst his men.

To declare equality was one thing. To live it was quite another, clearly, and accord wasn't going to come without a great effort on everyone's part—including Rhys's. The fact that Rhys was no more interested in camaraderie than the guard who faced him didn't help matters. But they did know each other, and he wasn't going to argue with Rhys tonight. Instead, he nodded and disappeared inside the newly-appointed women's solar in search of Catrin. The sleeping rooms lay on the floors above.

Rhys was grateful the queen was so far advanced in her pregnancy because it meant there was no chance he would be called in to speak to her. Rhys had changed in appearance in the years since he'd last stood before her, but Queen Eleanor was a perceptive woman. He didn't want to risk recognition. So far, he had successfully avoided any direct contact with either her or her husband. He didn't know how long that could last, but the sooner he resolved this investigation, the sooner he could disappear again into anonymity.

It took nearly a quarter of an hour, while Rhys cooled his heels in the corridor, before Catrin finally appeared, still fully dressed in the deep green gown she'd worn to the feast, but now wrapped in a thick cloak with her auburn hair loose down her back. It was April, but stone castles were cold. "What do you want?"

Her animosity was palpable, but Rhys resolved to ignore whatever was going on behind those hazel eyes. The queen would give birth, and then they'd all be gone again, and whatever Catrin thought about him wouldn't matter.

Catrin had spoken in French, probably to maintain the distance between them, but Rhys answered in Welsh. "A man was found dead."

"So I heard." She didn't take the bait, continuing in French.

Rhys smiled, not knowing whether or not to believe her, though news did travel fast in such a small community. He wasn't even impatient with her attitude. Since he'd returned to Caernarfon, he'd been insulted almost daily by real experts in superiority. She was trying too hard.

"Did you hear he was wearing the tunic of your dead husband?"

She tried to hide her shock, but Rhys saw the flash of fear in her eyes. Still, she managed to keep her voice level. "No. I did not know that."

She was a widow, so it was only mildly improper to add, "He was wearing your husband's colors and nothing else."

In the twenty years since Rhys had seen her, she'd learned to control her emotions well, because that elicited hardly more than a raised eyebrow. "What do you want from me? I heard you arrested a Welshman already." The sneer was back in her face and voice.

"He wasn't arrested, simply taken in for questioning—"

She cut Rhys off. "Which makes him as good as dead."

Rhys continued as if she hadn't said anything, "—but since he didn't do it, I need to discover as quickly as possible who did do it before Aron is hanged as an example and to make the investigation go away. If the dead man is Norman, the coroner will want to blame a

Welshman as a matter of course. I was hoping some information from you might help me find the real killer."

She stared at Rhys without speaking.

His brows furrowed. "What?"

"Nothing." She shook herself and looked into the room, told whoever was nearest that she'd been called away, and then turned back to Rhys, sounding for the first time like the Catrin Rhys had known, "How do you think I can help?"

He reached behind her and pulled the door all the way shut. Somewhere along the way, she'd started replying to him in Welsh, so he hadn't worried about the guard understanding their conversation. There was no reason to disturb any of the other women, however, so he took her arm and walked her along the corridor.

"For starters, I need you to look at the body, as difficult as that might be ..." His voice trailed off, suddenly thinking better of what a few moments ago had seemed like a fine plan. Then he halted abruptly. "Never mind. It was selfish of me to ask. I'll find someone else."

"Who else is there *to* ask?" She tsked through her teeth. "Guy fitz Lacy obviously didn't recognize him. I am lady to the queen now. I have no men of my own. They all serve my son or the Earl of Gloucester, and none of them are here."

The Earl of Gloucester to whom she was referring was Gilbert de Clare, a powerful Norman magnate with extensive lands in Wales and England. Catrin's husband had been one of Clare's men, chosen deliberately as a husband by Catrin's father as a means of alliance, since twenty years ago Prince Llywelyn had been allied with Clare against the English crown. In fact, for a brief period, Llywelyn, Clare, and Simon de Montfort, the leader of the Second Baron's War, had been in rebellion and conceived a plan to divide Britain and Wales amongst themselves. She'd been sixteen herself at the time, with no say in the matter.

Six months after her marriage, Clare had forsworn Llywelyn and Montfort, betraying them to gain favor with Edward and his father, King Henry. Thus began Catrin's twenty-year sojourn in England. By rights, it wasn't something Rhys should be holding against her. Up until now, she'd been making that hard.

"It won't be pretty." He found himself adopting a similar turn of phrase to the one the undercoroner had used with Guy fitz Lacy.

"As if that's unusual these days. Not that you care." The last half of what Catrin said was spoken in an undertone, and Rhys didn't know if he was supposed to have heard. Then she seemed to shake herself and asked, "What about it isn't pretty?"

"He's been dead two days."

"How do you know that?"

"Because he's cold and not stiff."

She pressed her lips together, and he began to feel more and more disgruntled with her attitude. They hadn't spoken in twenty years, but she *knew* him.

Didn't she?

Because he himself had doubts, he relented enough to add, "You will understand, I assure you, when you see him. I cannot apologize too much for asking you to come."

There was no need for them to pass through the great hall, since at the moment it was a free-standing structure, and Rhys escorted Catrin across the bailey to the King's Gate, which was the gatehouse that faced the town and the one he'd come through earlier. The church was located as far from the castle as it was possible to be and still be inside the town walls. Rhys had learned by now that nothing Edward did was by accident, so he assumed the symbolism was meaningful—he just wasn't quite sure what it was, since Edward was an openly pious man.

If the church appeared to be something of an afterthought in the town, the laying out room was even more so. It had become a necessary evil, due to the sheer number of deaths that had taken place in Caernarfon over the last year since starting to build the castle. The pace of the work was unprecedented, in that the workers had managed to construct all the walls and gates, and even some of the towers, in a single year. King Edward had called in every mason in England to work on his castles—not just at Caernarfon, but also at Harlech and Conwy. If some lesser magnate or bishop wanted to build his own castle or church, it was just too bad. Every available hand was currently in Wales.

But the unholy pace occasionally meant that proper caution wasn't taken. Winches weren't secured, men didn't take a moment to ponder before cutting with a saw or other blade, and weren't getting enough sleep. Six months ago, men were dying five days a week, and a fever of fear had begun to envelop the castle. Some said the project was cursed—which was one reason the existence of the incomplete hexfoil was so troubling to everyone.

In the end, although the castellan of the castle couldn't prove any of the accidents had been on purpose, he'd hanged two Welshmen anyway, and most of the Welsh workers had been ejected from the building works and servant hall.

Rhys had investigated every death that didn't immediately appear to be an accident, but hadn't found true intent in any circumstance. Rhys honestly didn't know if he could have told Guy the truth if he had discovered it. As with Aron, the Welshman Guy had wrongfully arrested tonight, one of the scapegoats had offered himself. He was a man only in his thirties, but he had a wasting disease that would have killed him painfully in a month anyway. The second man had been Guy's own decision, having come upon him in the dead of night in the old palace on the hill and taken a dislike to him. As he was a wife-beater and had a ferocious temper, he was little missed.

The number of deaths had decreased since then, and with the king here, the master mason had sent off the rest of the common Welshmen. Even the village headman, Gruffydd, had been told his services were not required this month. Only three Welsh people remained: Rhys himself, Dai (the undercoroner's assistant)—and Catrin.

6

Day One

Catrin

"I thought Welsh people weren't allowed in the town after dark." As they passed through the gate, Catrin's eyes tracked to the guard as he waved the pair through. She hadn't ever tried to enter the town before.

"They're not." Rhys eyed her for a moment before explaining. "While the coroner cleared the way tonight, I have worked to cultivate the guards throughout Caernarfon."

She stared at him. "You've done what?"

He threw out a hand to stay the protest on her lips. "I never bribed them or played favorites, but I have access to the countryside in a way they do not. So if a man wants anything—from a new cloak to a packet of fresh butter to flowers for his sweetheart—he can get them from me. Initially, I gave these items away as gifts, and then later I came to be known as someone who could get a man what he needed if he could pay."

Catrin didn't like the sound of that at all. What he was doing felt dishonorable. "So if I'd been alone, I would have been turned away, but because I am with you, they let me in?" She was disgruntled, and it showed in her face and voice.

"I have been very careful not to hide what I've been doing. I'm not a smuggler, and if I was ever told to desist, I would." He shrugged. "Since no Norman speaks Welsh, I was already the middleman between every Norman in this town and every Welshman outside it anyway. This is just an added service."

She could feel Rhys's eyes on her, and her lip curled for a moment before she managed to smooth her expression once again. But otherwise she bit back any further comment. Rhys really had changed, and if that was the case, better he didn't know what she really thought. As an adult, she had learned to hide her emotions from those around her. She'd just never had to do it with Rhys, and she was finding the ability didn't come naturally.

In the last six months of the war, after her husband's death and once Prince Llywelyn had thrown his support behind the rebellion started by his brother Dafydd, Catrin had begun tapping into her network of friends and, for lack of a better word, spies, who over the years had kept her informed about what was happening in Wales. She'd reversed the communication network such that she was able to send news to Llywelyn himself, to the point that she was conducting her own private campaign. It had been heady work, and rewarding, knowing she was one small thread in Llywelyn's network of patriots that stretched from Holyhead to London. Any news she thought might be of use to him, she sent, wending its way from Welshman to Welshwoman, all the way to Gwynedd.

In retrospect, the work she'd done for Llywelyn could have gotten her—and everyone who helped her—killed. But she had needed to do her part for her people, and it had given her purpose and strength.

After the war ended, Catrin had found herself faced with an uncertain future. Her son had married, agreeing with Gilbert de Clare that he was obligated to ensure the future of his name, which resulted in Catrin no longer being the mistress of her own household. When the invitation to join the queen's retinue had come within weeks of the marriage, it had seemed like a gift from God—until it became clear to her that, although she technically was well-favored and enjoyed a high station, in joining the queen's household, she'd become a servant. It was a new experience for her. She'd been born the daughter of a powerful Welsh lord. Though her marriage had been to a less powerful Norman, she had been queen of her own castle, so to speak. As a lady-in-waiting, she had no maidservants, no household to run, and no villagers to protect and oversee. Her entire purpose was to serve the queen.

She'd been unhappy in her new service—until she realized it made her invisible. As during the war, she began to use her role to protect her people: a servant girl being molested by a nobleman; a brewer who had been wrongfully accused of theft; an orphan for whom she found a position as a baby minder. It wasn't quite as meaningful as when she'd been working for Llywelyn, but it was what, with her limited reach, she could do.

Rhys, on the other hand, appeared to be helping *Normans*. She couldn't understand it. She had wondered since the prince's death at Cilmeri if Llywelyn's network of spies had a traitor in its midst, else how could he have become separated from the body of his army and killed? That someone close to him was feeding him false information made sense.

She didn't want that traitor to be Rhys. She didn't know if she could bear it if it was. But she had to know the truth.

To do that, she would need to get close to him and gain his confidence. By that light, her abrasiveness up until now was ill-advised, and she resolved to be more accommodating in future.

With hundreds of laborers working on the castle and town wall, plus the regular townspeople, more of whom arrived every day, the streets of the town were narrow and lined with huts. Ultimately they would be converted to stone or milled wood, but for now, they were akin to what her people built in the hills: round wattle-and-daub dwellings with thatched roofs. She didn't know exactly what incentives the king had dangled before these English immigrants, but they must have been desirable indeed—or their circumstances in England so dire—that they'd agreed to locate to what to them had to be the ends of the earth.

Either that, or, like the Welsh people within the communities he'd destroyed to build his castles, the king had moved them by force. She honestly didn't know which was the more likely.

Looking at Rhys now as they passed through the deserted streets of Caernarfon, the only two Welsh people in the entire place, she wondered how long she could continue in the queen's service, even for the slight benefit she could still provide her people, if the only Welsh people left for her to work with were people like Rhys.

Although, if her brother was right, and he usually was, with the world the way it was now, she didn't actually have a choice.

Again, and uncomfortably, she didn't share what she was thinking with Rhys, merely nodded her thanks as he propped open the door of the laying out room with a rock. Rather than gesturing Catrin inside, he did the polite thing, which in this case was to enter first to give her time to adjust to the smell and the idea of looking into the face of a dead man. He'd brought a lantern from the castle, and now he hung it on a hook above the table where the body had been laid.

Fortunately, the smell wasn't as terrible as she'd feared by his description. The dead man hadn't been in the shed long, and the building wasn't well constructed, so gaps remained between the slats that made up the walls. Even so, she hovered in the doorway, as yet unwilling to fully commit to the endeavor.

"Can you see his face well enough from there?" Rhys said.

"No." Catrin put to her nose the lavender sachet Rhys had provided for her but still didn't move closer.

It wasn't as if she hadn't seen a dead body before, but she didn't know that she'd ever seen a murdered one. Thankfully, he didn't push her nor tell her again how much he regretted asking her to come. They needed to determine the dead man's identity, and she knew as well as he did that he had no good way to do that without her. Of course, he could have left Catrin to Guy, and it occurred to her only now that this really should have been Guy's job. Perhaps

Guy had bowed out because of her earlier treatment of him. It seemed unlikely that Rhys had asked Guy for the honor.

With that thought, she stepped back outside and, for a moment, leaned her head against the rough planks of the wall, striving to get her bearings. She didn't want Rhys to think she'd left entirely, so she reached out her arm and waved a hand in the doorway. "Give me a moment, please."

"Of course," he said, as he would. He was absurdly understanding, and she found herself irritated by it. He was trading on the fact they'd spent the first sixteen years of her life together. But he didn't know her, and she didn't know him either.

She had to admit, however, even with her distrust of him, that he was still a better option tonight than any of the men in the castle, namely the newly arrived John le Strange, whom she despised, or Guy fitz Lacy, who was downright menacing. As a Lacy, even a bastard one, Guy was associated with the royal court. She'd met him once during her marriage and many times after, most recently a month before this current visit to Caernarfon.

In that instance, he'd behaved a little too familiarly for her liking and hadn't appeared to understand or care that she wasn't interested in his affections. Thus, she'd been more straightforward in rebuffing him here than she'd been before. He, of course, had been offended, and Margaret had given Catrin a cold look for what she perceived to be unseemly behavior from a noblewoman.

What Margaret didn't know was that Guy was the man who'd forced himself on a maid at Gilbert de Clare's castle in Bristol. Afterwards, the maid had come to Catrin in tears, and she'd helped her get a new position elsewhere, well out of his range. What Guy had done was commonplace, but his behavior had ruined any chance with Catrin.

Better to deal with Rhys than Guy, and that meant facing what lay in the room. Holding her breath, she forced herself through the door and up to the table, in order to look down at the man's face. Then she gave a single nod and walked back outside.

Rhys followed, eventually guiding her to the wooden front step of the church. She sat abruptly and put her head in her hands.

He sat beside her, close enough to provide comfort but not enough to touch her. "I gather you know him?"

"He was one of my husband's men, as you suspected, though I should point out that he's English, not Norman, if it makes a difference to anyone. Cole de Lincoln he called himself, descended from one of the few Saxon barons who managed to survive William the Bastard's conquest and subsequent purge of noble Saxon families."

"Do you know what he was doing here?"

She shook her head. "As far as I know, he was supposed to be in the south with Justin."

She glanced at Rhys, noting the momentary question in his eyes—before his expression told her he'd just connected the name Justin with her son. He gave her a nod. "Thank you."

"You met him, you know."

"Did I?"

"It was a few years ago. Justin accompanied my husband and Gilbert de Clare to a conference of barons during the five year peace between England and Wales."

Rhys's mouth quirked. "I'm sorry you weren't there to introduce us."

She gave him a wry look. "My husband didn't even think about bringing me, even knowing my family might attend."

Catrin was immensely proud of the man her son had become. He was brave and honest, upright in every way that mattered. For all that he resembled her husband, Robert, with a very Norman-looking face, light brown hair, and eyes to match, he had a kind heart and delighted in singing, as any Welshman should.

Thankfully, Justin hadn't been at the Battle of Llandeilo Fawr where Robert had died, though, like Robert, he'd fought against her people.

Still, he spoke Welsh like a native and had never tried to hide his origins. As far as she knew, he'd been smart enough and capable enough to make his origins not matter. If he continued to rise in Clare's service, despite the fall of Wales to Edward, he would be among the few nobles with Welsh blood who did so. Likely, he had benefited from the fact that her brothers had pledged their loyalty to Edward without reservation.

"Who was Cole to you?" Rhys said.

"Nobody." And then at Rhys's skeptical expression, she looked at him more directly. "Really. He is one of a dozen knights who served my husband but survived the slaughter at Llandeilo Fawr. Now he serves my son. I haven't seen him in a year. I have no idea why he was riding to Caernarfon."

"If I had to guess, he had a message for you."

Catrin found her hand clutching the fabric of her cloak as it lay over her heart. "Justin was well when I last saw him. The war is over! It couldn't be—" She stopped and tried again, fear constricting her throat, "I would know if—"

Rhys had been visibly hesitating about how to make her feel better, but he finally put his arm around her shoulders, squeezed once, and said soothingly, "It need not be something dire. Perhaps his wife has given him a son."

Catrin had her fist to her mouth, trying to calm her breathing, and barely noticed that he touched her. It felt natural, in truth, disturbingly so.

Rhys was still trying to comfort her. "If Cole serves your son, that means he also serves Clare. He could have been carrying a message for the king, and it could have nothing to do with you or Justin at all."

Catrin closed her eyes briefly, and when she opened them, the tears that had threatened to fall had receded. "I'm sure you're right."

Rhys made a disgusted sound at the back of his throat. "You don't have to pretend with me. I have no children, so I can't know what it's like to be a mother, but I know grief. And I know loss."

Catrin turned her head to look into his eyes, trying to really *see* him, to figure out what with him was a mask and what was real. He looked back at her with a calm expression, and she could see neither condescension nor deceit in him. She gave him a rueful smile— the first one she'd bestowed on him, in fact. "I have no idea what that message might have been. Did you find anything on the body besides that tunic?"

"No. And the barn was empty of everything else but hay."

She thought about that for a moment. "Does the coroner know what you know?"

"If he drew the same conclusions, he said nothing to me about it. He doesn't know Cole's identity yet, of course, since I just learned it from you."

She bit her lip. "The man he took into custody, could he be responsible for Cole's death?"

"It is highly unlikely," Rhys said. "I will question him in the morning and let him go if I can."

She glanced at him sharply. "You said that before. The coroner will want a scapegoat."

"He will, which is the reason Aron volunteered for the job. But I will do everything in my power to find the killer before Aron suffers for another man's crime."

Rhys was a bundle of contradictions, and Catrin didn't know how to interpret what he'd told her. On the one hand, the smoothness with which he interacted with the castle guards, bowed to the king, and stood at Guy's right hand was disconcerting. On the other, he'd just boldly confessed that Aron had volunteered to be arrested, he knew it, and was using the false incarceration as breathing room to find the real culprit.

The Rhys she'd known twenty years ago had been unable *not* to tell the truth in full at all times. This Rhys was apparently very good at hiding his real self, in that he was telling both her and Guy what each wanted to know. He still might not ever tell an outright lie, but one or the other of his faces had to be false.

She gave Rhys another piercing look, but he merely looked blandly back at her before he stood and held out a hand. "I will escort you back to the castle."

She didn't move. "And then what?"

"What do you mean?"

"What will you do after that?"

"I'll return here to see if there's anything else to learn from the body. Tomorrow I will go back to the barn and see what I might have missed in the dark. Now that I know who he is, I can work towards reconstructing the series of events that led to his death."

She took Rhys's offered hand but, as she rose to her feet, said, "Then I'll stay too. There's no sense in you going all the way to the castle only to come back again to finish your work." She gave him a quick nod. "Do what you have to do. I'll wait."

Catrin could tell that Rhys wanted to protest or even go so far as to override her entirely. But as he hesitated, she walked back to the laying out room. She was a grown woman, and she was right that it was already very late. If he wanted an early start tomorrow, the sooner he finished, the more likely he was to get one.

A moment later, he passed her, going right to the body and picking up one of Cole's hands.

Catrin had let him enter the room first, and now she slung the sachet around her neck, no longer holding her nose, and braved the smell and the sight of the dead body of the man she'd once known. "Please tell me what I'm looking at."

The proper reaction to such a request from a lady should have been *you're mad,* but Rhys seemed to have given up sparring with her, and he treated her request seriously. "As I told you, it is possible to know how long a person has been dead by the condition of the corpse. If it's been a few hours, the body is warm and not stiff. Closer to half a day, it'll be warm *and* stiff. By a day old, it'll be cold and stiff, and by two days, it will be cold and no longer stiff. That's poor Cole."

"What if it had been snowing this week?"

Rhys shot Catrin an approving look. "Very good. Yes, that would make a difference. And being completely frozen would make the timing of his death impossible to determine."

She smiled, not displeased to have reached a correct conclusion. "We arrived at the castle only yesterday."

"Indeed," Rhys said, "implying Cole rode all this way to see someone already here or someone who would be. Like the king."

"Or me."

Rhys pressed his lips together before nodding. "Is that why you're staying?"

"I'm staying because I have to know what happened. Does his death have something to do with me? Is it, in a sense, *my* fault?"

"You can't take that on," Rhys said immediately. "The man responsible for Cole's death is the one who wielded the blade. Nobody else."

She tipped her head back and forth to silently say *maybe.* "What else do you see?"

"Some things that don't matter, now that we know who he is."

"Such as?"

He lifted one shoulder. "He has long limbs. Longer than mine." He met her eyes. "He was a tall man?"

"Taller than most everyone I know."

"He might even have been taller still if he wasn't so bow-legged, I presume from so many hours in the saddle. Just as well he was a knight because those feet would have hurt." He gestured down the table to where Catrin stood.

She hadn't known how interested she would be, once she got past the fact that Cole was dead, but now she peered at the poor man's toes. He had protruding bunions, with big toes that turned unnaturally in. "He did often wear pointy-toed shoes."

"It can be better for shoving your feet into stirrups, but I prefer mine more rounded." Rhys drew her attention to his boots, which, though much scuffed, appeared of high quality—and rounded in the toes, as he'd said. She had a moment's gladness that he had landed on his feet, before she remembered her suspicions of him, and the corners of her mouth turned down again.

Meanwhile, Rhys had more to tell her. "From the depth of the wounds and the nature of the incision, I'd say we are looking for a knife with a four- to five-inch-long blade serrated on one side."

"Like might be used in a kitchen for cutting meat?"

Rhys turned his hand back and forth. "It's double-sided, with one side a regular sharpened blade."

"Why would a dagger be serrated on one side?"

"Serration is expensive when done well, but it protects the edge of the blade from damage when it cuts through armor, as seemingly occurred in this case. And it rips flesh."

Catrin shivered. "Ugly."

"Because of the location of the wounds on the right half of Cole's belly, it's possible the dagger was in the killer's left hand."

"That would be unusual, wouldn't it?"

"It's something to consider." He pursed his lips. "I'm not seeing any damage to Cole's hands. Either he didn't fight back, or he wore gloves."

Catrin allowed her eyes to travel slowly from the top of Cole's head to his toes. "To have stabbed him thus, the killer must have moved in close." She glanced up at Rhys to find him looking back at her with interest. "That says to me Cole knew his killer or, at the very least, thought he had no reason to fear him." She paused. "Somehow, that doesn't sound like a Welshman to me."

7

Day Two

Rhys

Rhys woke up cursing himself—not because of the lateness of the hour, even though it wasn't as early as he'd hoped to rise, but because he was sure he'd find the hangman's noose around his neck before the day was out. He'd heard Catrin snort in derision at him when he'd mentioned the way he'd cultivated the guardsmen, and he'd told her that Aron had volunteered to be arrested. He cursed again: *stupid, stupid, stupid.*

It had been a long time since he'd allowed his heart to get the better of him. He wanted Catrin to be on his side, and she was the one person up at that castle Rhys wished knew the truth about what he was doing for their people. Because of that, he'd showed something of himself to her out of weakness for their shared past, speaking at times too fervently and freely. Though he hadn't meant to undercut his carefully cultivated façade, he feared he'd revealed a little too much as a result.

It was too easy to treat her like they knew each other well. And, of course, he wanted her not to hate him.

But if he was to continue in the life he'd set for himself, he needed to protect her from the truth. From the comments she'd made, she was still highly partisan in favor of the Welsh cause, which was all very well and good as far as it went, but she hadn't lived in Wales since the war ended. She didn't understand the danger of a careless word. As a queen's lady, she was in a protected position. He was not.

To genuinely have her convinced he was a loyal servant to the English crown would be a significant triumph, because if *she*, who had known him as a youth, believed the lie, then everyone else would too.

The feeling of dread continued as he accepted a walking breakfast of bread and cheese from Sian, Gruffydd's wife, and headed down the road that led to the castle from the village. The Welsh settlement had a green in the center, with twenty houses spread around it, encompassing a distance of at least two hundred yards of the south bank of the River Cadnant. The Welsh had never been much for living in towns, but the village had sprung up in this location because of its proximity to the sea and the royal palace on the hill.

Once Rhys arrived at the castle, it was a matter of wending his way among the craft huts, winches, stray stones and other construction equipment, dodging workmen all the while, on his way to meet Guy fitz Lacy.

While he was relieved nobody looked at him oddly (or more oddly than usual), meaning his impending doom wasn't common knowledge as yet, his heart did beat a little faster when Guy himself stepped out of the great hall and moved to intercept him.

"Had a lie-in today, did we?"

Rhys didn't bother to deny it because, first, it would feel like he was giving Guy an advantage over him, and second, it was factually true. Guy wouldn't know how late Rhys had stayed up last night—and even if he did know, he wouldn't care.

Instead, he said, "May I be of service?"

"You're wanted in the gatehouse. The new captain of the king's guard arrived hours ago and asked to see you immediately."

The old captain had fallen ill and died on the journey to Caernarfon. Although Rhys was working with Guy at the moment, he was officially a member of Tudur's retinue—which meant he served the king as Tudur did, and Rhys's real commander was the captain of the king's personal guard, not Guy, who now pressed his lips together, implying irritation.

"I was not pleased to have to tell him I didn't know where you were. I couldn't even say where you were lodging, and he expressed irritation you didn't have a berth in the castle."

Guy said all this accusingly, as if his ignorance and Rhys's lack of housing in the town or castle was Rhys's own fault. It was true Rhys had deliberately kept that information from Guy as a matter of course. He hadn't wanted him to know where he was staying because he didn't believe it was any of Guy's business. And he made it a point never to lie. Perhaps it was splitting hairs, because his omissions resulted in deception, but to him it remained an important distinction.

But the real truth was, up until this moment, Guy hadn't thought where Rhys lay his head at night mattered. Besides, even if he'd been given the information, his knowledge of the surrounding countryside was minimal. The Normans defended the castle. They didn't risk themselves riding through the countryside except in parties of more than fifty. Guy knew his way to the barn where the body had been found only because Rhys had showed him. Up until now, Rhys had always been there when Guy needed him.

For once, Rhys felt compelled to defend himself. "Surely the captain knows why I have no lodging here."

Guy cleared his throat. "He does." For the first time in Rhys's presence, the coroner appeared uncomfortable. "He called you Rhys de la Croix. I didn't know of whom he was speaking at first. You didn't tell me you'd been on crusade with the king."

This last sentence was said in an accusing tone, so it wasn't actually an apology for his condescending and dismissive manner up until now. It was more that he was offended Rhys had kept such a vital piece of information from him.

"It was a long time ago." Rhys chose to be forgiving, even if Guy couldn't, and even though the dread in his belly was now a hundred times worse.

There was a certain kind of safety in being underestimated and despised. But in referring to Rhys as *de la Croix*, this new captain showed he *knew* who Rhys was, maybe even knew him well and, worst of all, was asking for him here in Caernarfon. There were a very limited number of people who had that information, most of whom were already in Caernarfon and were, in fact, Welsh. It made the importance of Rhys's approach to Catrin pale in comparison.

It was on the tip of Rhys's tongue to ask Guy the captain's name, but then he decided he would simply wait and see. Asking for the new captain's identity would reveal a vulnerability within Rhys and imply he cared who he was or was apprehensive about it.

And yet, despite the belligerence with which Guy had initially greeted Rhys, clearly something in his attitude had changed, in that Guy proceeded to personally escort Rhys to the guardroom in the King's Gate. It was one of the few mostly finished rooms within the castle walls and apparently was going to be the captain's quarters until the king moved on from Caernarfon.

When they arrived, nobody was present, but given the remains of a meal on the table, someone had been there recently.

And then, for the first time in living memory, and maybe as a sign of Rhys's new-found status, Guy left Rhys alone and unguarded in the captain's quarters. In the past, while Rhys had some freedom to wander the corridors and eat in Caernarfon's great hall, he was looked upon with suspicion every time he entered a room. Certainly, he had never been left alone in one.

With no recourse but to see the coming moment through, Rhys settled against the wall to wait, his arms folded across his chest and his feet crossed at the ankles. If nothing else, hours, days, and years of guard duty and stalking culprits had taught him patience. While he had work to do today, if he was to continue the investigation into Cole's death *and* serve his people, he needed to start out on the right side of this new captain, whoever he was. By arriving at the castle at mid-morning, Rhys was already on the back of his heels with him.

The king wouldn't be at Caernarfon for more than a month or two at most, depending on how quickly the baby came, if he or she lived, and the health of the queen. Then, the king and his retinue, including the captain of his guard, would move on. Rhys would be left in Caernarfon, responsible again only to Tudur and to whomever the king chose to replace Guy as coroner.

Rhys had every intention of handling the new coroner as he handled Guy. For the first time, in fact, Rhys was looking upon Guy's coming departure as a good thing, since Guy was clearly resentful of Rhys's history. Hopefully, he would soon grow bored with acknowledging it and return to treating Rhys with disdain. Rhys took this moment alone to ponder how to make that happen sooner rather than later.

Unfortunately, he wasn't given much time to think before the door to the guardroom opened and one of Rhys's closest friends, Simon Boydell, entered the room, a look on his face halfway between consternation and amusement.

"Rhys de la Croix, master of arms, defender of princes."

He said *Rhys* the Welsh way, with the breathy trilled *r* like Rhys had taught him thirteen years earlier on a ship to the Holy Land. Simon had spent a diligent quarter of an hour learning how to say it properly and then, out of pure contrariness, had never said it right again.

Today, Simon knew what he'd done, because he smiled as he spoke, though the pinching at the corners of his eyes told Rhys his amusement was just a bit forced. Simon had added the *de la Croix* because he wanted Rhys to remember their shared past.

As if Rhys could ever forget it.

"Simon." Rhys straightened from where he'd been leaning against the wall and allowed Simon to embrace him for the first time in more than four years.

Then they stepped back and studied each other.

"I thought you were dead."

"I was left for dead."

And then Simon went straight to the one issue between them that truly mattered. "What in the name of our blessed Savior are you doing here, Rhys?"

Again, he pronounced Rhys's name correctly. Because of that, Rhys couldn't fob him off with a jest or evasion. He knew exactly what his old friend was asking. He wanted to know what had happened at Cilmeri, where Rhys had been all this time since then, and why Rhys hadn't let him know he was alive.

"Prince Llywelyn died and, afterwards, I did what I had to do to survive."

Simon sighed, pulled out a bench next to the table, and sat. "You always were something of an idiot."

Of all the things he could have said, few would have made Rhys laugh. But laugh he did. Simon was speaking in that familiar manner that had been second nature when they were young men, thinking a crusade was an adventure worth having if ever there was one and not displeased with the idea of being absolved of sin for a lifetime. Both younger sons of minor noblemen, one Welsh, one

Norman, they'd joked and jested from Chester to Acre. There, of course, the jests had ceased. Or, if they'd found amusement still, it was in the macabre.

As a younger son, Simon had been shut out of his father's inheritance in favor of his older brother. Rhys's father had encouraged him to achieve everything he could on his own merits because it was the only honor that lasted.

"Given the way you've kept yourself hidden up until now, why are you involved in this investigation? Why didn't you leave Carnarvon as soon as you saw what this was about? You had to know you couldn't investigate the death of a man anywhere close to the king without calling attention to yourself."

Rhys gazed at his friend, understanding that Simon's question was coming from a deep well of anger—and it was an anger Rhys couldn't address, much less apologize for.

So he spoke the simple truth instead. "I hate murder."

Simon's lips twisted. "Don't we all. Any man would say the same."

"But not every man has seen what we've seen, Simon. We've lived through death in a thousand different guises. We've caused it ourselves. That is the reason every breath, even if painful, should be savored, and every life followed to the end, come what may—Welsh, English, or Norman, God help me. If the priests are wrong, and this world is all there is, then no man should cut another man's life short, not even that man himself. And if there is such a thing as heaven, then a man can only be well-served by living as fully as possible every heartbeat of the life he's been given, in preparation for the next one."

Rhys stopped. He hadn't meant to go on like that. In truth, He hadn't realized how much he cared until he'd started speaking. As he stuttered to a halt, Simon gazed at him with that pleased look Rhys had seen many times on his face when they'd been the best of friends. Rhys would start speaking, usually more earnestly than a situation called for, and Simon would allow him to ramble on until everyone around them was both glassy-eyed and awestruck at Rhys's forceful and elaborately reasoned argument. Simon would act like he'd invented Rhys himself or he was his prized heifer at the village market and suddenly they'd be drinking for free. If only to get Rhys to stop talking.

"Not everyone agrees with me," Rhys concluded, somewhat lamely.

"Clearly." Simon let out a puff of air that was almost a laugh. "Here I thought your silence had something to do with me, but it didn't, did it?"

"No. After Cilmeri, I couldn't—" Rhys broke off.

Simon allowed the pause to lengthen before finally saying, "You couldn't what?"

"I swore a long time ago that I would never lie to you, and I never will. But not all lies are overt. There are those of omission. It was better to absent myself from your life, to let you think I was dead, than to pretend to be something I wasn't."

8

Day Two

Rhys

Simon's left hand went to his chin as he studied Rhys. Rhys kept his eyes on his old friend's face. He would tell him the truth if he asked. And hang for it, if that was the price for honesty.

"Self-pity does not become you."

Rhys didn't pretend not to know what Simon was talking about. "Self-pity? Shame and guilt, more like."

"In your case, it's the same thing. And you have no cause to feel either—unless you've done something horrific in your exile. Did you have anything to do with this man's death?"

"No."

"So you failed to defend your prince. From what I heard, the force arrayed against you was overwhelming." He looked at Rhys curiously. "But you knew that, didn't you?"

Rhys gritted his teeth and didn't answer.

SARAH WOODBURY

Simon nodded. "You feel you should have died with your fellows, is that it?" He tsked under his breath. "We've been through this before in the Holy Land, though then you were counseling others."

Rhys knew he had to say something, and in the end it was the truth. "I won't pretend with you. My world ended when Llywelyn was killed."

"As it should have."

Rhys hadn't expected such understanding—which shamed him further. "I haven't figured out how to live without him to follow."

"Yes, you have." Simon gestured broadly. "Even in the short time I've been here, I've asked around about you. Since you returned to Gwynedd, your conduct has been exemplary."

"Such was my intent." Rhys took in some air, having spoken without thinking. "What I show of myself doesn't necessarily reflect what I feel."

They were skating dangerously close to what Rhys *actually* had been doing in the last year—that is, protecting his people from Simon's people. Rhys never lied outright, but he'd become very good at arranging things so his masters never learned the whole story.

Simon dropped his hand on Rhys's shoulder. "I hope never to put you in a position where you feel you must lie to me. I understand that you did what you believed you had to do."

Simon was speaking with more grace than Rhys deserved, and Rhys bent his head, acknowledging the sacrifice they were making for the sake of their friendship. Then he shook himself, thinking the sooner they put aside questions about what had pulled them apart the better.

"What are *you* doing here? You are the captain of the king's guard, but yet you still wear Prince Edmund's sigil?" He gestured to Simon's surcoat, which (like John le Strange's the previous night) showed the three lions and azure *fleur-de-lys* proclaiming him to belong to Prince Edmund of England, Earl of Lancaster, the brother of King Edward and a fellow crusader, hence the name he was known by: Edmund Crouchback. Both Rhys and Simon had served in Edmund's retinue on crusade, and Simon had continued in that service thereafter.

Simon looked down at himself. "It has been an eventful morning. I am still working through the protocol."

"This will be quite a change for you, serving the king instead of the prince."

"We all serve at the pleasure of the king, as you well know."

"Edmund must not have been pleased to give you up."

"It was he who offered my services."

"Only so the king didn't have to ask."

"If the king had known you were available, I'd still be in Chester."

Rhys scoffed. "Neither the king nor Prince Edmund were ever that fond of me. Besides which, I'm Welsh."

Simon's lip twitched. "The king doesn't have to be fond of you to respect your abilities, and he knows well your origins."

Rhys pressed his lips together, not able to reply in any kind of civil fashion. King Edward was Rhys's mortal enemy, which Simon should realize if he understood Rhys at all. But then again, maybe he couldn't understand it because the entire notion was inconceivable to one such as he. If anything, what the Normans around Rhys felt most these days was impatience with the Welsh lack of appreciation of the sacrifices made for them and the benefits that would accrue to them for being incorporated into the Kingdom of England.

For his part, Simon looked hard at Rhys. "You, however, have been sorted. I have spoken to Lord Tudur, Coroner Lacy, Sheriff Pulesdon, and the captain of the garrison here at Carnarvon. From now on, you will report directly to me, and if anyone wants the use of your services, those orders will also come through me."

"You have been busy." Rhys was attempting to jest, but he was impressed and a little daunted by Simon's thoroughness. But as Simon continued to bend his gaze on him, Rhys finally realized his friend's intentions and started shaking his head. "No. No, no, no."

Simon overrode his protest. "Before I left for Carnarvon, Edmund spoke of you in my presence, openly regretting your loss. I am being completely serious when I say he sent me to his brother to become the new captain of his guard because he believed he couldn't send *you*."

Rhys wasn't going to give up what little freedom he had without a fight. "Simon ... what is this about?"

"I need your help. And not this—" he waved his hand up and down in front of Rhys, "—version of yourself."

"My help?" Rhys laughed. "Surely you have dozens of capable men who would be happy to assist you in whatever capacity you require."

"Possibly, but things would go much better with you at my side. Nobody else brings your specific attributes to the table."

"Which are what, exactly?"

"You are the most intelligent—and cleverest—man I've ever known."

"Except when I'm an idiot, as you said yourself." Rhys didn't allow himself to be distracted by the compliment. "What exactly do you need my help with? Not this murder, surely. You could solve this blindfolded. You know it's murder. You know what to do even if Guy does not."

"This isn't about the murder."

"Then what?"

"In the past two months, there have been several incidents— each on their own viewable as simple accidents—that threatened the king's life."

For once, Rhys had no ready reply, just stared at his old friend.

Simon smiled sardonically. "That got your attention. And now Guy tells me this new man died over the top of an incomplete hexfoil."

Rhys wet his lips. "Even with the hexfoil, which I admit is unsettling, I don't see a connection to the king as yet."

Simon leaned forward, his hands flat on the tabletop. "That's just it. The incomplete hexfoil indicates it isn't simple murder, not that any murder could be viewed as simple so near the king's person. And that isn't the only incident, either. How is it the king's captain died in the first place? Everything could be related."

"Gerald was ill. He died. It happens." Rhys found himself defensive, though he wasn't entirely sure why.

"At such an important time, on the way to the castle that will be the jewel in the king's crown, within days of the birth of the king's latest child?" Simon seemed fond of waving his hand, because he did it again, this time indicating Rhys's appearance and his unhappiness with it. "Where's your sword?"

"I have been asked not to wear it in the castle, and I swore a year ago that if I couldn't wear it when it counted most, I wouldn't wear it at all."

"You are a crusader!" Simon's words came out with real force.

Rhys put out a pacifying hand. "Until you started talking, nobody here knew it, and I'd appreciate it if you wouldn't broadcast it any farther than you already have."

"Nobody?"

"Nobody."

"Rhys—"

He tried not to wilt under Simon's glare. "I have been very successfully hiding in plain sight for a full year now. Trust you to ruin everything."

"It was bound to happen eventually," Simon said. "I gave the coroner your proper name, so he will have everybody knowing your full identity by dinner time, and neither of us need ever say a thing."

"Alternatively, he could be so resentful of my station, he tells no one."

Simon gave Rhys a withering look and said, deadpan. "Oh sure. That's exactly what is going to happen."

He was right. Worse, it was likely the king would be even less pleased than Simon (though not as personally hurt) to have been kept in the dark. When Rhys had begun this charade, he'd hoped never to see either the king or Simon again. He had thought he'd put his past behind him. Like Simon said, he was an idiot.

"You do still have your sword, of course." Simon wasn't really asking a question.

"I do." Rhys thought about denying it, but it would be petty to lie. No crusader, no matter how low he'd fallen, would ever give up his sword. He'd bent a knee and kissed the hilt a thousand times in the Holy Land and after. It would be like casting away the cross of their Lord.

"What kind of oath did you make?" Simon's eyes narrowed. "Was it binding? Did you speak the words before a priest?"

Rhys shook his head, even more wary about where this conversation might be headed than he'd been when Simon had walked into the guardroom.

"So you could wear it, perhaps unsheathe it and wave it around threateningly? Maybe even defend yourself?"

"I suppose."

Simon gave a sharp nod. "Then you will wear your sword from now on. I will ensure it is not remarked upon." It was an order, not something Simon had ever given Rhys before. Now Simon looked at him with something like amusement in his eyes. "The coroner seems particularly taken with you."

It was a relief to laugh and a bit of the tension in the room was dispelled. "Your senses must be truly failing you if he left you that impression."

Simon smirked. "His attitude did improve once I called you by your rightful name." He gazed at Rhys for another moment. "I suppose it could have been worse. You could have become a monk."

"After Cilmeri, no monastery in England would have me, and none in Wales could afford me. I'm neither farmer nor herder, and I had no gold to buy myself a position. The war has ended, the roads are safe, so no monks need the services of a warrior to protect them from marauders. But my family did need me to protect them, so I came home."

Simon nodded at the most complete explanation Rhys had yet given him. "I'm glad you didn't leave your sister in the dark."

Rhys's head came up. "That's why you weren't surprised to find me here?"

"I stopped at Conwy on the way from Chester and spoke with her. At long last, she told me the truth: you were alive and in Carnarvon."

Rhys couldn't be angry at his sister. She'd always had a soft spot for Simon because he'd brought Rhys home from the Holy Land alive. "Efa has enough to worry about without me."

"I think she would disagree." Simon paused. "Your brother-in-law asked me to tell you he is doing as you suggested, against his better judgment. What did you ask of him, Rhys?"

Rhys gritted his teeth and almost didn't answer, but there was nobody else in the room, and Simon had saved his life—and Rhys his—more than once. That bond couldn't be denied, even if he wanted to. Simon couldn't know the full truth, but he knew Rhys too well to share Catrin's confusion about who he really was. "I told Huw not to listen to the hotheads around him. There is no future in disobedience. He needs to keep his head down and do as he's told. Just as I must."

"A mason isn't usually a profession that leads to rebellion." Simon canted his head, studying Rhys in that way he knew very well, even after all these years apart. "Is yours?"

Rhys wet his lips and didn't answer.

Simon continued as if Rhys hadn't just avoided lying to him, "Like Carnarvon, the castle on the River Conwy rises at a great pace, and there will be more castles to build once it is completed."

That was exactly what Rhys was afraid of, of course, though he didn't say so to Simon. It was one of the many things that made returning to Gwynedd to live and serve so extraordinarily difficult.

When again Rhys didn't respond, Simon tsked and changed the subject. "About this murder."

It was a relief to speak of something else. "What about it?"

"The coroner said he'd already arrested a villager, though the man claims to be innocent. Guy isn't so sure."

"Of course he's innocent," and then Rhys laid out what he knew so far, which wasn't much, though it did include the dead man's identity and the questions raised by Rhys's conversation with Catrin.

Simon rubbed his chin. "He's an Englishman, dead in a Welsh barn, which used to be part of your prince's palace, over the top of an incomplete hexfoil. I'm not liking the symbolism."

"Nor I."

"And Lady Catrin had no idea why Cole had ridden all this way from Bristol?"

Rhys shook his head. "He could have been bringing a message to her from her son or to the king from Gilbert de Clare. She fears for her son's life, of course."

Simon grunted. "I will have to send a messenger back to Gloucester to discover the truth."

"Meanwhile, if you still want me to pursue Cole's murderer, it is my intent to return to the barn and attempt to retrace Cole's steps."

Simon had been sitting on the edge of the table, but now he pushed to his feet. "And I am due for an audience with the king."

"Does he know about me?"

"Not yet." Simon made for the door.

Before he could leave, Rhys put out a hand to stop him. "You forget."

Simon made a noise of disgust. "Thanks for the reminder. It's been a busy day." He put up his arms. "Help me with it, will you?"

Rhys pulled the surcoat up over Simon's head, a task nearly impossible for an armored man to do on his own. It reminded Rhys again of how difficult it must have been to remove Cole's armor and gear after he was dead. It seemed unlikely he'd done it on his own when he was alive.

Throughout this last year, because he wasn't allowed to wear his sword, Rhys had dressed more like a man-at-arms, in leather instead of mail. He wore a dagger (unserrated) on one side of his waist and a knife on the other, belted around a plain ash-gray tunic. He hadn't actually put on his mail armor since Cilmeri, and his frame wouldn't be used to the weight of it anymore, even if it fit. Most likely it would hang loosely around his shoulders and chest. He had worked to maintain his fitness and strength of arm and leg, but he had no *teulu* to ride in anymore, and he knew he hadn't regained his fighting weight after his injuries.

But if Simon required him to wear his sword, regardless of his lack of other gear, it would mean detouring back to the village where he lived to collect it before going to the barn to continue the investigation.

Then Simon dropped the surcoat he'd been wearing, the one sporting Edmund's sigil, over Rhys's head. "We will start as we mean to go on. Edmund's colors will do for now until the king decides if he wants you to wear his."

Rhys didn't fight his friend's hands as Simon adjusted the fabric over Rhys's chest and rebuckled his belt, still minus his sword, of course, at his waist.

"Come find me after you're done at the barn," Simon said. "And we will see the king together."

9

Day Two

Rhys

Rhys was looking forward to some moments to himself at the barn, grim as the scene would be in the daylight, to consider his predicament, and was thus justifiably horrified to discover Catrin had arrived before him.

"What are you doing here?" The words came out of his mouth before he could stop them, a duplicate of what he and Simon had said to each other an hour before.

It was the second surprise encounter of the day, and Rhys couldn't say he was completely happy about either one, as much as he had once loved both Catrin and Simon.

He refrained from cursing like he wanted to, not because she was a lady, but because it would have betrayed his emotions too profoundly. When Catrin was nine and he eleven, in the loft of this very barn, they'd practiced saying every curse word they could remember, both crude and blasphemous, as emphatically as possible. As a soldier, Rhys had employed profanity many times since then. He was sorry he'd missed the last twenty years of Catrin's life, because he didn't know if she even remembered their escapades, much less allowed a choice curse to escape her lips every now and then.

She turned on him, ready to go on the offensive in an instant. "You are wearing Edmund's sigil *and* your sword today? I thought you weren't supposed to do that in Caernarfon."

She surely knew how to get to him. She always had. Despite his irritation—and her outrage at being questioned—when he looked at her she could have been that young girl in pigtails again, running after him and her older brothers.

So he didn't answer her question any more than she had his. "You shouldn't have come." He looked around. Fortunately, she'd arrived moments before he had, so she hadn't yet entered the barn. "Have you no escort?"

"You're saying I'm not safe outside Caernarfon's walls?"

"I don't know." He couldn't stop himself from being sincere with her. "A man was found murdered yesterday. I can't guarantee anyone's safety."

She didn't appear in the least bit concerned. "I have as much right to be here as you. And I expected you sooner. You slept later than I thought you might."

Rhys swallowed down another retort, which wouldn't have helped matters in the slightest, and attempted to rein in his ire. In truth, he wasn't angry at Catrin so much as at the circumstances in which he found himself. "The delay wasn't because I lay late in bed. My new captain arrived, and I was required to meet with him." He made an expansive gesture with both hands. "Thus the sword and surcoat."

Some of the obstreperousness left her, perhaps because she saw something different in Rhys's face. "He's that bad?"

"He's that good." Rhys didn't add *unfortunately*. Even if he should have meant it, he didn't.

His love for Simon had never turned to hate, no matter how hard he tried to make it so. That inability threw into sharp relief the fact that he shouldn't actively hate every Norman who crossed his path. Most were simply doing as their masters bid them—just as Rhys was and always had done. In truth, both sides were ignorant of each other. In the Holy Land, Rhys had come to learn that, at some point, every man was responsible for his own soul—and it was up to each man to decide what he would and would not do—what he *could* and *could not* do.

Catrin bit her lip. "Who is he?"

"Simon Boydell."

She shook her head. "I'm sorry to say I know very little about the life you led after I married. I don't know him." She paused. "But you obviously do."

"I served with him in Acre." Rhys didn't want to talk about that, and to head off whatever Catrin's next comment was going to be, he said, "How is the queen? Won't she be missing you?"

"I am among the lesser of her ladies and am not one who will be attending the birth. She was meeting with the midwives this morning and was so out of sorts she sent everyone but them and her kinswomen away. Likely, the birth is close. It's a relief, really. She has become so snappish."

From Rhys's personal experience, the queen was often snappish, though he supposed he would be too after giving birth to fifteen children, only six of whom still lived, and suffering now under pressure to produce another son, as backup to ten-year-old Alphonso.

"Even if you are safe outside the walls, that doesn't explain why you are without an escort."

"I am a widow, which means I am not a little girl anymore. When the queen does not need me, I can do as I like." But then she relented. "I knew you'd be here, which is what I told the guard who let me out the castle gate. He knows you, apparently."

Rhys didn't think he was mistaken to see her lip curling again.

"As I told you last night, they all do." Rhys didn't want to talk about his relationship with the guards, fearing the more he said, the more likely he was to defend himself against her disdain, which he'd resolved not to do.

Instead, he swung open the one intact barn door and then carefully propped wide the door that was partly off its hinges to let in daylight and as much fresh air as possible. The barn doors faced east, and with the sun shining today, he was able to see quite clearly the hexfoil drawn in the dirt in the middle of the floor.

Catrin frowned. "I thought you said it wasn't completed."

Rhys crouched before it, touching the ridge of soil thrown up by the knife that had carved the circle. "Last night, it wasn't." He swiveled to look up at her. "Likely one of the villagers returned and finished it."

Catrin glanced down at his face. "Doesn't that make you angry?"

He looked up at her, puzzled. "Why would it?"

"I was wondering if you were irritated to discover how far your authority extended—or didn't extend, in this case."

"Clearly not far enough, regardless. Though, as I said, I don't object because I understand."

"What if it was the killer?"

"Why would he return?"

"To finish what he started? Perhaps he was interrupted before he was done."

"Cole has been dead nearly three days now." Rhys let out a sharp laugh. "Believe me. The killer left the hexfoil unfinished on purpose."

"Are you troubled that whoever finished it disturbed the scene of the crime and made you less able to see what really happened?" She gestured to the interior of the barn. As Rhys had seen last night with the help of a lantern, there was very little left in it.

These were all good questions, actually, but Rhys didn't want to reward her by telling her so. "I suppose I could be, but it is also clear that Cole wasn't killed here anyway."

"How do you know that?"

"There are only a few drops of blood on the ground." He walked away from her and the hexfoil to a clump of hay and swept it across the floor to see what might be under or within it. The barn was still solid, so the hay was dry, but his action revealed nothing hidden.

Everything from Prince Llywelyn's time that could be used had been taken away long before King Edward had started building his castle.

Rhys circumnavigated the room anyway, more thoroughly than he'd done the previous night, and then climbed the ladder to the loft. A few more wisps of hay remained here too, along with a rumpled blanket, which told him where Iago and Mari had been lying before they discovered the body.

"I'll just have a look around the outside, shall I?" She exited the barn.

Rhys didn't like the idea of her going off by herself any more than he did her staying by his side. Thus, after another long look at the hexfoil, he joined her and found her crouched before a blackberry bramble, carefully moving a few of the prickly branches aside. Here in April, it wasn't fully leafed yet, and the berries wouldn't be ripe for many months.

"What have you found?"

"A boot."

Gingerly she reached among the branches and came up with a soldier's leather knee-high boot, longer and narrower at the toe than the one Rhys himself wore. The top of the boot would have ended just below the wearer's kneecap, and was similar to the boots he and every other knight of his acquaintance wore, whether they were Welsh, English, or Norman.

Catrin rose to her feet with the boot in her hand. "A man would not have left this behind over the course of a romantic evening."

"That does sound unlikely," Rhys agreed before turning the boot upside down to examine the sole. "No one would discard such a valuable item on purpose. At a minimum, he'd be walking around with one boot."

The boot was well-scuffed, but solid. If it belonged to Cole, and he'd lived, it would have served him another six months at least, depending upon how much walking his life required. For many knights, that was as little as possible. Rhys himself no longer owned his own horse. Last night, to keep up with Guy and because the summons had been urgent, he'd ridden to the barn on a mount borrowed from the castle garrison. Today, he'd walked. These days, his boots were well broken in.

"Could the killer have dropped it by mistake from the bundle of gear he took off Cole?"

"That's the obvious conclusion for me too." Rhys tried to look severe, but he was finding it helpful to have someone else with whom to talk things through, though he would never say so to Catrin.

In order to have removed Cole's clothing and gear, the killer would have had to have space and time undisturbed. As a retainer to Catrin's son and an Englishman in what he would have viewed as a hostile land, Cole should have been wearing mail armor consisting of at least a mail vest if not a full hauberk, like the one in Rhys's trunk that no longer fit him. Mail was expensive, however, and worth the effort to the killer to remove if the goal was monetary gain.

Then Catrin looked down at her feet, a rueful expression on her face. "I'm sorry to say I'm as much to blame as anyone for how muddled the tracks around the barn have become."

"We mucked it up last night, so it is hardly your fault." Rhys grimaced, more to remind himself of how he should be behaving than because he was particularly upset about the tracks. He had learned, belatedly, how little there was to gain from regretting what couldn't be changed.

Then he held out his arm to her. "May I escort you back to the castle?"

She blinked. "That's it? We're done?"

"Well ... I'm not. But it's time you were."

"Oh no, you don't! Cole could have been carrying a message for *me*. It will take weeks to learn what it was by sending to Gloucester for answers. Better that we discover it ourselves." She folded her arms across her chest. "What's next? What would you do if you weren't wasting time trying to get rid of me? After last night, you should know better."

For a moment, she was so completely herself it left Rhys breathless, and despite his best intentions, he found himself smiling. "I'm not trying to get rid of you. But you're a lady now and should not be companionable with one such as I."

The instant he spoke, he realized what a telling choice of words he'd used. He should have told her she shouldn't be tagging along after him like a puppy or some other more derogatory phrase that implied he didn't want her with him. It was certainly how her mother had described their relationship more than once. At that time, Catrin had declared she was doing nothing wrong and had come storming to him about it.

Today, he'd made it seem instead as if he thought he wasn't worthy of *her*.

By way of reply, she kicked out with one toe to show him her sturdy boots hidden underneath her dress. "No dainty slippers for me. I came prepared."

He couldn't help himself. He laughed.

10

Day Two

Catrin

Catrin had a glint in her eye, her face was alight, and she'd forgotten to damp down her enthusiasm. Damn the man for being so much like the boy she'd known, even after all these years. "If someone brought Cole here as you say, likely it was in a cart or thrown over the back of a horse—" she stopped abruptly.

He nodded, eyebrows raised. "Which begs the question, what happened to the horse?"

She deflated slightly. "You thought of that already."

"My guess is Cole was killed on or near the road, thrown over the back of his own horse, as you say, and brought to the barn. Why the killer stripped him of his gear and laid him out on the incomplete hexfoil remains a mystery. Unless Cole made a habit of riding naked through the countryside—"

"That does sound unlikely," she said, in mimicry of him.

He ignored her jest. "He *was* naked. What I do find likely is that his gear was stuffed into his own horse's saddle bags, which is how the boot could have fallen out without the killer noticing."

"But *why* any of this? It's seems so elaborate and unnecessary."

"It appears unnecessary to us. Killers, in my experience, have their reasons, even if those reasons make no sense on the surface to a sane man."

Catrin glanced away, not wanting to show him what was going on inside her head. She was becoming actively worried the killer was a villager, and his intent was to protest King Edward's rule. If so, ambushing what looked like a Norman rider on the road and bringing him to what had once been the barn of his prince's palace to lay him out so gruesomely made a certain kind of sense.

She really hoped that wasn't what had happened. If a viable candidate for leadership could be found, armed insurrection against the English crown would be one thing. Random protest that involved killing the nearest person to hand was quite another and would do none of them any good.

Even if Rhys supported King Edward, she'd seen with her own eyes his regard for their people and heard it in his voice when he talked. For the first time, it occurred to her that if he'd betrayed Llywelyn, it could have been out of love for Wales rather than hatred. Many other lords had preferred not to see Wales torn apart by war, especially one that dragged on through the winter, and decided to throw in their lot with the king in hopes the war would come to a quick end.

The thought made her stomach hurt, but she could see how he could have come to that conclusion. How could she not, seeing as how her own brothers had defected to King Edward before Prince Llywelyn's body was even cold?

She shook herself and refocused on the issue before them. "So why the incomplete hexfoil?"

Rhys canted his head. "Why do you think?"

Catrin's brow furrowed as she thought. "It's showy, isn't it?"

Rhys gave a quick nod. "Everything about it speaks to the idea that the killer *wanted* the body to be found. He wanted everyone in an uproar about it."

"Why?"

"That I couldn't tell you."

"If he really wanted everybody to see what he'd done, he should have left Cole in the middle of a crossroads."

Rhys tapped a finger to his lower lip. "You are right about that." He sounded reluctant to admit it. "Or possibly, he didn't want him found immediately to give himself time to get away."

"Or he *didn't* want Cole to be found," Catrin said, "and it really was a satanic ritual. You've been assuming it was a ploy because you don't scare easily yourself, but it's the reason the local people completed the hexfoil."

Rhys seemed surprised by her reasoning, but he nodded. "In which case, was Cole killed because of who he was and the message he was carrying, or was the attack random, for twisted purposes in the killer's own mind?"

"Making the killer a madman? Who in Caernarfon could fit such a description?"

"I find much of what the Normans do madness in itself, but it is of a different kind. This—" he gestured behind them to the barn, "—this is something else entirely."

"I imagine everyone in the village and town wants it to be a masterless man."

"That would be convenient, if nothing else." Rhys's lips twisted. "But I find it hard to believe any could be operating so close to Caernarfon. Masterless men rob a traveler and leave him for dead in the road, as you suggested. And if such a man wasn't local, he might not know about the barn in the first place."

Feeling the tug of interest again, Catrin was nodding before Rhys finished speaking. "So where is the horse? And where are his possessions other than the lost boot? And if we find them, do we find the killer?" She threw out a hand to stop him before he could answer. "If the killer did all this, would he be stupid enough to *keep* everything he took?"

"We won't know until we find the items and the horse. Horses are valuable, though. It might be hard to give up once acquired."

"One boot isn't going to do him a lot of good. If one of the villagers or a townsperson is walking around with mismatched boots, we have him." She started moving around the area, her eyes on the ground, looking for hoofprints, though, as she'd said to Rhys, with all the tracks from last night, things looked hopelessly muddled.

For a moment, Rhys stood gazing around with his hands on his hips, and she had a moment of impatience with him for watching her rather than helping, but then he moved purposefully towards the near corner of the barn and began pacing around a perimeter much wider than the one she'd been following.

It forced her to stop and ask what he was doing.

"I was here last night, so I have some idea of where everyone stood. Obviously the coroner's men and the villagers left their footprints, but the horses were tied over there—" He gestured to a rail fence that had been used to pen stock. "So why are there hoofprints over here?"

Catrin lifted her skirts and came closer, though if what he was looking at were hoofprints, he had a keen eyesight that eluded her. Rhys had been crouching beside the marks he found, and now he looked this way and that, surveying the ground around him, before abruptly rising and heading up the sloping track that would take them the back way to the prince's palace. Until a year ago, the palace had been the central point of the entire area, so all roads led to it, including this track.

The barn lay less than a mile east and slightly south of the castle. If not for the trees that had been allowed to grow, they would have been afforded a view of the whole region. That was, of course, why the palace had been built on the hill in the first place. Edward was building Caernarfon on the waterfront not because it was central or it made the castle more defensible, but so it could be supplied from the sea—and the defenders could retreat to the sea, or all the way back to England—if it was overrun.

Catrin followed Rhys without speaking, letting him concentrate on the ground before him. But once they reached the top of the slope, Catrin stopped suddenly, her heart constricted at the sight of the ruin before her. She had grown up here as much as Rhys, and though she'd had an idea of what to expect, she found tears pricking at the corners of her eyes. Because she'd arrived in Caernarfon from the other direction, on the new road that ran by the Menai Strait to the castle, she hadn't seen the palace earlier.

The prince's palace had been built over the remains of an old Roman fort, with encompassing walls that stretched roughly a hundred yards on each side. Part of the wall ahead of her had been knocked down, allowing her to see the blackened and ruined interior. By Welsh law, each commote—what the English would call a small county—was required to provide a palace for the prince, so he could have a place to stay when he administered to the local people. At a minimum, the palace had to include a hall, quarters for the prince, kitchen and storage areas, stables, a barn, a kiln, a dormitory for the prince's retinue, and a privy.

Today, none of those buildings remained intact.

Rhys stopped beside her. "They say the fire was caused by a lantern knocked over in the stables, and thus an accident, but I wouldn't know if the story is true. It happened over a year ago, before my time."

She nodded dully. The only building still with a roof was the prince's quarters, consisting of an anteroom and his private chambers, though the door was gone and the glass in the windows had been knocked out or salvaged.

They started walking again, following the farm track around the wall. Neither spoke, and she wondered again how Rhys lived with himself. To her mind, the shame in his eyes at the feast was now fully explained: even if he'd betrayed his prince with the best of intentions, the consequences to his people were so dire and long-lasting, he would live the rest of his life with the guilt of what he'd done to them.

The old Roman road had crossed the River Seiont to the south and then run directly north to the palace, where it intersected another road that headed northeast to Conwy. With Llywelyn dead and the palace abandoned, the roads north and south had been diverted around the palace to the west, intersecting now at Edward's castle and making the ancient paved highways nearest the palace only stems off the main road. What had once been a smooth stone surface was now split by vegetation and piled with debris.

To any observer, Edward's message spoke as loudly as if it had been shouted from a mountaintop like a passage from Hosea: *For Israel hath forgotten his Maker, and buildeth temples; and Judah hath multiplied fenced cities: but I will send a fire upon his cities, and it shall devour the palaces thereof.*

Catrin averted her eyes from the desolation before her and asked, "What was happening here three days ago?"

"We were preparing for the king's arrival." Rhys shrugged, and the tug of familiarity was back. To distract herself yet again, she sped up slightly in order to reach the entrance, now missing both great wooden doors that used to block it.

She touched the left-hand pillar, seeing in her mind's eye the hundreds of times she'd passed through the gate as a child, thinking it her right to come and go as she pleased. She'd been the daughter and granddaughter of stewards, cosseted and catered to. In retrospect, in spoiling her, her elders hadn't done her any favors. They certainly hadn't prepared her for her future life.

She found the anger and hatred she held in her heart for Edward rising, and she forced it back down. Those emotions could be useful at times in driving action, but they were ultimately more harmful to her than to Edward, who likely couldn't care less what she or anyone else thought of him. Focusing on how much she loved her family and her people produced the same result with less weight on her shoulders. Even now she could feel a stabbing of tension, like a large splinter, driving into her right shoulder. She stretched her back to ease the pain and in so doing, looked to the right of the road.

"More hoofprints." Catrin pointed to the edge of the path, prompting Rhys to bend to look.

"You're right."

If the horse had stayed on the road itself, it would have been impossible to make distinctions, since the surface was too hard-packed with stone and dirt. But these tracks were isolated and fresh.

"These even I can see." She bent forward too, with her hands on her knees. "When did it last rain here?"

His chin wrinkled as he remembered. "Four days ago, for most of the morning on and off."

"But not since?" Sometimes getting Rhys to impart information was like pulling teeth.

"No."

"If Cole rode here from the northeast, coming from Edward's castle at Conwy some twenty miles away, he would have traveled along the same road my company took. But if he rode towards Caernarfon from the south, he would have traversed the length of Wales and ultimately arrived here, where all roads meet. Or once did."

Standing at the ruined palace gates, Catrin looked south, imagining the scene, how the killer had come upon Cole at the very end of his journey, and what he'd done to him.

Rhys read her thoughts, or merely his were following the same course as hers. "Would Cole stop here only a mile from his destination, in the ruin of the palace at that?"

"You're asking me?"

"Who else do I have to ask? You knew him."

"Only a little." She canted her head as she thought. "Still, he might not have known he had so little distance to go."

"Perhaps he was looking for shelter."

"And even if he did know, he could have stopped to clean his boots and brush the dust from his garments before seeing me."

"Or the king."

She ignored that. "We should continue our search. If we find nothing of note, we can double back and try the more northern road. The barn is located in such a position that finding evidence here doesn't tell us from which direction Cole came. Both roads from Gloucester would have been equally long."

Rhys stepped through the gate and breathed deeply. "How many times were we here together as children?"

"It tugs at one's heart," she agreed, perhaps incautiously. The dappling of sunlight through the fully leafed trees made the palace more serene and inviting than she had feared. It was destroyed, but its spirit was at peace.

Inside the walls, the slate path was overgrown with grass and moss. His hands on his knees, Rhys moved deeper into the complex, shaking his head every now and again as he bent closer to the ground. "You look to the right. I'll look left."

Thus, turning their backs on each other, they progressed through the expansive space. Catrin allowed her instincts to guide her steps, and she fetched up ultimately at the prince's quarters.

As before, hooves had made a distinct impression on the grass and dirt just off the pathway. "Rhys! Come look at this!"

In a few moments, Rhys was beside her. At her pointing finger, Rhys shot her a twitch of a smile and a *thank you* and stepped through the doorway into the roofless house.

He froze.

She peered around him, but he put out his arm. "Give me a moment." Then he left her by the door and hastened into the middle of what had been Llywelyn's private solar. The wooden floor was gone, removed for a building somewhere else, maybe even Caernarfon Castle, leaving packed soil so long dry and sunless that nothing but a few hardy weeds grew there, even after a year.

The fine soil made it easy to see the large patch of earth that was darker in color than it should have been, and when Rhys crouched and swept his fingers through it, they came up adhered with sticky dirt.

Despite herself, Catrin recoiled. "Is that blood?" The sound of her own voice brought her down to earth, and she managed to speak next in a more normal tone, "Cole died here."

"I'd say so, though I can't distinguish human blood from animal." He straightened to his full height before drawing her attention to the ground around him. "Footprints, you'll note. Many of them. Someone was here recently—at least two someones going by the different sizes and types of boots."

"Cole's are the larger ones."

"It does seem they might be." He looked at her. "If the queen knew I allowed you to search with me, she'd have my head."

"Then we won't tell her." Catrin lifted her skirts and started across the room. "I'm having a hard time imagining a turn of events which leaves Cole stripped of his gear and dead in a barn two hundred yards away."

"I'm sorry to say I can think of quite a number of scenarios, none of which I want to share right now without more evidence." He shot her a wry look. "That was just in case you were going to ask."

"I do want to ask, but maybe I won't just yet, like you said, until we know more." She moved to a far doorway, which led to Llywelyn's sleeping quarters. This room was smaller and more intact, in that the floor hadn't been pillaged, requiring her to step up from within the building's foundation to get inside. Footprints were visible on the dust of the floor here too, some of them small, as if children had come here to play, which she didn't doubt. She and Rhys would have, had they been children now.

It felt awkward to be here, as if they were invading Prince Llywelyn's privacy, though nothing of him remained. The room had been stripped long since by either the Normans or the local people, once they knew neither he nor any other prince would be coming back. Catrin followed the interior wall, which it shared with the solar, until she reached a narrow door that stood ajar. Pulling it wide exposed a passage, three feet deep at most, between the two rooms. The back wall was entirely made up of shelving, empty like the rest of the room.

"What was stored here?" she asked Rhys.

"It was the prince's treasure room. He brought his gold with him wherever he went, though his wealth was in cattle more than coin."

"I would have thought it stayed at Aber."

"The piece of the true cross was kept there, too precious to be transported around Wales," Rhys said, "but the prince couldn't leave behind his gold and silver. He had a treasure room in each of his palaces, every one guarded day and night while he was in residence."

Rhys spoke with sadness but no rancor. Their back and forth conversation over the last hour was making her think—and maybe it shouldn't have been a surprise—that their understanding of each other was incomplete. But revising her opinion of him could be dangerous, in case she'd been right all along, and he was as loyal to his Norman masters as she supposed.

And she might not be wrong about him. It could be instead that he was resentful of the fact that his betrayal of Llywelyn had netted him nothing: no station, no land, no wealth. Not even, apparently, gratitude, since her queries about him over the last two days—other than to her brother Hywel—had resulted in shrugs and dismissal. Nobody knew who he was or had been. Nobody cared either.

"My husband had a cupboard such as this. It was accessible only from his counting room where he kept his books and ledgers."

Rhys sighed. "All gone now."

"Not all gone." She bent to the ground and came up with a single silver coin that glinted in the palm of her hand. "Hard to believe this has been lying here all this time."

"It is hard to believe." Taking it from her, Rhys held the coin up to the light coming from the window, which was open to the elements. With the doors gone, there wasn't much point in closing the shutters. "If not impossible. It's shiny still." He rubbed his thumb across it. Then he held it closer to read the lettering. "Minted last year, in fact."

They exchanged a look and then both swept their feet through the accumulated dust. Their search discovered nothing more, however, and as one, without needing to speak of their mutual decision, they turned to leave. But as they stepped outside of Llywelyn's quarters, a gray horse, sixteen hands high at least, greeted them from the grass a few feet away. Its reins were still tied to a stake, which it had dragged to its current position.

"There you are, my beauty." Rhys reached for its bridle. "Did you hear us talking and came to say hello?"

The horse held steady, making no move to run away.

Catrin followed the trampled grass around the back of Llywelyn's quarters to the old stable, which still had a water trough in front of it with two fingers of water in the bottom.

Rhys followed, leading the horse. "She's still wearing saddle bags."

Pleased to have more of the mystery solved, Catrin unbuckled the straps, but her initial excitement dissipated almost immediately when the contents proved to be less than momentous, consisting of a bedroll, a change of clothing, a cloak for rain, and a wrapped cloth containing the remains of a simple meal of bread and cheese, now hard and stale. The strap of a water skin was looped around the saddle horn.

Rhys studied the animal. "I confess to have been assuming the killer used Cole's own horse to transport him to the barn."

Catrin walked all the way around the animal. "I see no blood."

"No," Rhys said heavily.

Catrin shot him a sharp look. "Why does that concern you?"

Instead of answering, Rhys boosted Catrin onto the horse's back. "Up you go."

She settled there, gathering the reins. It was reaching a point where they couldn't continue as they were. She was going to have to confront him, regardless of the consequences, and make him answer all her questions, not just this one.

"It's time I got you back to the castle. At least Cole's horse will have a stable to sleep in tonight."

"Talk to me, Rhys!"

Rhys looked away, obviously reluctant, and began leading the horse with Catrin on it out of the palace. "If Cole wasn't brought to the barn thrown over the back of this horse, the killer had his own, didn't he?"

Catrin gave a little gasp. "Making him a knight or nobleman? It *would* narrow the pool of suspects."

"Alarmingly so." Then he lifted one shoulder noncommittally. "Maybe I'm jumping to conclusions. A farmer with a cart is just as much a possibility."

"Or a wheelbarrow."

"Though I see no wheel tracks."

They headed down the ruined road to where it intersected with the good one coming from the castle. Wide enough for two carts to pass, the road saw a great deal of traffic, though likely less in the middle of the night, if that's when Cole had been killed.

The sound of pounding hooves came to them from the direction of the castle, prompting Rhys to swear under his breath. "We don't have time to hide."

"We're not doing anything wrong."

"I'd rather not draw attention to anywhere we've been, particularly when that place is the scene of the murder."

Rhys brought the horse with Catrin astride it onto the main road, presumably to give the impression they'd been traveling along it all this time. Catrin held the horse steady near the edge, and Rhys stayed with her.

A moment later the horseman came over the western rise.

"It's Dai," Rhys said to Catrin, with surprise in his voice. "He's the assistant to the undercoroner."

At the sight of Rhys and Catrin ahead of him, a look of sheer relief crossed Dai's face, and he reined in to speak to them. "Can you come with me? We've found another body."

11

Day Two

Rhys

The River Seiont emptied into the Menai Strait on the southern side of Edward's new castle. Following the river upstream meant at first heading southeast but then the river looped around the entire region, sometimes heading north, sometimes south, but always east, ultimately originating at Llyn Padarn near Prince Llywelyn's castle of Dolbadarn. Consequently, the road from Caernarfon Castle followed the river initially, but after it merged with the road coming from Llywelyn's former palace, it turned directly south and crossed the river.

Ancient stone footings, presumably also Roman in origin, had once stuck up from the bank above the natural ford. Llywelyn had never seen fit to rebuild the bridge, since the ford was a good one and impassable only in flood. But since the coming of the Normans, the bridge had finally been rebuilt, using the footings as a base as they had not been for centuries.

Their destination turned out to be the sawmill that lay down-stream from the new bridge. Dai followed the mill race before turn-ing into the yard. These days, the mill ran night and day, providing wood for the castle and town. The sawmill was still run by Welsh-men, though with an English overseer.

Catrin had again refused to be left behind, but she kept the horse well back as Dai pointed Rhys to the body and Math the Wa-terman, who was crouched beside it.

Math was seventy years old if he was a day, but he insisted on going out on the river every day, checking his lines and fish traps. Before Llywelyn's death, he'd kept the palace kitchen stocked with trout and salmon. These days, he had a stall in Caernarfontown's market, on the green just outside the town walls, and made three times as much—most of which was tithed to the king before he closed up shop for the day.

"They found him among the reeds in the shallows of the mill pond," Math said in Welsh.

Rhys turned to Dai. "See if you can find the coroner, will you? He needs to know we have another murder."

"Of course, my lord. Should I bring him here?"

Rhys pursed his lips as he considered the issue. "Just warn him we found it. I'll notify him when I've brought him to the laying out room."

Dai nodded and urged his horse back down the road to the castle. Catrin chose at that point to dismount from Cole's mare, but still remained at its head, holding the bridle.

"This is none of my doing!" The overseer of the mill was an Englishman named Robert, a Norman name, but one that was becoming more common among the English populace.

"Please tell me what happened." Rhys took a few steps closer, making appeasing motions with his hands.

His unaccusatory tone calmed Robert, who dropped his arms, having run his fingers through his hair in his agitation. "We heard a clunking sound, and I sent Owen outside to see what was the trouble."

"This is in the waterwheel itself?"

"At the entrance to the mill race." Robert pointed Rhys to the wooden track that took the water from the millpond and sent it into the waterwheel. One sluice gate, which controlled the water in the mill pond, could be opened and closed, depending upon how much water was needed to fill the pond. A second sluice gate controlled the amount of water running from the pond, down the mill race, and into the waterwheel. Then the water flowed out the bottom of the wheel, down another course, and back into the River Seiont.

It was where the water entered the mill race that the body would have stopped, too big to pass the sluice gate. This told Rhys the body had been dumped into the millpond deliberately because, like Cole, the killer had wanted him to be found. Eventually anyway.

Rhys looked at 'Owen', whose proper Welsh name was Owain, and whom Rhys knew from the village where he himself was living. "Is that what happened?" he asked in Welsh.

Owain nodded. "I found the body. The boys and I dragged him out."

"Do you know who this is?"

"No."

Rhys glanced at Owain's fellows, all of whom were Welsh, and all of whom shook their heads. Rhys had the odd realization that he didn't believe them. A job at the mill paid well and was a skilled position that none of them wanted to lose by being implicated in murder. Rhys had the idea to try again later, when the men were alone and Robert wasn't watching. Rhys dismissed the mill workers to their jobs.

"You told Dai it was murder. Was he drowned?" Once they'd gone, Catrin spoke from where she stood, a good ten paces back. She seemed to finally realize the less anyone noted her involvement the better.

"He was stabbed, much like Cole."

Returning to Math, who was still crouched over the body, Rhys looked more closely at the wounds in the dead man's belly. There were three. Again. "Or rather, exactly like Cole."

"Was it the same type of weapon?"

"I wouldn't want to bet against it, though time in the water hasn't been helpful."

The man lay as Owain and his fellows had left him, dragged free of the pond, but not far enough to prevent the water from lapping at his feet. This victim was younger than Cole, perhaps thirty, though with a similar Norman haircut—not cropped short and spiky like Rhys's but longer, with hair past his ears—and shaved chin. Rhys was learning, however, that just because a man looked like a Norman didn't mean he was one. Cole had been English.

The man was also naked, like Cole had been, and even larger than Cole, with huge muscled arms that could have lifted Catrin one-handed and maybe Rhys himself. His body was cold—not just from the water—and his limbs flaccid. Rhys rose to his feet, and one of his knees cracked as it straightened. "Do either of *you* recognize him?"

Catrin made no move to come closer, but her view was unimpeded, and she shook her head. "No."

Math stood too, with a grin at Rhys at how *his* knees were still spry and said, "No reason why you should know him, my lady, but I do. Those boys should have told you the truth, because some of them must know him too."

"Who is he?" Rhys said.

Math let out a puff of air. "At one time I would have said no self-respecting Welshman would have worn his hair like that, but he's one of them ... what do you call them?" He snapped his fingers. "A mason." He said the word as a Norman would. "His name was Tomos."

Welsh people, either by custom or cussedness, had always distinguished themselves from the English and Normans by their appearance. Math apparently thought they should continue to do so. But sooner rather than later, it might be increasingly hard to tell a man's identity by what he looked like. Any man could dress enough like another to be confused for someone he wasn't—at least until he opened his mouth.

And even then, languages could be learned and accents altered. Rhys already knew of several Welsh noblemen who'd changed their names and their appearance when they'd submitted to Edward.

Owain ap Gruffydd ap Gwenwynwyn, a former Welsh lord who'd once tried to assassinate Llywelyn, was now Owen de la Pole.

"Do you know anything more about Tomos?" he asked Math.

The riverman shrugged. "The master mason brought him in at the start."

"I didn't know any Welshmen were still working on the castle these days."

"He was the last. The master mason trusted him, and he was a devil with a chisel. He could turn any stone into something beautiful." He paused. "Tomos had to sleep outside the town at night though, just like you."

As far as Rhys knew, all the rest of the masons were Englishmen and billeted inside the castle grounds or in the town. Rhys's brother-in-law, Huw, was a Welsh mason working at Conwy Castle. If Huw had spoken the truth to Simon, he was keeping his head down and doing as he was told. He had a family to protect, in the form of Rhys's sister, Efa, and their children, so he had more to lose than Rhys himself, which was why Rhys believed him. But Rhys couldn't help seeing Huw's face as he looked down at Tomos's body.

"You also need to see this." Math made a motion to indicate that Rhys should help roll the dead man onto his stomach.

At the sign of the incomplete hexfoil carved into the man's back underneath his left shoulder blade, Rhys recoiled.

Catrin could see too, and she gasped. "It *is* the same hand, Rhys."

He met her eyes, which silently spoke the same words he was thinking: *Oh, that is not good.*

Math looked from one to the other. "I thought it was bad, but you two look like it's worse."

Rhys made a gesture that he meant to be dismissive, but he nonetheless told Math the truth, even if not all of it. "We've seen the symbol before."

"Underneath the other dead man. I heard."

That Math had heard wasn't any kind of surprise. A dead nobleman in their former prince's barn was catastrophic news, which was why Rhys couldn't believe a Welshman was the killer. He would not have left him there unless he hated his own people. Rhys had plotted out a hundred ways to murder several of the Normans of his acquaintance. In every case, he would have made sure the body was hidden permanently rather than putting him on display, lest the reprisals from the castle touch everyone he cared about. That would have been contrary to the entire point.

It wasn't all that easy to get rid of a body, however. Perhaps the killer realized as much and had decided to go in the opposite direction.

"Should we be afeared for our lives, do you think?" Math didn't seem particularly concerned by the idea, even as he broached it.

"I hope not," Rhys said, "but someone killed two men in a single night."

"Two men who, by all appearances, were entirely unrelated to one another," Catrin added.

This was not going to go over well in castle, town, or village. In the years he'd served as Prince Edmund's *quaestor* after returning from crusade and before he joined Prince Llywelyn's retinue, Rhys had brought to justice in the vicinity of fifteen murderers—but only a single instance of a killer who was responsible for more than one death. That investigation had been ugly and difficult, with six murders of street urchins over a two month period. In the end he'd caught the man only because the people themselves had ultimately put aside their reluctance to become involved and stepped forward to identify him.

"Do you have a canvas I can wrap him in?" Rhys asked Math. "I'll get it back to you cleaner than it was."

Math stumped away, heading to a little hut near the dock where he moored his boat—not in the mill pond but on the adjacent river. He went inside and came out with a folded hemp canvas, which he proceeded to lay out on the bank. Then, with a bit of a struggle, convincing Rhys that Tomos weighed as much as both of them combined, the two men manhandled the dead mason away from the millpond, rolled him in the canvas, and heaved the body onto the back of Cole's horse, Rhys doing most of the work, despite Math's determination to help. Rhys could have asked for help from the millworkers, but the less they were involved with Tomos's death, the better.

Breathing harder than he wanted to admit, Rhys glanced at Catrin. "We'll have to walk."

"I am not fragile."

"I can see that." On one hand, he didn't want to encourage her. On the other, she'd been helpful so far, and she was right that she wasn't a girl anymore. He would be wise to stop treating her as one.

They set off, at first in relatively companionable silence—or so Rhys thought—but as the journey wore on, he sensed a growing tension in Catrin that after two hundred yards finally burst out in the form of anger. "How could you?"

"How could I what?"

He spoke before he thought, which perhaps he shouldn't have done. He could guess that this question wasn't about the murder investigation.

"How could you *work* for them after everything that's happened? After what they've done and are doing daily?"

Rhys was taken aback and didn't know how to defend himself or even if he should. If he'd thought at all about the consequences of deceiving her, he should have known she would eventually challenge him on his allegiances. But as the afternoon had worn on, he had forgotten she didn't know.

So he asked carefully, "How is what I do different from what you're doing?"

"How do you know what I'm doing?"

"You are lady-in-waiting to the Queen of England."

"Do you think I had a choice in the matter?"

"Do you think I did?"

She'd been walking with him beside the horse as he led it, but now her stride lengthened, and she got ahead of him. He could see Caernarfon's towers now, so he let her go, though not before calling after her, "Peace be upon you."

It was an old blessing from his time in the Holy Land, and an appropriate counter point to the well of irritation and anger that had risen within him at the way she continued to question and distrust him—which wasn't fair of him since he'd encouraged her to do so and had spent the day trying to get rid of her.

She glanced back, surprise and confusion in her face. But she had the required response to hand anyway. "And upon you, my lord."

Then she hurried off. Rhys kept up enough to make sure she came to no harm, staying within sight behind her. Once she passed into the palisade that protected the tent village on the way to the Queen's Gate that guarded the eastern entrance to the castle, he felt able to turn towards the town gate, bringing his second dead body in two days to the laying out room.

Cole's body was gone, having been transported first thing that morning to the new burial ground on the other side of the river from the castle because there was simply not enough room for a graveyard within the town. Edward's priest had blessed the designated ground, and Cole would lie in his coffin inside another little hut, out of the elements, until his burial as the sun set that evening.

Rhys had attended burials in that graveyard before, and he had to admit that on a fine day like today, with the sun setting into the sea, it felt as if the dead—whoever they'd been and whatever they'd done—were on their way to heaven.

12

Day Two

Catrin

After the discovery of the body at the millpond and her conversation with Rhys, Catrin needed answers more than ever. After some deliberation, she decided the best place to get them was from Aron, the wrongly arrested villager. The fact that Rhys knew Aron was innocent and had arrested him anyway was deeply troubling. The injustice scored her heart. If that was the way he worked, he really wasn't the man she'd known, even if the moment-to-moment experience of being with him was tugging her in the other direction.

Catrin had to know the truth of Rhys before she spent another moment in his company. If his head was truly as bowed as her brothers', who were now serving Edward as wholeheartedly as they'd served Llywelyn all those years, then she really had no place else to turn in this world.

But even as she made her way to Aron's cell, she acknowledged the extent of her own hypocrisy. She'd accepted her brothers' decision to bend the knee to Edward immediately after Llywelyn's death. Why couldn't she accept Rhys's?

Because she expected better from him. Maybe it wasn't fair. But it was how she felt.

She expected better from her brothers too, but she could forgive them for wanting to save their family. She half-believed Tudur—and even more Hywel—that Llywelyn himself had told them to change sides, knowing that Tudur had spent too many years despising Dafydd, Llywelyn's younger brother, to follow him as Prince of Wales after Llywelyn's death. Dafydd's rebellion had been more about *him* and his pride, as everything always was, rather than the people he led. They all knew he was a fraction of the man Llywelyn had been and had himself betrayed Llywelyn too many times.

And she also knew that if her brothers had continued their resistance, all three of them would have died in the aftermath of Cilmeri, along with many of their people. If Llywelyn really had given Tudur permission to abandon him, he was a better leader and man than even the most loyal partisan had supposed.

As Catrin crossed the threshold of the guardroom, the man on duty looked up from where he was leaned against the wall, his stool tipped back on two legs. It took a heartbeat for him to realize he was looking at a noblewoman, after which he leapt to his feet. "My lady!"

"I would like to talk to your prisoner," she said in her best French.

The guard's face lost all expression as he tried to figure out if she was serious. "He speaks no French."

"But I speak Welsh," Catrin said in Welsh.

"So you are one of them." The guard nodded, not so much implying something untoward about her identity as acknowledging a truth, and Catrin had a sudden thought that his accommodating attitude might be the result of Rhys's efforts to cultivate good relations with members of the castle garrison.

Regardless, without further ado, he led the way down the spiraling tower steps to the basement, at which point they were faced with a door composed only of metal bars, which he unlocked with a large key. The cell was round like the room above, with a stone floor, likely necessary so close to the sea, to deter seepage of groundwater. Several sets of chains were attached to the walls, giving opportunity to have more than one prisoner in the cell at a time. The castle might be years from completion, but the prison was in full working order.

The gate swung wide, and Catrin stepped inside the cell. At the moment, it held only one prisoner, and Catrin blanched at Aron's unkempt condition, even after less than a day in chains. Instantly, she realized she'd made a mistake—not in coming, but that she should have brought food and water with her.

"I'm so sorry," she said in Welsh to Aron, and then she turned to face the guard, who still stood in the doorway. "Thank you for letting me see him. Now I need you to fetch food and clean water."

The guard's face lost all expression. Having lived in England for many years, with many English in her employ, she recognized the look as one which meant he was deciding whether or not to argue.

"If he murdered Cole, he will hang, but as Cole was *my* man, I want his killer going to the gallows whole. Please," she paused, determined to convince him but unsure as to how. "The queen would be dismayed that a man would be kept in such condition in the same castle in which she is about to give birth."

This was entirely untrue, of course. There was perhaps no person alive more vindictive than Queen Eleanor—and that was including King Edward. Fortunately, the guard was part of Caernarfon's standing garrison, so he didn't know how little Queen Eleanor cared about any of her people, English or Welsh. She cared about the king, her children, books, and money, not necessarily in that order (though it was true the king always came first).

To Catrin's relief, after another moment of dithering, the guard nodded and disappeared up the stairs, leaving Catrin to crouch in front of the prisoner. "I was a fool not to have brought you something to eat and drink myself. Forgive me."

To her surprise, Aron looked at her with bright eyes. "I confess to being thirsty, my lady, but I am perfectly well, all things considered."

"Do you know who I am?"

"We all do. Welcome home, my lady. We are glad to see you back where you belong."

"I don't know that I will be staying. I'm in the service of the queen now."

He bent his head in a sign of respect. "As are we all, my lady."

"So, how can you say that you are well?"

"Ach, I am not without hope. Iôr Rhys will be seeing to me soon." *Lord Rhys*, he'd called him.

"You can't know that."

"Of course I do." He looked at her with narrowed eyes. "You knew him well once, my lady. How can you not know he will move heaven and earth to get me out of here alive and well if he can?"

Before Catrin could answer, the guard returned with water and a loaf of bread, and such was the effort he'd made that the bread was still warm.

She took it from him with genuine relief and a smile. "Thank you."

He backed out of the doorway. "I'll be in the guardroom."

Once he was gone, Aron sneered and said, "*Mochyn.*"

She frowned. The guard had gone out of his way to help. At the same time, given Aron's current position, it was easy to understand his disdain. "I think he has some English blood, actually."

"Ah, then he is *defaid.*" A sheep.

"I'm sorry you've been caught up in a crime not of your doing. I wish there was something I could do to help."

Aron had already taken a long drink of water, but now he set down the flask. "The fact that you're here is more than enough."

"What do you mean? You are in chains for a crime you didn't commit."

"But it was my choice, wasn't it?" He made a gesture with one hand, rattling his bonds. "The more we are able to take the world for what it is, the more we'll be able to stand with straight backs. Rhys taught us that."

She was glad of the opening. "Tell me about Rhys."

He tipped his head. "Can I trust you? Perhaps you were sent here by the coroner to learn what you could from me."

Catrin drew back in genuine shock. "I wouldn't!" Then she took a breath, completely understanding why he would question her presence. It was pernicious, this lack of trust—and not knowing whom to trust. Anyone could be genuinely working with the king, like her brothers were, and report to him even the slightest infractions of correct thinking. Come to think on it, such was her situation with Rhys.

Aron smiled, having been watching her face closely and reading what she showed there. "Ah, you see it now. Do you understand why I had to ask? Iôr Rhys is risking *everything* for us."

Catrin eased out a breath, endeavoring to get her heartrate to slow. This was what she'd come to hear, and she didn't want to ruin the moment by displaying too much urgency. "How so?"

"You really don't know, do you?" Aron studied her for another long moment. "You think he betrayed our prince." It wasn't a question.

"Didn't he?"

"My lady, he was badly injured and left for dead. It's a miracle he survived."

"Do you really believe that?"

Aron shook his head at her, not to deny but because he appeared to have no words in the face of her suspicions.

"How is it that nobody in the castle knows he rode in Prince Llywelyn's *teulu* and was with him at Cilmeri?"

At the mention of the prince, Aron's hand jerked towards her arm, and he gripped it tightly. "Shush, my lady."

Her lips pursed. "You don't say his name?"

"They know it when we do. Better to make them think we have forgotten him. Submitted."

She couldn't let his dismay deter her. "How can they not know?"

"Who is going to tell them? He was hiding in plain sight—and doing it well—until you arrived." Aron laughed derisively. "The only man any of these *mochyns* ever look directly at is Lord Tudur."

She thought back to her conversation with Hywel. He'd been evasive, even as he'd encouraged her not to judge Rhys.

Aron relented. "We didn't need him to explain that building the castle for Edward would be like allowing ourselves to be conquered all over again, but he was the one who told us to stop sabotaging it."

"Now I really don't understand."

Aron relaxed against the wall, cradling the loaf of bread to his chest. "We resist, my lady, in every way we can, but it does us no good to get caught or lose so many of our number that we are left with only widows and orphans. We resist by teaching our children who we are."

"And who is that?"

He threw out a hand the best he could given the length of chain with which he had to work. "We are part of this land, and it is part of us as long as we don't forget or neglect it. We resist by living. And we resist by not allowing that coroner to put an innocent boy in chains to assuage his pride and because it's convenient." He bounced the flat of his hand off his chest. "I am an old man. Iolo is eighteen, and he is too sweet to survive a day in here without blubbering."

"So you took his place."

"I did." There was unmistakable pride in Aron's posture and voice.

"And Rhys let you?"

"Of course."

"He was never one to lie before."

Aron laughed. "Is he lying? I have never heard him tell a lie. It's more a matter of shaping events so they make sense to those who rule us while leaving us room to maneuver and breathe."

"He has befriended all the guards in Caernarfon. He told me so himself." She was trying to be matter-of-fact.

"And look how it has benefited me. Because the guard knows Rhys, they let you in to see me, and here I am with a nice warm loaf of bread." He tore off a piece and ate it, his expression dissolving into one of pure pleasure. He swallowed before speaking again. "They like him. And that makes them hurt us less."

Catrin was finally beginning to understand the scope of what Rhys was attempting. The risk to him left her breathless.

"What about my brothers? Do they know what Rhys is doing?"

Aron's expression turned into a mockery of innocence. "Know what, my lady?" Then he sobered. "They know he was at Cilmeri, of course. Rhys thinks Hywel suspects he is using his position to protect us, but he hasn't pried, and nobody is going to tell any of your brothers what is better for them not to know for certain. Best that nobody has to lie to the king."

13

Day Two

Rhys

What he was going to say to the king when he went before him with Simon was preoccupying Rhys's thoughts more than the poor fellow before him. Tomos was dead, stabbed the same way Cole had been. Rhys didn't really have much more to say about it than that, but he was doing his due diligence anyway. The king was a far more daunting puzzle.

A shoe scraped on the threshold of the hut. "Another body, eh?"

"Yes." Rhys endeavored not to sigh at the sight of Guy. After all, he had told the guards at the gate to send for the coroner, and here he was.

It was Guy who sighed instead, and though he spoke of the body, his eyes were clearly on Rhys himself, taking in his surcoat with Prince Edmund's crest and the accompanying sword at Rhys's waist. If possible, the corners of his mouth turned down even farther. "Do we know who he was?"

"A mason, working on the castle. According to Math the Waterman, his name was Tomos."

The frown firmly fixed on his face, Guy clearly didn't want to step closer but knew it was his duty. "He looks worse than the last one. Is that because of the water?"

Rhys decided there was no harm in explaining. Guy was going to be the Sheriff of Denbigh, and anything he learned here might be of help to the people there. "Because he was in the water, I am forced to be less clear about the day of death than with Cole's body, but the combination of lack of rigor and decomposition indicates to me he's been dead more than two days and closer to four. In fact, if we ultimately discover that he died about the same time as Cole, I wouldn't be surprised. The question before us now is what these two men have in common that would have led to their deaths?"

"Nothing, surely."

"But they had to, else why would they both be dead?"

Guy gestured to the stab wounds in the man's belly, almost identical to those that had killed Cole. The similarities were unmistakable, even without Cole's body to compare them to. "I see he didn't drown."

"He did not. It's worse than what you see there too." The body had been placed on the table face up, but now Rhys pushed up on the dead man's shoulder to show Guy the incomplete hexfoil carved into his back.

Guy swallowed hard. "The man you sent to find me didn't mention that."

"I didn't tell him. If the people think a crazed acolyte of Satan is loose in Gwynedd killing people, there will be panic. But there is no doubt these two were stabbed in the same way and are both associated with the incomplete hexfoil. It is impossible their deaths are a coincidence."

A satisfied look crossed Guy's face. "The king will be pleased we already have the killer in custody."

Rhys gaped at Guy for just a heartbeat, but then closed his mouth and looked back down to the body. "Did you talk to Aron?" If so, it hadn't been with Rhys to translate.

"Since you were nowhere to be found, I took Dai. The man refused to confess."

"That would be because he didn't do it, my lord."

Guy's chin stuck out. "Of course he did."

"There are witnesses who can vouch for his whereabouts the night these men died. Besides which, it was always unlikely that the man who discovered the body was the killer anyway. You might as well blame Owain or Math for finding the body in the millpond."

Guy's eyes narrowed, and Rhys cursed inwardly for putting the idea into his head. Because of that, he spoke more exasperatedly to Guy than he ever had before. "If you start accusing every man who finds a body of its murder, the people will learn not to report a body when they find one."

Then he cleared his throat, endeavoring to calm himself. He hadn't wanted Guy to know who he really was, but now that he did, Rhys couldn't shy away from using it. Not with a man's life at stake.

"With the king in Caernarfon, any evidence will have to be presented to him, because he will be the one to pass any sentence. If you bring Aron before him as the killer, I will have to speak the truth myself as I know it."

As Rhys was speaking, Guy's face lost all expression. It was almost more disconcerting than if he'd been furious, but Rhys figured if he was going to go down, it might as well be in defense of Aron.

At the same time, Rhys decided that he could throw a bone— and, if he was honest, one for himself as well. "My lord, Aron is a small man, aged. If you look at him closely, he isn't in the best of health either. Will anyone really believe he could have overpowered either Cole or Tomos?" He gestured to the dead man before him. "Look at him!"

Guy didn't like those conclusions, Rhys could tell, but if he was picturing a trial in the hall, as Rhys was, Aron's slight form would provide a sharp contrast to the description of either murder victim.

"They *were* stripped of their clothing and gear," Guy said musingly, "and transported some distance."

"I was barely capable of lifting Tomos onto the horse's back with Math's help. We have to look elsewhere for the murderer." Rhys spoke with a finality he hoped would be compelling.

And to Rhys's relief, Guy was looking more resigned than mutinous. Rhys had a terrible feeling that at some point he was going to pay for disagreeing with Guy. Or he would have done if Guy hadn't been preparing to leave for Denbigh. The moment of departure couldn't come soon enough.

But then Guy ruined everything yet again. "As it is, we will have to report these events and the state of our investigation to the king as soon as possible. This man was a king's mason. Cole was a messenger from the Earl of Gloucester. We can no longer put off our duty."

Rhys kept his eyes focused somewhere near Guy's chin, having noted Guy's *we* and *our*. "When we spoke this morning, Lord Simon mentioned the need to see the king. With the discovery of this new body, I haven't yet had a chance to return to the castle to report what we know." His *we* twisted a bit on his lips as it came out, but Guy didn't remark upon it any more than Rhys had.

In truth, he supposed he might as well get it over with. Even if Simon hadn't arrived at Caernarfon, with this second death, being recognized might have been impossible to avoid.

"May I take it you will release Aron?"

Guy grunted his reluctant assent before adding, "When Lord Tudur offered you to me as my quaestor, he said you'd investigated death before, but he should have told me you'd done so for the king himself."

"Pardon, my lord, but it was in the service of his brother, Edmund." Rhys spoke very carefully, trying to tread the narrow path where he was respectful but also correcting Guy's error.

Guy's expression was still pinched, but he didn't counter that Rhys was splitting hairs. Instead he said, "So what is our next step?"

It was on the tip of Rhys's tongue to mock, to say *it's about time you asked me what I think,* but he refrained and simply answered the question as straightforwardly as he could. "We know his name and where he worked, so we can begin to question the other masons and Tomos's family, if he had one, as to when they last saw him. Did he sleep in his own bed his last night? Was he drinking with his mates?" He grimaced before adding. "Did anyone have any reason to hate him enough to kill him?"

"There has to be something. I'll set my men on it."

"Oh, and also, my lord," Rhys finally looked up and met Guy's eyes, "Lord Simon is concerned that the death of his predecessor, Captain Gerald, wasn't a genuine illness and his death could be related to these other two."

Guy stopped in the doorway, staring. "Do you really think so? Gerald died of the flux."

Rhys shrugged. "So we thought. No hexfoil there, incomplete or otherwise, anyway, and it wasn't as if he was stabbed to death."

"True, but our killer could be getting a taste for murder." He paused. "I think that's an important line of inquiry. You should pursue it as best you can."

Rhys was a little taken aback by Guy's sudden enthusiasm, but the conversation had been so productive, Rhys didn't want to object. He even felt he could venture another suggestion. "If the master mason or his second could come visit me here, we could get some of these questions cleared up right away, so I would be able to pursue this other line of inquiry."

"You should have asked him to come when you sent the guard to find me." Guy's expression reverted in an instant to being superior. It had to have become a habit by now, and Rhys was pleased to see how little time it had taken, a matter of one heartbeat to the next.

"My apologies, my lord. I didn't want to take that step without your approval."

"Wait here for him. I'll send him along." Then he departed.

Rhys heaved that sigh of relief he'd held all this time to have Guy finally gone. He had a headache from all the back and forth; he couldn't imagine what Guy himself was feeling.

Then he pulled his journal, pen, and ink from his satchel and set to work, describing the state of the body and his observations of it so far. He made an attempt to draw the incomplete hexfoil, but he had no hand for it, so he did his best with words.

He was about to throw a covering sheet over the body when his next visitor, Mark, the mason's second, an Englishman, appeared in the doorway. He was closer to Rhys's height, some six feet, than Tomos's greater size, though he shared Tomos's broad shoulders and barrel-like chest. His hands were thick and stubby, and he had what looked to be gray granite dust permanently fixed in his hair.

The last time Rhys had encountered Mark was a few months ago, when Rhys had been investigating the theft of some tools.

"Coroner Lacy sent me to identify the body," he said stiffly in English. "Sir."

In conquering England, the Normans had brought the French language to Britain, making it the language of government and law. The English had proved stubborn, however, and insisted on keeping their own tongue, which gave Rhys hope that the Welsh could keep theirs too.

"Thank you for coming." Rhys put down his pen and picked up a secondary lantern from the table against which he'd been leaning and held it above the dead man's face.

Mark bared his teeth. "That's Tomos all right." He harrumphed. "He was a journeyman dresser and an expert sculptor. I knew as soon as he didn't show up for work that something was wrong. Up until then, he had been very reliable."

"How long ago was this?"

Mark screwed up his face as he thought. "I last saw him at the end of the work day the evening of the day before the king arrived."

Rhys had to pause a moment to work out the day Mark meant. Cole's body had been found in late evening the day after the king had arrived, and it had already passed through rigor. For that reason, Rhys had put his time of death two days earlier—making it possible Cole and Tomos died on the same night. If he hadn't been looking at his second murder, he would have been pleased to have guessed correctly.

"Had he a family?"

"He did. His wife died with their child. That's why he came all the way out here."

"From where?"

"Rhuddlan."

Rhuddlan was a castle and town on the River Clwyd, some distance east of Conwy but still in Wales. King Edward had begun Rhuddlan Castle in 1277, so a mason who worked on it would be well known to his fellow workers, which explained how Tomos had ended up in Caernarfon.

"My lord! My lord!" The high tones of a boy speaking English rang in the street outside the door, and then the third visitor of the day filled the doorway. "Oh." He stopped as his eyes adjusted to the lower light, and he realized who was in the hut and what they were doing in it.

"Can I help you?" Rhys threw the sheet over the corpse. Rhys knew most of the children in the town, few enough of them as there were, and the messenger's name was Johnny.

"I was sent to find you." Johnny's eyes were fixed on the body, even though it was now completely covered. It was unlikely to have been the boy's first dead body, but Rhys didn't want to be responsible for any child's nightmares.

"You're speaking to a crouchback." The mason cuffed him upside the head. "Show respect."

Johnny ducked his head in acknowledgement of the censure. "Sir Reese, I was sent to find you."

By this point, Rhys was torn between wanting to throttle Simon for his meddling and thanking him.

Strangely, Rhys also felt somewhat embarrassed. Before two years ago, he took his station as a knight for granted. Then, when he'd returned to Gwynedd a year ago and deliberately hid his past from the conquerors, their disrespect had made him alternately angry and bemused. Now to be treated well was creating an itching between his shoulder blades, as if he was under intense observation. He always had been watched, of course, but shedding his mask created a situation where more would be expected of him, and he would be even more of an oddity than before. Welsh crusaders were few and far between.

On top of which, the truth was worse (or better, depending on one's perspective) than they knew. It was only a matter of time before the entire castle heard the rest of the story—from Simon in a pinch, but even possibly from the king himself: Rhys wasn't just any crouchback. It might be dawning on Guy only now that Rhys knew the king personally and had been Prince Edmund's personal quaestor. But what he might not yet know was that Rhys had saved Edmund's life at Qaqun in the Holy Land and had been knighted on the spot by the prince himself.

Some part of Rhys wanted to see Guy's face when he found out. The rest was urging him to *run*.

But all he did instead was reassure the boy. "It's all right, Johnny. Why were you sent to find me and by whom?"

"Cole de Lincoln is to be buried at sunset. Lady Catrin awaits your escort to the funeral."

14

Day Two

Catrin

Catrin could have had her pick of a half-dozen men, any one of whom would have jumped at the chance to escort her to Cole's funeral. Guy was one such suitor, John le Strange another. She couldn't shake the feeling, however, that the real reason they were interested in her was not because of her wit, intelligence, or charm but because of the small settlement she'd inherited from her husband. The vast majority of her husband's estate had gone to her son, as was appropriate, but he'd made dispensation for her too.

Even with all that, she had to ask herself why she'd sent the boy to find Rhys. Was it to torture herself? By going to the barn this morning, she'd put herself in his path on purpose, to try to discover the truth about him and what happened at Cilmeri. Now, after her conversation with Aron, at a minimum, she owed him an apology. She'd treated him badly, openly questioning his honor, and he probably never wanted to speak to her again.

She had hardly finished the thought, however, when he appeared before her, with his wise brown eyes and a not-quite-smile that hovered perpetually around his lips. The relief she felt at the sight of him had her turning to put away her needlepoint, but really to hide her welcoming expression, which she had been unable to prevent from transforming her features.

In this case, it wasn't Rhys she was trying to hide from but the other ladies in the room.

By the time she turned back, he was bowing over her hand. "I'm sorry I'm late. I was seeing to the body."

Safe to say, no man of her acquaintance had ever spoken those words to her before. And yet, it felt normal that he would. That opening also provided an opportunity for her to talk about something external, even if it was his murder investigation, and she leapt to take advantage of it. "Were you able to speak to anyone about Tomos?"

"One of the masons came down to the church to identify him."

She had been waiting for him in the women's solar, and they'd been speaking in Welsh, so none of the three other women present could understand them, though they were all looking on with evident curiosity. Remembering her manners, Catrin introduced Rhys, and then allowed him to raise her to her feet and help her with her cloak.

Thankfully, Margaret, the senior lady-in-waiting, was not present, so no more explanation than she was going to Cole's funeral was required. But she could still feel their eyes on her back as Rhys escorted her from the room.

Rhys appeared to take the entire scene in stride, and not until they reached the water gate did he remark on the circumstances of his reception. "You looked surprised to see me."

Her expression turned rueful. "I suppose I was."

"But it was you who sent for me, wasn't it?" His words came not as a retort but somewhat blankly and told her he'd never considered refusing her call, no matter how badly she'd treated him.

Her heart warmed, and she finally acknowledged that her brother had been right: she *knew* Rhys, even after twenty years apart. The needed apology formed on her lips because she didn't want to go another moment with him thinking she distrusted him. But before she could get out a single word, they were interrupted by the arrival of Rolf le Strange, as evidenced by the green chevron on his shoulder.

She pressed her lips together instead.

"My lady." He bent over her hand in greeting. Even without the chevron, she would have known who he was by his slightly oily tone. John was equally abhorrent, but more laconic in his speech pattern.

As Rolf straightened, his eyes slid first to Rhys, who nodded back, and then fixed on her other hand tucked into the crook of Rhys's elbow. Rolf's nostrils flared in annoyance for just an instant, before his expression smoothed. His recovery was so quick, in fact, she almost wasn't sure she'd seen it.

Math the Waterman was ready for them, having brought his boat to ferry mourners across the river to the graveyard. Rolf stepped into the boat first and then held out his hand to Catrin. Since she and

Rhys were still on the dock, she couldn't reasonably refuse, so it was Rolf who helped her to a seat in the bow.

Rhys took the usurpation in stride, though he kept checking Catrin's face. She was trying to keep her expression impassive for Rolf's sake, but also let Rhys know she wasn't happy. With a slight movement of her left hand, she indicated the seat next to her and, without further ado, Rhys stepped into the boat without help, by-passed Rolf, to whom Math had just handed one of the mooring ropes, and plopped himself down next to her. He put one arm behind her, reaching for the rim of the boat to her right, and held onto the rim next to him with his left, stabilizing both the boat and them, and behaving as if he couldn't imagine a better spot in which to find himself.

Rolf turned around and visibly balked at the sight of them sitting so closely together. At first it appeared he was going to try to stand for the journey until Math said, in heavily accented French, "Sit, my lord, or we might go over."

While Rolf obeyed, no happier than before, Rhys leaned in to Catrin to whisper in Welsh in her ear, "Math hasn't allowed one of his boats to capsize in living memory. But I would give a great deal to see Rolf end up in the river." Then, as she hid her smile, he bobbed his head at Rolf and said, "Can you swim, my lord?"

Rolf's chin jutted out. "No." He sneered. "I suppose you can."

"Yes," Rhys said simply.

Catrin elbowed him in the ribs. "That was petty."

"Around him, I can't seem to help myself, and his brother is no better."

"No."

Being united in opposition to someone else was better than not being united at all, but it was a cheap way to foster camaraderie. Unless they found genuine common ground, their friendship would fail in the end. She thought again about apologizing, but even if Math was a friend to Rhys, she didn't want to speak of important things in front of him.

Catrin shifted to try to get more comfortable on the hard wooden seat. Fortunately for her rear, the journey was a matter of yards, and then they reached the little dock on the southern bank.

When the priest had announced the time of the funeral, she had supposed the mourners would consist only of her, Rhys, and the priest. But when they arrived at the grave, they were greeted by a genuine crowd. In addition to Rolf, not only was Guy fitz Lacy present, but he'd brought a half-dozen guardsmen from the castle along with him. Oliver the undercoroner was there as well and Richard de Pulesdon, the new Sheriff of Caernarfonshire. He and Guy were the two halves of the law in the county, with the sheriff responsible for overall order and the coroner primarily interested in the monetary value the king could derive from a death.

To Catrin's mind, it was typical of Edward, who was always strapped for gold, to see even death in terms of money and power. Heaven forbid a man die without the king extracting whatever he could from the loss, usually at the expense of the bereaved family.

The system had been established after the arrival of the Normans, whom, in the early years of the conquest, the English were killing wherever possible. When a corpse of any stripe was reported, the coroner levied a heavy fine on the inhabitants of the associated village, on the assumption that the dead man was Norman. The fine could only be avoided by proving he was English.

So far, here in Caernarfon, neither dead man was Norman, so Catrin wasn't at all sure what role Guy was going to be playing in collecting the king's due. To her, the system of levying fines seemed a good way to encourage local people to immediately bury any body they found and not tell the coroner at all. It was a wonder the villagers hadn't done that with Cole rather than risk pauperizing themselves more than they already were. It was testament, perhaps, of their trust in Rhys to protect them.

The day had dawned sunny, but was ending gray. Gray days in Wales were far more normal than the few sunny ones they'd had, but she would have liked Cole to go out with a sunset.

The actual mass for Cole's soul had happened after she'd spoken to Aron, a service Rhys had not attended. His absence had surprised her initially, until it occurred to her that nobody had told him it was happening, including her. From the few words he'd said, he'd been examining Tomos's body up until the moment she'd summoned him.

Once the gravediggers set to work covering the body, the small group of mourners dispersed.

The priest, accompanied by Rolf le Strange, then approached Catrin. "Thank you for coming, child. You didn't have to."

"I wanted to, Father. I knew Cole for many years, and I would like to tell my son I attended his burial."

The priest bent his head in acknowledgment and moved away. Rolf le Strange bowed also, but when he came up, his eyes were on Rhys. "Your services are no longer required. I will escort the lady home."

Rhys became like an ice statue at a feast. Catrin herself was more than a little confused by Rolf's behavior, since up until now it had been John who'd expressed an interest in her. The men's eyes met for a momentary contest of wills before Rhys actually smiled. "Thank you very much for offering to relieve me of the duty, but the lady herself asked me to escort her to the graveside and back, and that is what I intend to do."

Catrin felt her own shoulders squaring, and she again slipped her arm through Rhys's. "As Rhys said, my lord, thank you so much for your kind offer, but it would be improper to arrive with one man and leave with another, even at a funeral."

Rolf couldn't actually argue with that, but his features became somewhat frozen too, his jaw tight, and he gave her a sharp nod. "Of course. Forgive me for overstepping."

"There is nothing to forgive, my lord," she said sweetly. "I appreciate your gracious offer of escort."

Frustration entered Rolf's eyes, but he could do nothing in the face of her relentless politeness. He turned on his heel and strode after the priest.

Rhys immediately swung Catrin around and began walking with her in the exact opposite direction. The narrow track followed the southern bank of the River Seiont and would eventually take them to the bridge upstream from the mill where the mason's body had been found. It was a bit of a walk, some of which was uphill, and, now that the sun had set, it would grow dark, but he seemed to understand as well as she that anything was better than returning to the castle in the same boat as Rolf.

Catrin went along with Rhys for some distance, until they were no longer visible from the graveyard or the castle, before finally coming to a halt in the middle of the road. "Enough, Rhys."

He stopped too, eyebrows raised. "Enough of what?"

"Don't pretend you don't know."

"But I don't know."

Somehow, yet again, she found herself digging in her heels rather than giving him the apology he deserved, but when it came down to it, the words stuck in her throat. She was angry at him rather than contrite. "This game you're playing."

He faced her. "Game?"

He really was making this difficult.

"Yes. Game. The most dangerous one I have ever encountered, more along the lines of chess than *ring the peg*."

Rhys's tipped his head back to look up at the darkening sky. His hands were on his hips, one foot higher than the other on the sloping road. Then he looked down at her, his eyes searching.

She didn't look away this time and, after a count of three, through which he still didn't say anything, she finally said what she'd wanted to say to him but hadn't been able to. It wasn't an apology for doubting him, but rather a desperate plea: "You were a member of his *teulu,* as your father was before you. On your father's soul, tell me what happened."

She was talking about Cilmeri, and this time he didn't pretend not to understand.

"We were ambushed."

"Ambush or accident? I heard that Prince Llywelyn was separated from the bulk of his army, and the English came upon him unawares. At first they didn't even know who it was they were attacking."

Rhys laughed mockingly. "That's what you were told happened because the truth is rather less noble."

She bit her lip. "Please tell me. I can't bear not to know a moment longer."

Rhys bent his head in a posture she recognized as indicating he was gathering his thoughts, and when he finally spoke, his voice was harsh. "Roger and Edmund Mortimer sent a letter to Prince Llywelyn, begging his forgiveness for opposing him and asking him to meet them to receive their homage. They said they were ready to switch sides and come to terms."

Catrin stared at Rhys, barely breathing. "No. They didn't. That's not what—" At his dark look, she swallowed down her denial and nodded. "Go on."

"The night before Prince Llywelyn's death, we toasted to what we hoped was imminent victory. In retrospect, we were foolish to hope the Mortimer brothers were telling us the truth, but at the time, it hadn't seemed like an outrageous proposition. They had shared ancestry, being descended, with Llywelyn, from princes of Wales. And King Edward had slighted Edmund Mortimer on more than one occasion, even going so far as to refuse to confirm him as earl and as heir to his father's estates, even after he'd confirmed Roger in his. There were few things more important to a lord of the March than his pride, and King Edward had hurt Edmund's.

"Instead of driving a wedge between Edmund Mortimer and the king, the king's disdain moved Edmund to further heights of sycophancy, striving to prove to the king—and maybe to his brother as well—his steadfast loyalty."

"So Llywelyn went to the rendezvous." She couldn't keep the sadness out of her voice.

"Llywelyn had positioned his army to oppose the English forces at the bridge across the Irfon, only a short distance from Buellt Castle. He designated his captains and made his preparations, but then went himself with eighteen of us to meet the Mortimers. We rode blindly into the ambush they'd laid.

"That day, I fought to what I believed was my last breath. In the midst of the melee, I was battling one man when a second confronted me. A blow to my head from the first, followed by a thrust through my midsection from the second, convinced my attackers I was dead."

The look on Rhys's face was so anguished, Catrin knew he was telling the truth, not that he could have lied about something as important as this. Her heart twisted that she'd made him retell it. "But you weren't dead, obviously."

"The blow rendered me unconscious. The thrust to my belly, while bloody and deep, wasn't enough to kill me just yet. I awoke in darkness, face down in the snow, among dead friends and the headless body of our prince." He wet his lips before continuing. "With my own hands, I carried Prince Llywelyn's body away from the battle-field to the Cistercian Abbey of Cwm Hir."

Her head came up, and her eyes were wet, threatening to spill tears down her cheeks. "That was *you*?"

He nodded. "I was ill for many months. By the time I recovered from my wounds, Prince Dafydd had been captured and the war was over."

Dafydd was Llywelyn's younger brother, who'd taken up the fight after Llywelyn's death. Though Dafydd had betrayed Llywelyn multiple times, it was King Edward he'd betrayed in the end, and Llywelyn to whom he'd remained loyal, up until the moment Edward had hanged, drawn, and quartered him and dragged his lifeless body through the streets of Shrewsbury. To this day, both his head and Llywelyn's slowly rotted on adjacent pikes at the Tower of London, a warning to all who dared go against the king. King Edward and Dafydd had been friends since childhood, so Dafydd's betrayal had been all the worse in the king's eyes.

Catrin took a step closer and then another until they were no more than a foot apart. "Why then, when you looked at me in the hall that first night, did I see shame in your eyes?"

"I failed him, Catrin."

She tsked. "If you failed him, then we all failed him. I know now without asking that you did everything you could to save him." At his nearly imperceptible nod, she continued, "How would your death have made anything better for anyone, especially him?"

"Many a day I wished I had died on that field." Rhys's eyes returned to his feet.

It was such a simple statement, but in so much error, and she tried to tell him so, putting all of her own twenty years of sorrow and loss into her voice. "It would have been easier to have died, but then who would have been left to return to Gwynedd, to raise the flag, and to carry on in his name?"

He lifted his head. "Is that what you think I'm doing?"

She put a gentle hand on his arm. "I know you are."

His eyes narrowed. "You *know*?"

"I've asked the right people the right questions."

His expression cleared, and he surprised her by laughing. "Aron. You talked to Aron."

She reached up to put both hands on either side of his face. "Daily you are striving to help our people. And now, I'm going to help *you*."

15

Day Two

Rhys

Perhaps Rhys should have been horrified that Catrin knew all—or at least most—of what he'd been doing since Cilmeri, but instead he found himself delighted—and a little bit impressed—that Catrin had discovered the truth on her own. Still, he was going to have to speak to Aron about letting her in on his secret without his permission.

Not that it could really be called a *secret*. Any piece of information that was known to as many people as knew of Rhys's recent activities didn't deserve the name. It might be that those to whom he reported had an inkling of what he was attempting—some like Hywel, or possibly Simon—and chose to work with the devil they knew rather than the one they didn't.

It was something to consider while he figured out how to make Catrin think she was helping while really he was protecting her too. Of all his endeavors, that might be the trickiest.

"How do you think you're going to do that? Help me, I mean."

"I'm going to help you solve these murders, for starters, and then I'm going to be your eyes and ears in the castle." She frowned. "Since I returned to Wales, I have let my emotions get the better of me. It may be that some of the other women realize I am less than fond of what the king has done to my country. I am sure the queen knows, because she told me so, even if I didn't admit it. In future, I will work to temper my impulse to be so open."

"No." Rhys was firm. "Don't change a thing. You must be yourself at all times." He started walking towards the bridge again. "They'll know something is wrong if you suddenly change who you are. It might be better, however, if you spent less time with me."

She had started walking with him, but now stopped abruptly again. "Is that what you want?"

He stopped too and found himself unable to lie. He'd become good at evasion over the last year, but outright falsehoods still eluded him. "Of course not."

She hooked her arm in his again. "Then to snub you would be to contradict what you just told me to do, wouldn't it? We are child-hood friends, and you are conducting an investigation into the death of my son's retainer. It would look odd if we didn't associate."

Rhys had to admit that was true.

"So let's start as we mean to go on. It seems we know how these men died, but we are no closer to understanding why they died and who could have done it. And the incomplete hexfoil?" She shook her head. "It makes me fear there will be more deaths."

"I'd be happier if you didn't say that out loud." They reached the bridge, crossed it, and then turned downhill, heading towards the castle. "Unfortunately, I also fear you might be right."

"So what's our next step?"

"It's usually a matter of poking my nose into the business of as many people associated with the victims as I can. In this case, that's a little more difficult, since Cole's only known associate was you, and Tomos the mason had no family. I suggested to the coroner that he speak to Tomos's fellow masons. Given that Guy was at the funeral, I am unsure if he took my suggestion seriously."

"Why don't we do it now?"

"They will have finished work for the day, and I am expected in the hall. Finally." He grimaced. "I have a long-awaited audience with the king."

She glanced at him, undoubtedly noting the grimness of his tone. "You don't sound very happy about it."

"This may be a very difficult meeting, at least on my end. I kept him in the dark about my whereabouts and even that I was alive. I find it unlikely he will take kindly to being deceived."

"You didn't lie to him, though, did you?" Her brow furrowed. "You never do actually lie."

"The finer points of deception will mean little to the king, I assure you. He will view it as a lie, even if only of omission, and not understand."

"Is that because he's known you so long? You served him before?"

"I did."

"Will you tell me?"

It wasn't something he had ever really talked about before, but he found himself telling Catrin anyway. He'd never set out to become a quaestor, and his first foray into investigating murder happened on Rhys's own initiative, because he was a meddler, as Simon would say and had said at the time. One of the king's men had been found dead in Acre, and while the impulse had been to blame a Saracen for the murder, the actual killer had been a fellow soldier, a rival for a woman's affections. The killer had taken the man's purse and left him for dead in an alley to make the death look like a random robbery.

Rhys had tracked down a witness to the crime, a ten-year-old boy, who'd seen the killer leaving the alley with blood on his tunic. But a ten-year-old Muslim boy was no valid witness. Rhys knew who'd done it, but had no proof until, confronted with a blood-spattered tunic, the killer gaped and incautiously said, "That isn't mine! I burned it after—"

Too late, he realized what he'd said. Truly, though the actual insult had been petty, the man's grudge had been great. If he hadn't confessed, Rhys would have had to let the matter go.

Prince Edmund, in whose service both murderer and victim had served, had been impressed with Rhys's cleverness, having known about the false evidence in advance. Simon and Rhys had been of relatively low rank at that time, and both had been promoted, which had placed Rhys in a position to save Edmund's life a month later.

But that had been in battle, a skirmish really, and all Rhys had been doing was fighting for his own life. The fact that he'd saved the prince's in the process was sheer coincidence and blind luck.

Simon refused to allow Rhys to say that out loud, and both had then been knighted for their bravery. Edmund had kept Rhys close after that, and he'd investigated for both princes in the years afterwards. War changes men, and for some, killing starts to come easy, as it did for the man in the alley. Still, even at those times, Rhys's association with the king had been peripheral and only at the behest of Edmund.

"So that's why you're not looking forward to seeing the king," Catrin said. "I think the king has more pressing concerns than punishing you."

"I hope you're right."

When they arrived at the great hall, Simon motioned them to where he was sitting near the top of one of the long tables. Even were a dozen lords not attending the king at Caernarfon, Simon was not high-born enough to sit at the table with him. And as the captain of his guard, it wasn't his place anyway.

Rhys held the back of the only chair, set at the end of the table, for Catrin, who accepted it. "Simon, this is Catrin ferch Goronwy, sister to Lord Hywel and Tudur. Catrin, this is my friend and long-time ne'er do well, Simon Boydell."

Simon stood to take Catrin's hand, and when he sat again, his eyebrows were nearly in his hairline, but he didn't comment in the dozens of ways he could have. If he had, Rhys would have kicked him under the table, whether or not Simon was his boss now.

What Rhys really didn't want was to be teased. Yes, Catrin was a widow and lovely, at least to him, though she wasn't conventionally beautiful by current standards. Her hair was red, for starters, which was deemed less desirable, and very curly, a second mark against her. Her eyes were neither green nor brown but somewhere between the two and outlined by dark lashes. She was freckled, and she had a bump on the bridge of her nose, which she'd broken before the age of ten, thankfully not Rhys's fault, though he'd been there.

But when she smiled, the room filled with sunshine, no matter how late in the day. She was smiling now, and Rhys had to forcibly turn himself away in order to think. He motioned towards the high table, which was full of diners, but the king's chair was empty. "Where is the king?"

"You just missed him. He has retired to the queen's quarters for the evening and isn't to be disturbed. You have a temporary reprieve."

"But he knows I'm here?"

"He does."

Rhys took a long drink of his mead, trying to settle his thoughts. "How did he take it?"

"He showed little emotion beyond a slight narrowing of the eyes."

That couldn't be good. Putting down his cup, Rhys rested one elbow on the table and his chin in his hand. "You never finished our conversation yesterday. What can you tell me about these three *incidents* that endangered the king?"

Simon's mouth opened, his eyes flicking to Catrin and back to Rhys.

"Catrin is lady-in-waiting to the queen. She isn't the one who perpetrated them. You can trust her."

"If we are talking about what I think we're talking about, I already know something of what you speak," Catrin said softly. "At least I think I do."

Simon's own eyes narrowed. "According to Prince Edmund, the king tried to keep them quiet."

"I was present for one. The queen confided in me and Margaret about another." Catrin tipped her head. "I confess I didn't know about the third."

Rhys turned to look at her. "The queen must really trust you."

Catrin's expression turned dubious. "I suppose she does. I haven't much thought so, but she knows that I don't gossip with the other women." She looked back to Simon. "My man was the first of the dead. And I have already helped Rhys in the investigation. Guy is next to useless, so why not take help from wherever it's offered?"

Simon laughed under his breath. "You always were unconventional, my friend."

"That's why I got results." Rhys suddenly found that he was starving, and he pulled a trencher off the stack and started loading it with roast mutton and sautéed parsnips. "Speak."

Simon sighed, resigned, it appeared, to his fate. "In the first instance, the king's horse nearly threw him—and would have if the king weren't such a great horseman. The beast was found to have a burr under his saddle."

"It could happen to anyone," Rhys said.

"It could, but the stable lad was flogged anyway."

Catrin wrinkled her nose in distaste. "I assume he claimed it wasn't there when he saddled the horse."

"As he would." Simon said. "It wasn't until the second instance that we began to rethink the first: the king's cook found hemlock root amongst the parsnips intended for his table."

Rhys froze with his fifth parsnip halfway to his mouth. He set down the knife with the parsnip still stabbed onto it. "And the third?"

"It was another incident while out riding. A hunting arrow narrowly missed him and killed the guard behind him."

Rhys was gaping at Simon. "Where was this?"

"On the road to Conwy from Rhuddlan."

Rhuddlan was where the king had proclaimed his new statute annexing Wales to England, so it was no wonder someone had taken a shot at him. Still, it was shocking how close the king had been to death.

"That's the one I knew about, which prompted the queen to tell me about the incident with the horse," Catrin said. "I didn't know about the hemlock."

"Did you catch the archer?" Rhys asked. "I'm assuming it was an archer rather than crossbowman, and you really do mean *arrow* rather than *crossbow bolt*."

"It was an *arrow*. And no, we never even found his roost."

"But you think it was a Welshman?"

"The arrow came from a bow."

"You don't have to be Welsh to loose an arrow. And he wasn't a good enough shot to hit his mark."

"True. In addition, no Welsh cooks were preparing the king's food when the hemlock incident happened, and the one with the burr took place in England, without a Welshman in sight."

"I suppose it's some consolation that the perpetrator doesn't appear close to the king or embedded in the royal court itself," Rhys said.

"Which brings us to the incomplete hexfoil," Simon said. "Could it be related to the incidents you investigated in the Holy Land that also touched upon the king?"

"Surely not. That was years ago and half a world away." Rhys's first instinct was to deny, though in retrospect he wasn't sure why.

"You always thought, even at the time, that we hadn't destroyed the nest." Simon gestured with the stem of his goblet to encompass the hall, but he was referring to the murders. "I'm inclined to think you were right."

"The Baphomets wanted to bring down the Templars. Any wrath directed at King Edward was a sideline, a product of his support for them."

Catrin had stilled beside them and now raised her hand to ask, "Baphomets?"

Simon eyed Rhys. "You are the one who insisted we speak openly in front of her. You tell her."

Rhys looked at Catrin. "The Baphomet were a group of rogue Templars who were accused of worshipping Satan."

Simon scoffed.

"You didn't believe it?" Catrin asked.

"Neither of us did," Rhys said. "Even with the loss of Jerusalem to the Muslims, the Templars are one of the most powerful and influential organizations in Europe and the Holy Land. Kings and princes throughout Christendom owe the Templars vast sums of money, and the Templars control great tracts of land—entire kingdoms when all put together. Some of their number—more than those who became the Baphomets—think they've lost their way and need to be reformed. The Baphomets we encountered in Acre distrusted the Templars' excesses to the degree that they wanted to bring down the order."

"Have you ever met a Templar?" Simon asked Catrin.

"Only once or twice in passing."

Rhys gave a little snort at the memories he had in abundance. "Many are arrogant."

"Like any knight," Catrin said mildly. "A knight must be a little bit arrogant to do what he does."

"That may be, but some say they have grown too powerful for a monastic order and threaten the reign of kings and popes alike."

"France, in particular, is not a friend," Simon said. "King Louis died on crusade before Edward and Edmund arrived in the Holy Land."

"Of dysentery, wasn't it?" she asked.

"Yes," Rhys said. "But some blame the Templars for failing to act sooner to contain the Saracens."

Catrin appeared to take the explanation in stride and merely said, "Cole never went on crusade. He certainly wasn't a follower of Satan."

Rhys let out a puff of air. "Of course he wasn't, any more than any of the men we captured in Acre were. Baphomet doesn't refer to anything at all—a god or otherwise. It was a society created to deflect attention from the dissenters, to disguise their identity and numbers. Their intent was to distract from their true purpose. While a big show was going on over here," Rhys wiggled the fingers of his right hand, "nobody would be looking at what was going on far more quietly over here." Now he wiggled the fingers of his left hand.

Catrin straightened in her seat. "That I understand."

As it was exactly what Rhys was doing every day, he hurried on. "*Baphomet* itself is a corruption of a name the Templars sometimes called the followers of Muhammad."

Simon made a shushing motion with his hand. Rhys's voice had risen as he'd been speaking. "Our opinions on the Baphomets are not universally shared."

"They aren't shared by anyone," Rhys said. "That doesn't mean we're wrong."

"What makes King Edward support the Templars if he resents owing them money?" Catrin asked. "I would have thought he'd want them weakened."

"A weak Templar order might call in his debts," Simon said matter-of-factly. "Edward knows that. And the Baphomet know that with Edward gone, his son Alphonso would be malleable."

"Which is all very well and good," Catrin said, "but it doesn't explain why they might care in the slightest about a messenger from Gilbert de Clare or a mason at Caernarfon Castle."

"Because their intent then and now is not only to kill the king, but to make him fear their coming," Simon said firmly. "A follower is here. Someone we missed."

Catrin sat back in her chair. "And the incomplete hexfoil?"

"The renegade Templars etched the symbol at crossroads or on walls," Rhys said. "Sometimes they paid beggars to do it for them. Their intent was to spread fear and expose the impotence of the Templars to control them."

"The opinion at Temple Church at present is that the Baphomet threat has been neutralized," Simon said.

"But the symbol remains." Rhys tipped his head to Catrin. "Fear of it is truly widespread when people in a village at the end of the world know what it is."

"They know it's an incomplete hexfoil," she pointed out. "They don't know where it comes from or its original meaning."

"She speaks the truth, Rhys."

"Which is why I still am not ready to concede the Baphomet are here," Rhys said.

Ironically, it was the crusaders themselves who brought the symbol home from the Holy Land. By talking about it, they had perpetuated it.

The first time Rhys had seen it, only a few weeks after he and Simon had returned to Britain, someone had drawn an incomplete hexfoil five feet wide in the dirt at a crossroads. A priest had pushed his way through the crowd that gathered around it, and Rhys had still been innocent enough, despite his sojourn in Acre, to tell him exactly what it was supposed to represent and where he'd last seen it.

He should have claimed not to know, though likely it would have done no good. It was already too late to stop the symbol's spread and the fear its supposed meaning engendered. But even that first day, Rhys hadn't seen an attachment to Baphomet in the minds of the populace, if the association had ever been known. It became a sign of Satan, used by some as a warning that a demon was close, and by others—few enough, he suspected—to summon one. It was the kind of thing two young lads might dare one another to draw, since cursing another person was the worst thing they could imagine doing.

Simon was still explaining for Catrin. "After we returned from crusade, as was often the case in situations like this, the initial hysteria eventually died down."

Rhys shifted in his seat. "I certainly don't like the idea of it rising again—"

"—especially not in the vicinity of the king," Simon finished for him, "who will know exactly what it is and what it means." He sighed. "Now, more than ever, we have to tell him what we know."

"We'd better have a plan for how to proceed before we do so. Anything less and it will look like we are as incompetent as I feel right now," Rhys said.

Simon grunted. "If either Cole or Tomos had something to do with the Baphomet, we will root out the conspirators. And if either was killed by a Baphomet—" Simon left the sentence hanging.

Rhys nodded. "We will root out him too."

Catrin, however, was no longer listening, her attention having been caught by a commotion at the door. Then the voice of Gruffydd, the village headman, bellowed in Welsh above the heads of everyone in the hall. "My lord! The townspeople are marching to burn the village!"

16

Day Two

Rhys

In an instant, Rhys was on his feet and racing toward the door. Only he and Catrin had understood the Welsh Gruffydd had spoken—and he hadn't said *townspeople* either, but *defaid*, sheep, the Welsh slur for Englishmen. Gruffydd knew little to no French—certainly not enough to convey what needed to be conveyed in the heat of the moment.

Rhys's presence might not have been enough to stop the guards from marching Gruffydd to the dungeon for disturbing the peace of the hall, but Simon's arrival hard on Rhys's heels was another matter entirely. They released Gruffydd, and he went to Rhys, grasping him by the upper arms in his urgency. "I was at the Queen's Gate to inquire about returning to work, like you said I should do, now that someone more reasonable is in charge—" here Gruffydd bobbed his head in Simon's direction, "—when my boy found me. He'd been to the city gate and seen them gathering, hundreds of them, he said, with torches, saying they were going to burn out the evildoers."

"How did he know that was their purpose?" Catrin had appeared on Rhys's other side.

"He speaks a little English, does my boy. Impossible language, if you ask me, but he knows it. He can count too, thanks to Sir Rhys. I sent him back to the village running, but I can only hope he'll be in time to warn everyone."

Rhys turned to Simon and explained what Gruffydd had said. Simon's expression, already grim, darkened. "Just what we need."

Rhys cast around the hall. "I don't see Guy or our new sheriff."

"They retired when the king did," Simon said. "You and I will deal with it."

"May we be of assistance?" Rolf le Strange came to a halt a few paces away, flanked by his brother, John. Even side-by-side, Rhys couldn't tell them apart but for the chevron on their shoulders.

"By the saints, yes! Gather your men. Every last one of them." And Simon quickly explained what was happening.

Rolf frowned. "We could let them—"

Simon turned on him, glaring so hard it was like flames were shooting from his eyeballs. It wasn't Simon's place to berate a lord of higher rank, but he did it anyway. "This is a land of law and order. The king does not countenance anyone taking justice into their own hands. And he certainly doesn't approve of the murder of innocent women and children."

Rolf took a step back at Simon's adamancy, but he also nodded. "Of course." He began sending men and guards every which way, most to saddle up and be prepared to ride.

Now Simon turned to Rhys. "Go now. I know you can ride without a saddle, and you're not in armor. Take whatever horse is free first. Get your people out. They'll listen to you, and none of us could make ourselves understood anyway."

Rhys was out the door in a flash, as he perhaps should have been the moment Gruffydd had told him the news—except, without the help of Simon and, God help him, Rolf, he could have done little beyond affirming the warning of Gruffydd's boy. But if he knew a higher authority was on the way, Rhys could possibly delay the vigilantes until help arrived. He would have hauled Gruffydd after him, but he had been on a horse's back maybe five times in his life and would only slow Rhys down.

He ran towards the Queen's Gate. Someone had just arrived because a stable boy was walking a horse towards the hitching post. Rhys intercepted him and took the horse, mounting just inside the gate. The stables themselves were located outside the castle because there was simply no room inside for anything that wasn't strictly necessary to either the king's retinue or the castle's construction.

And then Catrin caught the bridle. "Take me too. The horse can carry two that far, and I can help."

His first instinct was to keep her safe, but she was right that the two of them could cover more ground once at the village, which didn't have a bell or any kind of central alarm (an oversight he would remedy tomorrow). And unlike Gruffydd, she'd learned to ride as a child.

He reached down and hauled Catrin onto the horse's back behind him. Then he spurred the horse through the gate, and they raced between the lines of workers' tents and huts towards the entrance to the encompassing palisade.

"Open the gate! Open the gate!" He shouted the words in his best French, and the guards hastened to obey, not knowing in the dark whom they were obeying but assuming anyone on horseback wearing Prince Edmund's sigil had the authority to tell them what to do.

Then the horse was through and faced with an immediate choice as to which direction to ride. Catrin swung out an arm to point north where lights bobbed along Edward's new road. Those lights appeared to belong to stragglers to the main party of townspeople, but it was enough to tell him that, since the vigilantes were taking the northern road by the River Cadnant, he should take the southern one along the River Seiont, past the old palace and St. Peblig's church. The little Welsh village lay almost due east of the old palace, at a lower elevation along the River Cadnant. It was reachable by a lane off both main roads.

The crowd of vigilantes had a significant head start, but they were hampered by their numbers and the fact that they were walking, while Rhys's borrowed horse could cross the distance at a gallop. Which it proceeded to do. Coming down off the rise on the other side of the church, he raced through the village to the far end and pulled up at the last, most western, house. When the party of townspeople arrived, it would likely be the first house they threatened.

There was no sign of Gruffydd's boy, but in the distance to the west, lights bobbed, still a good half-mile away. They had less than a quarter of an hour to get everyone out.

Catrin slid off the horse. "I'll wake the people here. You can cover more ground with the horse, and they know you anyway. They'll heed your voice."

Rhys didn't argue. They were here now, and the whole point of her coming was to split up the work.

"Awake! Awake!" He urged his horse back up the lane, shouting as he rode, and by the time he'd ridden back to the green, he could hear people stirring. Not everyone would have been asleep already, but people did tend to settle in once the sun went down because they rose with the dawn to work.

"What is it?" Aron appeared at his front door, scratching the back of his head.

"You're free!" Rhys's spirits lifted at the sight of the older man. Something had gone right today.

"Thanks to you, my lord."

Rhys dismounted, talking as he did so. "The townspeople are marching towards the village. They intend to burn it to the ground." There didn't seem to be any point in breaking the news gently.

"Right." Aron spun on his heel. "I'll see to my lot. We'll get to the church, yeah?"

"Yes." Rhys hadn't thought that far ahead, but it made sense. Even vigilantes might be hesitant to burn St. Peblig's with people inside.

His heart was pounding in his ears as he went from house to house, waking some and rousting others. He hadn't ever noticed how aged the villagers had become, but it shouldn't have been a surprise. After Llywelyn's death, it was Gwynedd that experienced some of the worst of the fighting. With so many men dead in the war and widows and children fled, life only now was beginning to return to what could even remotely be called *normal*. The number of elders meant fewer than he'd hoped had heard his shouting. Many would have to be woken by hand.

Iago and Mari, the courting couple, were not together as it turned out, but Iago took it upon himself to wake her and the rest of her family, since Gruffydd remained back at the castle. By the time Rhys emerged from a third house, Gruffydd's son had arrived, limping on an apparent sprained ankle but joy in his face to see the entire village on the move.

"Rhys!" Catrin's call came from the western entrance to the town. "They're here!"

Rhys turned to look just as a flaming arrow arched through the air and hit the dirt a few feet from where Catrin stood. Rhys shouted at her to come to him at the same moment she did the exact opposite, lifting her skirts and running towards the oncoming townspeople, screaming at them in English to stop, that they were going to kill innocents. He ran after her.

None of the townspeople appeared to be listening or maybe even hearing her because a second arrow flamed, this time hitting the thatched roof of the last house. Villagers were wailing all around him, and then Rhys found a girl of ten arresting his headlong run by hanging onto his arm.

"My granny won't come!"

"What?" He looked down at her as she tugged on his sleeve.

"She says no *defaid* is going to drive her out of her home, and she'll die in her bed or nowhere."

Cursing, Rhys followed the girl into a house not far from the one currently in flames. The girl fell to her knees beside her grandmother's bed. "You have to come, *Mamgu!*" That was Welsh for grandmother.

The woman was skin and bones. "I won't!"

Rhys bent to her. "You're not going to die today, not by their hand, not on my watch."

"They won't force me out of my home!"

"It can be rebuilt." Rhys spoke gently. "She's not ready to lose you, not this way."

The grandmother glanced at her granddaughter, who had tears streaming down her cheeks. Then her wrinkled chin firmed. "Where are we going?"

"To the church."

Taking her words as tacit permission, Rhys scooped the grandmother into his arms, noting that his saddle bags would have weighed more than she did, and carried her from the house.

17

Day Two

Catrin

Instinct had made Catrin run toward the oncoming crowd of angry townspeople, and instinct made her stop twenty paces from them. She had her arms out wide, waving them, and she was close enough that the leader, a tall black-bearded fellow, could see her by the light of the torch he carried.

"Stop! You have to stop!"

She spoke in English, which he understood, and it seemed the sight of her was enough to at least slow the horde's progression. It was helpful too that the people behind him had already walked a mile from the castle to reach the village. It wasn't a difficult walk by any means, but it might be that a few of them had sobered up in the time it had taken.

The man flung out his hand to their sole archer. "Light another one, John!"

The fact that the young man in question had almost killed her a moment ago didn't seem to daunt him, since he obeyed instantly, laboriously lighting the shaft of another arrow. He wasn't a very good shot, but if he shot enough arrows, he would eventually kill someone.

"Stop it! Stop it!" Catrin planted herself in front of the archer instead of the leader. "Why are you doing this?"

The young man laughed, despoiling her air with the smell of ale. "They're murderers! All of them!"

"They're women and children!"

By now the group had started moving again, some already past her, and she hiked up her skirts and got in front of them again. Ahead of her, she could see Rhys emerge from a hut with an elderly woman in his arms. His horse was being held on the green by a tall woman, which likely was the only reason it hadn't bolted, given the flames.

By now, the townspeople had reached the first hut, the roof of which was engulfed in flames, and their leader began pointing people towards other houses. "That one!" he said, gesturing a torchbearer to the house from which Rhys had just come.

Catrin ran to the horse and scrambled onto its back, cursing the length of her skirt, which she had to tuck up around her knees.

Then she urged it directly towards the initial torchbearer, whom she took to be the leader. She could hear Rhys shouting in Welsh from behind her for her to stop, but it was as if all her suppressed loss and anger and grief was on the surface. She couldn't stop for him. She couldn't stop for anyone.

That is, until a bellow came from behind her, this in French. "By all that is holy, you will go no farther!"

She couldn't help but rein in and turn. It wasn't Rhys's voice but one she knew better, simply because she'd spent the last year in the company of the man's wife.

King Edward was standing in his stirrups, gesticulating and shouting, now in clipped English with a few of the words he knew—chief among them being, "Stop!"

A host of mounted men flowed around him, already starting to corral the townspeople. Three huts were alight, but more men had dismounted, Simon among them, and they were organizing a chain of buckets of water from the river.

The king settled back in the saddle, and because his eyes were on her, Catrin trotted the horse to where he waited.

"Thank you, sire," she said simply. "If you hadn't come—" She found her throat closing at the thought.

"I will not have disorder!" He was angry, but then he put out a hand to her. "Where's that truant, Reese?"

Catrin couldn't lie. "There, sir." She pointed to where Rhys was just passing off to a young man the elderly woman he was carrying and called his name.

Rhys turned, saw the king, and, to his credit, didn't hesitate or waver. He made his way straight over, striding out with his long legs. When he reached them, he caught the bridle of Catrin's horse before bowing his head. "Sire."

King Edward glared at him. "After you see to your people, you'll be finding out who incited the townspeople to violence."

"Yes, my lord."

"Damn fools. As if I didn't have enough to worry about. And you!" the king turned to Catrin. "What were you thinking?"

Catrin swallowed hard. "I was trying—"

"It's just a house. Not worth losing your life over." His anger was cooling, and he spoke his next words more calmly. "Homes can be rebuilt, but you are irreplaceable. I can't have Eleanor upset."

"No, my lord."

Abruptly, the king turned his horse's head and trotted it to where Simon was conferring with three other men. At the sight of the king coming towards him, Simon detached himself too. Catrin couldn't hear what they said to each other, but then Simon snapped his fingers, and four of the cavalry aligned their horses with the king's in a protective stance, and rode away south, heading for the church and, ultimately, the castle.

Rhys put a hand on Catrin's calf. "You should follow."

"No." She looked down at him, and then slid off the horse as if she was snow melting off a roof. A heartbeat later she'd wrapped her arms around Rhys's neck. He clenched his arms tightly around her waist.

"I was so scared for you," he said into her hair.

"And I for you."

18

Day Three

Rhys

It was going to take more than a few hours to recover from the night before. The smoking ruins of the burned huts in the village would ensure that. But nobody had died, thank goodness, and Simon had passed out coins from his own purse, probably totaling an amount of far more value than what had been lost. Rhys would have given out coins himself had he any to give.

One house was a total loss, but the other two were only damaged, and their inhabitants had found beds amongst their neighbors. Simon had taken the ringleader and the archer into custody and promised they would be locked up until they could get to the bottom of what had happened. The rest, much chastened and subdued, even if only temporarily, had returned to the town. Whatever the end result, Rhys didn't have much hope for improved English-Welsh relations, if such a notion had ever been possible.

Though Rhys gave up his bed to Catrin, he managed a few hours' sleep on a pallet on the floor in the kitchen, before rising at dawn to begin work again. He returned some hours later, having, among other things, been to see Simon at the castle. He found Catrin sitting at the table at breakfast with Sian, Gruffydd's wife. It was a sight he could easily get used to.

Before, as a noblewoman and lady-in-waiting to the queen, Catrin had been uncertain of her welcome in the village, but her actions had transformed the villagers' perceptions of her, and she was now one of them, as she had been as a girl. Gruffydd's wife appeared to be treating her like a long-lost noble cousin. Rhys had some hope the events of the night would make Catrin feel like she had done enough that she wouldn't see the need to involve herself any more in his investigation.

He had a terrible feeling, however, it would make her only want to help more.

"My lord Rhys!" Sian was around the table to greet him with a totally unexpected hug. As a rule, the Welsh were more demonstrative than the English, but she had never hugged him before, as if he were family. "You and Lady Catrin bless our house with your presence! It is wonderful to see you together again. I well remember the two of you rambling the lanes as children."

Catrin smiled too, but then the light in her eyes dimmed a little. "It was a long time ago. So much has changed."

"Very little for the better, my lady," Gruffydd said, "except for you."

Catrin shook her head, but Gruffydd wasn't wrong, and it had nothing to do with what she looked like. Perhaps that was all the royal court cared about, but if it was, they were missing the entire point.

At sixteen when she'd married, her red-hair and freckles didn't fit the feminine ideal, but she'd had a slender figure, dainty wrists and ankles, and pale skin. Among the nobility, the more slender a woman was the better. With childbirth and maturity, Catrin had developed a woman's curves, and Rhys had been pleased to see her set to her food last night with a genuine appetite.

And that was really the best thing about her: she was fully and totally *alive*. Since Llywelyn's death, much of the time Rhys himself had felt like a walking dead man. In his conversations with his countrymen, few could see the point of doing much more or hoping for much more than to keep body and soul alive. Even the children's play was more subdued than he remembered.

Not Catrin. Her innate joy filled not only her but the room, and from the reactions of Gruffydd's family, it wasn't just Rhys himself who realized it.

In his mind's eye, he saw again the way she'd thrown herself between the townspeople and the village, careless of her own wellbeing, and he shuddered. That had been too close. He could feel his hair turning grayer at the temples just at the memory.

Catrin made room for Rhys on the bench beside her.

"I should be escorting you back to the castle."

"There will be time enough for that."

"The queen has no need of you in the mornings?"

"I never know when she's going to need me, morning, noon, or night. The last few days, she's been awake on and off all night and very out of sorts. Her back aches. I sometimes sing to her."

"The babe's time is near then," Sian said knowingly.

"So the midwife thinks."

"She'll have missed you, then," Rhys said.

"Perhaps. I will apologize."

"You have nothing to apologize for, my lady," Sian said. "You saved us. Surely the queen can appreciate that."

Rhys wasn't so sure, but instead of arguing he said, "You won't be going without an escort again."

"I am perfectly capable—"

"Not after last night, not to mention the fact that there's a murderer on the loose."

She sobered instantly. "You are right. I didn't think."

Somewhat mollified, Rhys turned to his adopted family. "The unrest amongst the townspeople shouldn't have been a surprise to anyone, and we can't let it distract us from *why* they attacked us. We have had two deaths, one a Welshman and one an Englishman, both of whom appear to have been alone on the road in the night. Everyone in the village should be careful until we get to the bottom of this. I've already been with Simon this morning. He interviewed the ringleader, a man named Vincent, who claims nobody came up with the idea to attack the village—or if anyone did, it was he himself."

"It was brave of him to admit it," Catrin said.

"Brave … or stupid," Gruffydd said. "What will be his punishment?"

"He's already been released," Rhys said. "He was fined a week's wages to the king and must pay for the loss of the three huts. Two dozen townspeople came up with the money this morning, and it's already been paid to the coroner. I will see that it gets to the affected villagers."

A thoughtful look entered Gruffydd's eyes. "The town's mayor has been in office for only a fortnight. I should take your advice and speak to him." He looked a little contrite. "Perhaps if I'd done it sooner, when you suggested it, this might have been avoided."

"Anything that results in less hatred can only be a good thing." Rhys spread his hands wide. "I need you to be careful. All of you."

"We will." Gruffydd bobbed a nod.

"As will I," Catrin said.

"You still shouldn't have done what you did last night," Rhys said, with a side-eyed look at Catrin, some of his disgruntlement returning.

"Then you shouldn't have pulled me onto the back of the horse."

It was true. He had nobody to blame but himself.

"You were gone when I awoke," Catrin said, "and Gruffydd couldn't say where you went. What else have you been doing?"

"I went to the millpond to look for tracks to tell me where Tomos was put into the water. Instead, I think I found where he was killed."

Everyone at the table stared at him. "Blood again?" Catrin said.

He nodded. "More than enough of it, on the far side of the pond from the mill."

Catrin harrumphed. "You should have asked me to come. You know I could have helped."

"You have helped, and I am grateful."

"I can help more."

"And I value your assistance, but for now it needs to be from within the confines of the castle itself. I was already planning to do a great deal there today."

At her glare, Rhys sighed and set down his spoon. The rest of the family was listening with rapt attention. "It is likely I will have to see the king today, and I cannot predict what his response will be when we truly meet face-to-face. I know we talked about you assisting me, and I value your company. I really do. But I cannot allow you to be caught up in whatever punishment the king has in store for me."

Catrin eyed him. "I suppose I knew that. Last night's encounter was only the first song in a longer set. You're trying to protect me still, aren't you?"

"If I can."

"There's no need. Really. I can take care of myself."

"I'm sure you can," Rhys said. "Or at least you could when you lived in England. But you're in Wales now, and even though everything looks familiar, it isn't."

Sian, who was sitting at one end of the table adjacent to Catrin, put a hand on Catrin's arm. "What he's trying to explain to you is the same thing he has said to us time and again: if he goes down, he doesn't want to take anyone else with him."

Catrin pressed her lips together before nodding. "I will be careful. I promise."

It wasn't an assurance that she would stay in the castle and tend to her queen, but Rhys knew when to quit while he was ahead. Even with the horrors of last night—or maybe, because of them—it was all he was going to get today.

19

Day Three

Catrin

As Rhys had promised, he welcomed Catrin's company and help with the investigation as long as it was confined to the castle. After breakfast, they began with the castle workers, much to the annoyance of the deputy mason. They'd received permission from the master mason, of course, but Mark was really in charge of the overall workforce, and he didn't like seeing it disrupted more than it already had been in the aftermath of the attack the previous night.

"You're wasting our time, my lord." Mark ended with the honorific as if it was the most natural thing in the world. Everyone in the castle had learned by now that Rhys was a crouchback. They didn't know the full story—Catrin herself knew only the minimum Rhys would tell her—but they knew enough. "None of my men did this. Questioning my people won't do you any good."

"Were any of the other masons particular friends of Tomos?" Catrin asked.

He looked at her, and his expression softened slightly. "They say not, my lady." Then he lowered his voice. "Should you be involved in this? Surely after last night—"

Catrin supposed everyone knew what she'd done too. She'd assumed Mark favored the vigilantes, but to think so would have done him disservice as he was looking at her with respect rather than disdain.

"My presence isn't a judgment on Rhys's abilities. Cole was my son's man, and if I can be of any assistance, I will."

For a moment Mark looked helplessly at Rhys, who smiled blandly back. Catrin was grateful that Rhys himself had given up arguing.

The first group they interviewed consisted of five masons who worked the stone, as Tomos had done. The men were different sizes and shapes, but they all shared the thick arm muscles and hands of the dead man. Rhys gathered them together and began by asking what he felt to be the first important question: "When did you last see Tomos?"

The first to answer was the youngest, a tall, thin apprentice with a shock of blond hair that stuck straight up from his head, full as it was of stone dust. "We ate in the mess before going our separate ways."

An older man, shorter, with a craggy face, nodded. He appeared to be the younger man's overseer. "We sleep in tents within the palisade, but Tomos found lodging elsewhere, outside the castle. Welsh aren't allowed inside the town or castle after dark." He made an apologetic gesture and looked embarrassed. "Excepting nobles such as yourselves, of course."

"It's the law," Catrin said simply, "and not your fault."

"Do you know where he was laying his head?" Rhys asked. "Have you ever visited the place yourselves?"

As one, the men before them shrugged. Truthfully, if Rhys didn't know where Tomos was staying, perhaps nobody did. Given the Welsh emphasis on hospitality, it was more than surprising that nobody in the village had taken him in.

"Do you know of anyone who had a grudge against him?" Rhys asked.

"Because he was Welsh, you mean? Last night was a long time coming?" The older man shook his head. "Last night shouldn't have happened, and Tomos was liked by all of us. He did his job well and minded his own business." Among laborers, both were high accolades.

The masons shared another quick glance amongst themselves, and then a third man, also a journeyman, embellished the answer. "Tomos was mourning his family. He didn't call attention to himself, and as long as a man does good work, we don't care where he's from."

"Might someone else have done? Someone who didn't know him as well?" Catrin said.

The masons considered the question, even as the journeymen kept glancing towards the building works, impatient to be back at it. Finally the same man raised one shoulder. "I don't know anything more."

Over the course of the morning, nobody else did either. Finally, Rhys appeared to grow tired of speaking to unhelpful workers, and he moved on to the guards at the gates. The King's Gate allowed access to the town, so he chose the Queen's Gate as the most likely egress point for Tomos.

They were almost there, having crossed the length of the bailey, when a page skidded to a halt beside them. "Lady Catrin!" He was breathing hard. "The queen requests your presence."

Catrin let out a sigh at being summoned, not that the morning's work had been particularly entertaining. She turned to Rhys. "You intend to continue your inquiries?"

"I have to. I also want to know why Gruffydd never mentioned Tomos to me. It's very odd."

"You, at least, should be happy, since you'll be rid of me."

"Catrin—"

She shook her head, cutting him off. She'd been teasing, but maybe only partly. At his horrified look, she took pity on him and smiled. "It's all right. Perhaps I will see you this evening?"

Rhys blew out a breath. "Yes. If I survive the meeting with the king later today, that is."

"It may not be as bad as you think. It isn't as if he doesn't know you're here."

Rhys groaned. "Last night may well have made everything worse."

"I doubt it. But like any trouble, best to face it head on."

"You are irrepressible!" he said, but she'd made him smile.

Smiling herself, she turned away, following the page, who escorted her as far as the Eagle Tower. One should never keep a queen—particularly this queen—waiting.

One step inside the foyer, however, she was stopped by John le Strange, of the blue chevron, who was leaned up against the wall, slicing an apple with a knife and eating it.

"My lady." He straightened and bowed. "I am glad to see you well after last night's horrors."

"And you, my lord," Catrin said, being polite. "Thank you for coming to our rescue."

"Of course." John scratched a bug bite on his neck under his right ear. The bite was red and inflamed, and if Catrin hadn't been in a hurry—and preferring not to speak to him at all—she might have suggested he see a healer.

"If you will excuse me, the queen has summoned me."

"She has not, actually." He put out a hand to her, almost touching her arm and had the temerity to look rueful. "I apologize for the ruse, but that was me."

"What are you saying?" She stared at him.

"I needed to get you away from that—" he appeared to just stop himself from cursing and swallowed instead, "—crouchback. It won't do you any good to be associating with the likes of Sir Reese. Look what he led you into last night!"

She couldn't be polite in the face of his criticism. "Last night," she bit off the ends of the words sharply, "was an act of horror perpetrated against innocent men, women, and children. Perhaps you would be better served trying to discover who it was who incited them."

He put up both hands at her onslaught. "Sir Simon already talked to the ringleaders! It has nothing to do with me!"

"Nor Sir Rhys."

He deflated slightly. "No, I suppose not. You do appear to know your own mind."

"That should not surprise you." She paused, wondering how to continue, and still displeased with his disparagement of Rhys, even if he'd walked it back a pace. "Sir Simon speaks of Rhys with liking and admiration."

John scratched at the bite again. "You must realize you cannot trust him." He meant Rhys, of course.

"I can't imagine why you'd say that." Catrin endeavored to breathe easily and without displaying ire.

John looked for a moment as if he was going to say something that was genuinely constructive—and revealing—but all he ended up doing was adding lamely, "It would do your standing at court no good to marry someone of such low rank."

"But he is my friend," she said gently, knowing no good would come from antagonizing John. If she knew anything, she knew that. "As you may know by now, Rhys served in the crusade with the king himself."

"So I've been told." John was scowling as he bent over her hand. "But you still deserve better."

"Have no fear for me, my lord." She wanted to pull her hand away from him, but he was holding it tightly. She didn't know what she would do if he actually tried to kiss her. *Scream?* But then John straightened, and she was finally able to pull her hand away.

"If you need anything—anything at all—please call on me."

"Thank you, Lord Strange."

"Please call me John."

"Of course, my lord," she said, steadfastly not doing as he asked, "have a pleasant day."

He grunted, brushed past her, and left the tower.

She watched him go, both a little stunned and concerned by his forwardness. First Guy, then Rolf at the funeral, and now John. The latter two in particular presented a problem, in that they were brothers. Even had she liked either one, it would have been bad policy to come between them. Thankfully, as a widow, she had some say in the matter of whom she would marry next, if she married at all. Even with the constraint of serving Eleanor, she had more freedom today than she'd had since she was sixteen.

"Was that Rolf?"

Catrin whirled around at the voice of Adeline, one of the queen's ladies. "It was John."

"Oh." The relief in Adeline's voice was evident, even in that single word.

Adeline was small, blonde, and very pretty. She had set her mind—rather than perhaps her heart—on winning Rolf, and she kept her eye on any woman who drew his attention. And truly, there was no reason Rolf shouldn't have been interested in her more than Catrin. For much of the journey to Caernarfon, Rolf had been attentive to Adeline more than to any other lady, which was why Catrin had been so surprised to find him wanting to escort her yesterday.

"Have you seen Rolf today?" Adeline asked.

"No, I'm sorry. I have not."

Smiling now, Adeline approached. "John is a good catch too. He likes you very much."

Catrin endeavored to be polite, but she couldn't help saying, "I have done nothing to encourage him."

Adeline put a hand to Catrin's cheek. "You don't have to, my dear. You are so lovely, even with that hair." Then she frowned. "I must say John is a better choice than the crouchback, even if he is in the king's favor. Margaret was just questioning your association with him this morning."

Adeline said *the crouchback* as if it were Rhys's name. Catrin couldn't wait to tell him and watch him roll his eyes at her.

"Nobody needs to worry about me," Catrin said, hoping to end the conversation quickly before it went any further down this road. How anyone felt about Rhys—and who Rhys really was—was not something she wanted to discuss with Adeline.

"Margaret referred to him as a *quaestor*. I'm afraid I don't know what a quaestor is." As with her comment about Catrin's hair, Adeline spoke straight-forwardly, asking a genuine question and looking for a genuine answer, so Catrin didn't take offense. With Catrin, Adeline had always been level-headed, but she was one of those women who behaved differently around men than women, in that amongst men she pretended to be less intelligent than she really was. Catrin respected her approach as a strategy that worked for her in navigating the court. Catrin herself was terrible at pretending to be anything other than what she was—a fact Rhys had pointed out just the day before.

"It's someone who investigates murder."

"Like a coroner, then?"

"A coroner investigates death so as to determine the potential revenue accruable from it to the Crown. A quaestor investigates death to attempt to bring the murderer to justice."

"You mean like our lord sheriff." Adeline tapped her lip thoughtfully, clearly ruminating on the newly appointed Sheriff of Caernarfon, whose brother was the Sheriff of Anglesey. Both had been appointed at the same time the Statute of Rhuddlan had been read out. Neither man had struck Catrin as suited to their new position any more than Guy was to his. The appointments were rewards for services rendered. She couldn't say that to Adeline, however, because of its implied criticism of the king.

So Catrin again endeavored to answer as plainly as possible. It was something she'd learned during her marriage. She'd been a child, still, in many ways, though she'd thought herself grown up and the equal to her husband, despite the fact he was twenty years her senior. He'd gone into the marriage with his eyes open far more than hers, seeking an heir and someone to run his household while he was away in his service to the Earl of Gloucester.

Though it had taken some doing—and some hard lessons in how to comport herself—she'd gained the respect and trust of the men and women she commanded. She'd also given Robert a son, as required. By those lights, their marriage was more successful than most. She'd overheard Robert say as much many times over the years. He'd been content with what he had.

But she had wanted a partner and a friend, even a lover, if such a thing was even possible. Truth be told, she wanted what the king and queen of England had together and didn't see why, now having achieved the age of thirty-six, she should settle for anything less.

"As I'm sure you understand, often a sheriff is a favorite of the court and thus has not investigated murder before his appointment. He relies on his coroner and quaestor, if he has one, for advice and to do the detail work of finding witnesses and hunting down culprits."

Adeline hummed under her breath. "It would be better for everyone if the coroner could catch this murderer soon. Likely he's a vagabond anyway and has nothing to do with us. Pursuit of him is taking up altogether too much of everyone's time."

She meant, of course, that it would be better for her, and it was Rolf who was preoccupied, though Catrin wouldn't have said the investigation was a particular concern of his. Catrin didn't yet know which of the lords had alerted the king to the vigilantes, but Rolf had been among those to ride to the village. It made her uncomfortable to think she might have to be grateful to one of the Stranges.

But again, Catrin spoke with patience. "The identity of the killer is what Sir Rhys intends to discover. High or low, he's the best one to catch him."

20

Day Three

Rhys

"My lord!" Johnny, the boy who'd come to find Rhys in the laying out room the day before, appeared in the doorway to the guardroom. "Please come quickly! Madam Alice has found a body in her latrine."

That was momentous news indeed, not to mention unwelcome, and Rhys was at the door in three strides. Johnny seemed startled by the speed at which Rhys moved, but he backed out of the doorway. Rhys was followed by the guard, a man named Richard, whom Rhys had been interviewing, not terribly successfully, about the goings on at the castle.

This particular guard was fond of mead, much to his chagrin, since it was a local drink. He'd been mocked mercilessly by his fellows for it, but Rhys quietly supplied him with a flask or two every week. So Rhys, on the whole, thought the information Richard was providing had been as accurate as the man could remember.

The general consensus that had developed over the course of the afternoon seemed to be that Tomos had left by the Queen's Gate as the sun set as he usually did.

Piecing together what the residents of the castle remembered, Rhys had discovered that a dozen people had passed through the gate either coming or going near the same time as Tomos had left, including Coroner Guy, Catrin's brother Tudur, and Rhys himself. Rhys vaguely remembered seeing the other two in the hall at some point during the afternoon and evening that day, but he couldn't be sure. Since Tomos had died the evening before the king and his party had arrived, there was little to distinguish it from any other day that month, other than that the castle's steward had been running around like a headless chicken in his quest to prepare the castle for the king and queen.

Because of that, Rhys had to accept how unreliable any information he gathered about what may or may not have happened five days ago might be. He himself could barely remember what he ate yesterday.

Before hustling both Johnny and Richard through the King's Gate, he spoke to the guard on duty, asking him to send someone to find Simon. The man bowed his head in acknowledgement of the request. Overnight, Rhys had been transformed from lowly knight, to someone to be respected and obeyed. Of course, he wore a sword now. And though he still hadn't hauled out his mail, he wore a leather vest and bracers and Prince Edmund's colors, in the form of the surcoat Simon had given him, belted at the waist. Really, it was as if Simon was standing at his shoulder.

"Do you know who is dead?" Rhys spoke to Johnny in English.

"She didn't say." Johnny shook his head vigorously, doing a skip step every few feet to keep up with Rhys's strides. "She just sent me to find the coroner, and one of the workers near the King's Gate told me he was with you."

"I haven't actually seen him today." Normally, Rhys couldn't get rid of Guy. But then, Johnny spoke no more French than Guy spoke English. Rhys had become the middleman at Caernarfon in more ways than one.

That said, since Simon's arrival, Rhys hadn't exactly gone out of his way to confer with Guy either. The coroner was still officially directing the investigation, but it was Simon to whom Rhys reported, and Simon with whom Guy had to confer. These Normans were all about protocol, and Rhys had learned that nothing good came from overstepping.

Once inside the town, they turned right, left, and then right again, ending up at an inn, one of four in Caernarfon. This one was within a stone's throw of the east gate of the town. Each of the inns, and the taverns associated with them, served a slightly different clientele. The one closest to the castle and the King's Gate was frequented most often by members of the castle garrison. Most of the masons spread themselves between a tavern near the church and another on the western side of town. The East Gate inn, which was, in fact, this establishment's name, catered to visitors who did not find food or lodging at the castle. The inn had been at full capacity nearly continuously since it opened six months ago.

Even if Rhys hadn't known in advance about the death, he would have realized something was very wrong by the screams emanating from the rear of the inn and the crowd of citizenry that had gathered in front of it.

Rhys turned to Richard. "Calm these people the best you can. And afterwards, see if you can find either Coroner Lacy or Lord Simon."

"Yes, my lord, though I have no English."

"*Stay back* and *everything is under control* should suffice."

Richard repeated the English back to Rhys in halting, accented tones. Rhys clapped him on the shoulder. "Well done."

Because he believed he would be unwelcome, Rhys had never frequented any of the taverns in Caernarfon, but today he pushed through the door to enter the common room as if he knew where he was going and then walked straight through the building to the rear door. Several men stood in the yard, scratching their heads and muttering. They were laborers associated with the inn, judging by the flour on one man's apron.

Further screams reached him. Now that he was closer, it was clearly a woman's throat they were coming from. He followed the sound until he swung around the stables that took up the entire right side of the yard and arrived at the latrine. It appeared remarkably well maintained, because he could smell the lime used to cover the waste but not the waste itself.

The screaming woman was now gasping for breath, standing well back from the latrine with her hands to her mouth. Another woman, much older than the first, had her by the upper arms and was telling her to calm herself. Because the inn had an associated tavern, where copious amounts of drink were consumed every day, the latrine was a four-seat affair, with an additional stall, separated from the rest, set aside exclusively for the use of women.

It was the latter door which was propped wide, revealing the body of a man slumped on his right side with his head near the latrine hole. His legs were splayed in front of him, and his back was to the right-hand wall. Blood from wounds to his belly had pooled on the floor beneath him. He wasn't nude, though his pants were around his ankles. If the same man—not yet determined—was responsible for all three deaths, he had changed his method in that he hadn't taken time to strip the body. Doing so would have increased the chances of him being caught in such a public place.

The blue chevron on the shoulder of the dead man's tunic told Rhys he was looking at the body of John le Strange. It was clear now why the citizenry were keeping their distance. Not only was this murder, but the dead man was a Norman nobleman.

"Did anyone touch him?" He looked at the older woman, who had the aura of someone accustomed to her own authority.

"No." She, in turn, took in Rhys's appearance. "My lord."

Then she encouraged the younger woman to leave, guiding her away with gentle yet firm hands, before turning back to Rhys. "I sent the boy to bring the coroner. Excuse me, my lord, but I don't know you."

"My name is Rhys." He moved to crouch in front of the door, five feet from the body, just looking.

The woman gasped. "My apologies, my lord!"

Rhys glanced back in time to see her bob a curtsey.

"I didn't recognize you as the crouchback!"

For once, he found it easy to be forgiving. "There was no reason you should. And it's perfectly understandable how finding the body of a dead Norman in your latrine could put everything else from your mind."

It was one thing for Cole and Tomos to be dead. It was quite another, as he'd just said to her, to be standing over the body of John le Strange. If Rhys were she, he'd be terrified of being thrown in chains, just like poor Aron, just for being the one in whose establishment John had died.

"Are you Madam Alice?"

"Yes, my lord. I own this tavern."

Rhys straightened from his crouch. "You have no husband or father?"

"My father was one of the first to come to Carnarvon, and I came with him. He died three months ago."

Rhys acknowledged her grief with a bent head. "It was a hard winter."

"My father was obsessed with cleanliness." She gestured to the latrine, made of a lattice of sticks, which had then been packed with clay. The roof was thatch, the better to absorb smells and prevent them from wafting across the entire yard. Rhys was impressed with the care taken with the building of it and said so to Alice.

"He learned about such things in the Holy Land. When the ordinance on latrines came down from the castle, he was already doing what was necessary."

Since the conquest of Wales, ordinances about controlling refuse had been strictly enforced. After dark, the town's nightmen would drive through the region, collecting waste in their carts to be disposed of elsewhere. They collected it from the Welsh village now too. It wasn't any wonder the farmland in Gwynedd, little of it as there was, had higher rates of production than it had ever had before.

"Your father was a crouchback too?" Rhys had been arrogant enough to think, before the arrival of the king and Simon, that he was the only one in Caernarfon.

"He was the supply master for William Longspee."

Rhys blinked at the mention of the man who'd become a hero and saint in the annals of the Crusades, though his war had been before Rhys's time.

"Why Caernarfon? Why not Denbigh?" Coroner Guy's brother Henry, the ruler of Denbigh in eastern Wales, was married to Longspee's granddaughter. "I would have thought it would have been a more natural choice."

Alice lifted one shoulder in a half-shrug. "He liked the sea."

It was as good a reason as any. "I would have been honored to meet him, and I am sorry he's gone." He gestured to indicate they had a more pressing issue to discuss. "If you would tell me what you know?"

"I was in the kitchen all morning, and here he was, dying in the back." Her face took on a fierce expression. "Nobody I let into the inn could have done this."

Rhys was in the business of eliciting answers and didn't care to antagonize her, so he didn't bother to deny her claim. He had a great deal of practice in ignoring absurdities. "Did you serve Lord Strange yourself?"

"The barman brought him his drink, which he took to a table, before coming to tell me that a nobleman had graced us with his presence. I immediately went into the common room to greet him and asked if he wouldn't prefer to retire to the salon."

Rhys canted his head. "You have one?" Salons were found in the most upscale establishments on the road to London.

"Many noblemen have darkened our door. Some would come to drink with my father and reminisce about the wars they shared. You're a crusader yourself, so you know that such men are often most comfortable in the company of those who shared their experiences."

"But not this man?"

"He declined my offer, saying he was meeting someone."

"I assume he didn't say who?"

"No, my lord, but I can tell you that no other nobleman came through the door, only good Englishmen. No Welshmen either." Then she put out a hasty hand. "No offense meant, my lord."

"None taken," Rhys said mildly and found that it was true. "Is there another way into the yard except through the front door of the inn?"

"Yes." She made a motion to indicate that Rhys should look around the corner of the latrine.

He stepped to do so and saw a gate, half closed, which when fully open would be wide enough to admit a cart. It led to a narrow alley that ran between the rows of buildings.

"So anyone could have entered that way?"

She looked down at her feet. "I suppose." But then she looked up. "Neither I nor my people had anything to do with this. We would never be foolish enough to murder a Norman. A scuffle in the common room is one thing, but a man stabbed in the belly in my latrine is quite another!"

"Who is this barman who served him?"

"That would be Tom."

At Rhys's raised eyebrow, she curtseyed and disappeared around the stables, hastening away, now that she'd been given permission, as quickly as possible.

Rhys studied the way John's body was arranged, aware that he had to go closer to it. At the very least, he would have to examine it—if briefly, since it was obvious how he died—as well as his possessions, if he had any on him. None of the other bodies had been left with their belongings. These missing items could lead Rhys to the killer, provided he didn't plant them on some poor unsuspecting soul. Rhys had already begun to wonder why he hadn't, at least in the case of items that were less valuable.

He moved closer, finally picking up John's wrist and turning over his hand. It was warm and loose, indicating a very recent death. John also had tissue and blood under his nails. Rhys's heart beat a little more quickly. Perhaps they'd finally caught a real break in that it looked as if John had marked his assailant.

Footsteps crunched on the gravel yard, and Rhys turned, expecting to see Alice and her barman returning. Instead, Simon took in the scene with a sweeping glance. At the sight of the blue chevron even he, who had seen death at Rhys's side in a hundred different ways, paled. "I thought this was a simple tavern brawl. I can see now why you sent for me."

21

Day Three

Catrin

"**I** have summoned you, Catrin, because Margaret tells me she spoke to John le Strange earlier today, and both are concerned that you have taken up with that Welsh quaestor named Reese. Is this true?" The queen plucked at the blanket, adjusting it over her large belly, and continued speaking before Catrin could answer. "I knew a quaestor named Reese, once, but he died. Maybe they are all named Reese."

Catrin was tempted to tell the queen it was none of her business who one of her ladies-in-waiting had *taken up with*, as Eleanor had so crassly put it, but she would be wrong. It was precisely the queen's business.

"Yes, I have been associating with Sir Rhys, but it is because I am concerned about the death of my son's man, Cole." She wasn't going to give anything away, particularly how she felt about Rhys, if she didn't have to. King Edward knew that Rhys was alive and here. Simon had told him yesterday, and the king himself had spoken with

Rhys at the village. That Eleanor seemed completely unaware of these facts and unconcerned about the events of last night (and Catrin's role in them) was odd—but maybe nobody had told her. On further consideration, Catrin found this likely.

Eleanor pointed to a cup of wine on the bedside table, and Catrin stood to hand it to her. The queen could have reached for it herself, so Catrin well understood the implications: she served at the queen's pleasure, and she'd best remember it.

And because of that, Catrin took it upon herself to tell the queen the truth. "All quaestors are not named Rhys, madam. As far as I know, there has been, and maybe only ever will be, one."

Eleanor stared at Catrin for a moment and actually leaned forward slightly, interested in the conversation beyond the pleasure of chastising Catrin. "What are you saying?"

"It is my understanding that this Sir Rhys with whom I have been associating saved the life of Prince Edmund in the Holy Land. He served as quaestor amongst the crusaders and then continued in the role for Prince Edmund for several years, once he returned to England."

All Normans, but the ladies especially, had perfected the art of not showing surprise. It was more than a little gratifying, then, to have actually said something the queen hadn't expected. She was rendered speechless for a count of three, after which she said, "The Sir Reese in question is the same Reese de la Croix of our acquaintance? He is here?"

"Yes, my lady."

Eleanor's face flushed red with anger, in a very unladylike way, and she hitched herself higher on the bed. "Why has he not made himself known to us?"

"He was in the hall that first evening and made his obeisance with the others." Catrin didn't want to put words in Rhys's mouth, but she thought she was beginning to understand some of what was going on under the surface between Rhys and the king. "I can't speak for him, but perhaps he feared he would not be remembered fondly."

"That is not for him to decide. He was the one who left *us*, after all." It was a sin of the first order. "We thought he died with Lewellen."

Catrin looked down at her hands.

"You don't have to say he meant us to think that." Eleanor actually snorted.

She was so agitated, in fact, that she threw off the blanket and made a move to rise to her feet. Instantly, Margaret, who'd been sitting near the window working on her needlepoint, was there to help her, with Catrin on the queen's other side. Once upright, Eleanor threw off their hands. "Leave me be. I'm pregnant, not elderly."

Now she rounded on Catrin, who couldn't decide if she was better off looking at her feet or in the queen's face. "You are to find him and bring him to me immediately!"

Looking down appeared to be the best approach, and Catrin curtseyed. "My lady, it was my understanding he intended to speak to the king last night, with Simon Boydell, whom I believe you also know from that time."

Before the queen could reply, Margaret handed her the wine goblet, now replenished, and Eleanor took a long drink. Then, holding the cup in both hands and resting the stem on her protruding belly, she studied Catrin. "Simon has served Edmund faithfully these many years. I was glad to hear the king had brought him to Carnarvon to captain his guard. But Reese—" she broke off, shaking her head.

"My apologies, my lady. I truly cannot speak for him."

"The king thought he was dead."

Catrin lifted her head and was able to say with absolute truth, "We all did. According to my brother, who confirms the story, Rhys almost died in the ambush at Cilmeri and spent many months on the edge of death in a monastery infirmary."

Eleanor harrumphed. "He still should have made himself known to us as soon as we arrived."

"In hindsight, I do believe he regrets his neglect of you and has been searching for a way to make up for it ever since."

The queen took another long slug of wine. Catrin wouldn't have said being drunk for the birth of one's child was necessarily the best way to manage the proceedings, but then, Catrin herself had birthed only one child, not sixteen. When Eleanor held out the goblet to Margaret to refill, her eyes were still on Catrin. "He served Lewellen from the time he left us until his death, did he not?"

"Yes, my lady."

"Was he a loyal servant?" She made a dismissive motion with the goblet, almost slopping the wine it contained over her hand. She didn't appear to notice. "Of course, he was. The Reese I knew had honor."

"He was loyal to the end, my lady. That is how he came by his wounds."

Catrin held her breath, watching the queen's face. She was more expressive in this moment than Catrin had ever seen her.

"Then he has been punished sufficiently for his mistaken allegiance. My husband has been in a forgiving mood of late." She rubbed her belly. "We owed Reese a debt, once upon a time. Perhaps we still do."

The queen's words brought genuine relief to Catrin, who didn't reply, thinking it would be better to say nothing than the wrong thing. She was glad she'd had no idea when she woke up this morning that this conversation was in the offing. It could have so easily gone terribly wrong if she'd overthought it.

Eleanor wasn't finished. "I have fond memories of those times. I will no longer be dining in the great hall, not with the baby due so soon, but you will bring Reese to me here, as soon as he is able."

Noting the change to a more accommodating tone, Catrin curtseyed yet again. "I will tell him, my lady, the first moment I see him."

22

Day Three

Rhys

"I didn't actually know the dead man was John le Strange when I sent for you because I hadn't yet seen the body," Rhys said, "but news of a death in the town seemed like a time, if there ever was one, to call for backup immediately."

"It's rather unlike you, actually."

"I suppose so. The old me, anyway."

Simon crouched before the body, his hands relaxed between his knees, as Rhys had done earlier. His expression was wry rather than revulsed as he observed the stab wounds. "I confess, I did not see this coming."

"If it's any consolation, I don't immediately see a hexfoil." Rhys hesitated. "That doesn't mean there isn't one."

"So no consolation at all."

"You know how this goes," Rhys said. "We keep moving forward until something stops us."

"Why are you here instead of Guy?"

"The boy the innkeeper sent to find the coroner found me instead."

"Three murdered men. Why John? Why any of them?"

"I have no idea." Rhys looked over at his old friend, realizing he hadn't actually told him about how he and Catrin had gone to Llywelyn's palace and found the place where Cole was murdered. Nor that he'd found blood at the millpond indicating Tomos's murder site. Now wasn't the time for further explanations either, and he wasn't sure how important these discoveries were anyway, not with John's murdered body staring them in the face. "Three days have passed since we started investigating, and while I know what happened, I have no actual suspects."

Gingerly, Simon peered into the other side of the latrine, next to where the man had died. Rhys had already looked there and knew the planks of wood that made up the floor of the latrine were stained. He didn't feel the need to guess with what—though it wasn't blood. Alice was right that the latrine had been well-maintained.

Then Simon's eyes tracked again to John's body. "I can't tell you anything at all about why those other men died, but John isn't a casualty in the same way the others are."

"He's a nobleman," Rhys said simply, "a servant specifically of Prince Edmund, unlike his father who serves the king directly. I spoke to John two days ago before examining Cole's body. He'd just arrived in Caernarfon moments earlier."

"Are you aware of the news he brought the king?"

Rhys shook his head warily.

"Prince Edmund is on his way. He should be here tomorrow."

Rhys found his shoulders sagging.

"Ah, you hadn't heard that yet?"

"I've been a bit busy."

Simon's gaze returned to the body. "So you have."

Rhys tried to take the news of Prince Edmund's imminent arrival in stride. Things could hardly be worse, in truth. Bad enough that King Edward was ensconced in the castle with his very pregnant wife, who also knew him because she'd been on that sojourn in the Holy Land. Until now, it had really been Prince Edmund whom Rhys had served. He could hide himself from King Edward—though he would surely face the consequences for that—but Edmund was a different story entirely.

Simon scuffed the toe of his boot in the dirt, apparently able to read Rhys's mind. "About your absence all these years."

Rhys glanced over at his friend, seeing Simon's face transformed by an intense expression that matched his tone. He was surprised they were talking about this now, but he couldn't refuse to respond when replying clearly meant so much to Simon. "Yes?"

"I never wished to oppose you."

"I know that. I can be grateful we never had to fight against each other directly." Rhys eyed his friend and then finally succumbed to the question he'd wanted to ask him for the last year and a half. "Was your absence at Cilmeri that day by design or just bad luck?"

"Prince Edmund was not aware of the Mortimer ruse to lure Llywelyn into an ambush."

Simon had said he wouldn't lie, so Rhys believed him. "It was underhanded, so they kept him out of it?"

"He's a crusader. It would have been beneath him."

"Did *you* know?"

The corners of Simon's mouth turned down. "I knew something was afoot, but nothing specific. Perhaps if I'd dug a little deeper, twisted some wrists—"

Rhys made a slashing motion with his hand. "Better that you didn't know, because even if you had, you couldn't have warned me. Don't apologize for what couldn't be helped. We are both crouchbacks."

"That we are. We serve with integrity or not at all." Simon's brow furrowed for a moment, indicating concern, but then his expression cleared, as if he'd decided something or had something confirmed that he'd had questions about. He nodded slowly, his eyes on Rhys's face. "You should also know, even if the prince might not want me to tell you, that John was Edmund's spymaster, privy to many secrets, though, interestingly, he did not know about you. It seems he had very few informants in Gwynedd."

Rhys stared at his friend, truly surprised. Before he could pursue that line of thought, however, the sound of voices came from behind them. Not wanting to expose John to just anyone's view, Rhys grabbed the edge of the door to the latrine stall and closed it—and then took in a genuinely shocked breath at the sight of the incomplete hexfoil carved into the front of the door.

Simon's response was more prosaic: he swore and said, "Who in the hell curses a latrine?"

"At this point, I'm far less concerned about the hexfoil than the hand that carved it. We have to assume it's the same killer now."

Simon glanced at Rhys, a puzzled expression on his face. "You thought otherwise up until this moment?"

"I still think it's a possibility. It has been five days since those deaths, both of which appear to have occurred in the same night. Someone could be hoping to piggyback on the other two murders. At the very least, it's something we should consider, simply because of John's station and the sheer number of people who might have wanted him dead—particularly now that you tell me he was a spy."

Simon grunted. "You always did have a twisty mind." Then he jerked his head. "We must see the king before another hour passes. You should throw yourself at his feet, beg forgiveness, and then tell him everything that has happened here. You can't avoid it now."

Rhys bent his head for a moment before finally accepting that the life he'd made for himself this last year was over. "I do know that."

Simon's dark look continued. "With John's death, I will be taking the lead on the investigation personally. The coroner means well, but he is inexperienced. I'll need you at my side, of course."

"Of course." Rhys spoke formally because Simon had done so. There was no rank between them except when imposed from the outside, but sometimes it was good to observe the forms. Rhys also knew (as did Simon) that the coroner *didn't* mean well. Guy had accepted the position for the power and wealth it brought him. The fact that investigating death was part of the job was an inconvenience, not a calling, as it was with Rhys.

If Guy hadn't been leaving soon to take up his position as Sheriff of Denbighshire, he might object to Simon taking over, not liking to be outranked by the son of a lesser nobleman, even if Simon's ancestor had come with the Conqueror. Then again, Guy had displayed little interest in this particular investigation so far and, as the Sheriff of Denbighshire, he was about to vault above the heads of many others. It was a great opportunity for an illegitimate son.

At long last, Alice came around the stables with Tom the barman. Because Rhys had been contemplating all the ways the incomplete hexfoil's presence, coupled with three bodies in three days, complicated the investigation, he had forgotten about closing the door. Thus, he didn't respond as quickly as he might have and was too late to swing the door wide to hide the mark.

Alice gasped from behind Rhys, and by the time he turned around, she had averted her eyes, both from him and from the door.

Tom was less circumspect. "It's here too? That won't be good for business!"

It was the one thing he could have said that could have made Alice respond forcefully. "It wasn't there before. I'd swear to it! I wouldn't have none of that in my inn."

"You didn't see it earlier when you came to view the body?" Rhys asked. "The door must have been closed for the corpse not to have been discovered sooner."

"It was one of the serving girls who found him. I only saw him after."

"Is that the same serving girl who was here when I arrived?"

Alice scoffed. "No. The first one was sensible and ran to tell me. This one came later, being a curious nit, and lost her head. I told everyone to stay away, but of course she wouldn't listen. She never does."

Rhys wasn't much concerned with Alice's staffing issues and turned to Tom. He looked exactly as a barman should, with a thick mustache and beard, a little gray at the edges, and almost no hair on top of his head. He was heavily muscled throughout his arms and shoulders. Though a bit shorter than average in height, he would have little trouble dealing with a patron who'd had too much to drink.

"Alice says you served this man when he arrived."

The barman wrinkled his nose. "He drank ale and ate a plate of bread and onions. He turned up his nose at the cheese. I don't know why."

Alice stepped in. "Some of these fine lords think the cheese we make here is too hard and tart. They want those soft Hereford cheeses they're used to." She sniffed. "The Welsh know how to make cheese, I'll give them that."

The Welsh had lived on milk and meat from cattle, sheep, and goats for as long as they'd been Welsh. They made bread too, but their expertise was in cheese and butter.

"You can't tell us anything more about him than that?" Simon asked.

"No, my lord. I'm sorry, my lord." Tom gave Simon the double honorific, indicating he was nervous. "I didn't know who he was then, not to look at. He didn't speak to anyone that I saw. The dining room was crowded, so I didn't notice when he left to use the latrine."

He gestured to the incomplete hexfoil on the door. "We should burn that bit right now."

"We can't burn it," Simon said. "It's evidence."

"I don't want it in my place." Alice glared at Rhys. "Does it have to stay?"

"No," Rhys said. "We've seen it as it is."

"Take it to the church," she said forcefully. "Father Mathew will know what to do with it."

Father Mathew was the priest at St. Mary's, whom Rhys did not know as well as Father Medwyn, the priest at St. Peblig's. Still, Rhys saw the sense in keeping it inside the town. Then it remained a Norman problem—and Rhys prayed it stayed that way.

So he nodded to Alice. "I will take care of it. You may go if you have things to see to."

"I do!" She gave a sharp nod. "I'll tell Duggan to cut that part out." Then she bent her head, "My lords," and departed with Tom to return to the inn.

Once retrieved from the other side of the yard, Duggan made short work of the plank that had formed one of the slats that made up the door, probably acquired from the sawmill off the River Seiont where Tomos's body had been found.

As he and Simon passed through the main room of the inn, finally able to leave, Alice approached once again with one more request: "If you don't mind, my lord, could you ask Father Mathew when you see him to stop by here after?"

"Certainly." Rhys frowned. "May I ask what for?"

"I'd like his blessing on the latrine, once I've installed a new door."

It felt good to laugh. If someone could curse a latrine, the priest could also bless it.

23

Day Three
Rhys

Rhys arranged for the body to be sent to the laying out room near the chapel, which was still the best place to put John, even if he was a nobleman, and then they set off for the castle, plank in hand. Simon walked beside Rhys, matching him stride for stride.

"Such has been my self-absorption that I haven't asked how it goes with you and your family," Rhys said, welcoming the feeling of camaraderie with Simon. It really was starting to feel like old times. "You have a new son, I hear?"

He'd caught Simon by surprise—at long last. "How did you know?"

Rhys grinned. "Just because I didn't reach out to you doesn't mean I haven't been keeping up."

"He is well. My wife won't let anyone else touch him, not even me most of the time. He eats night and day."

"As he should. Your second, yes?"

"Second son. Third child." His chin jutted out. "I would do anything to protect them."

"As you should." Rhys paused. "That's probably why I haven't married."

Simon shot Rhys a sharp look. "Prince Edmund wouldn't—"

"—hold my family hostage to my good behavior? Maybe you're right about Edmund, but the king *would*. There is *nothing* he would not do if it served his interests. I temper my speech with everyone but you, but do not mistake me or my thoughts." Rhys's tone had hardened, involuntarily at first, but he let it continue. *No lies,* they'd said, and by God he was sick of hiding. It scourged his soul daily. Simon would never know how many times he'd been a hair's breadth from letting him know he was alive. Always he'd held back, telling himself it was better the way it was.

It wasn't.

Simon had to know the truth if they were to continue in each other's company as more than just old companions thrown together one more time. "Just because words are not spoken does not change who I am and what I feel." Then, in Welsh, Rhys added, just to be provocative, "Every nobleman in that castle has the blood of my people on his hands."

Simon threw out his own hand. "Do I have to remind you where you are?"

Rhys felt a frisson of satisfaction. "So you do understand more than you let on."

"I understand you. It's speaking Welsh that eludes me."

Rhys continued to stand his ground. "You are Norman, descended from a knight who rode with the Conqueror. I am Welsh, of a lineage that has opposed yours for over two hundred years. We have to accept we have differing opinions about the way things should be—and let it go. Even as I chafe at this new station I've had forced upon me, I have accepted you and your loyalties. I need you to accept mine."

Simon opened his mouth to speak, but they'd reached the castle gate, and the commotion beyond the barbican brought them both up short.

Rhys swallowed hard at the sight of men and horses crowded into the small bit of space that wasn't under construction and thus available for them to mingle in.

"Prince Edmund has come early," Simon said softly.

"Are you sure you want to come with me?" Rhys said.

"I am no fair-weather friend, Rhys." There again was the proper pronunciation.

Sure enough, three paces into the great hall, Guy fitz Lacy met them with a furrowed brow, and his words were for Rhys. "Prince Edmund wanted to see you the moment you appeared. I am to take you to him." He looked Rhys up and down. "He will be pleased you are wearing his colors." He strode away, expecting them to follow.

"It wasn't as if I had a choice," Rhys said as an aside to Simon. "I actually feared he might be angry I was wearing them without permission."

"I find that unlikely," Simon said prosaically, "but soon you will be before him, and then we will know."

From in front of them, Guy laughed mockingly and then turned around, walking backwards and talking at the same time. "What's that about?" He gestured to the board.

"Come with us to speak to the prince, and you will see about that too," Simon said.

Rhys was prepared for humiliation, which was the last thing he wanted Guy to witness, but now that Simon had included him, he couldn't prevent it. The corridor to the receiving room seemed very long. It irritated Rhys that he felt like he had as a youth, when he'd been caught up with Hywel in one infraction or another, and marched to see Hywel's father.

Rhys told himself he didn't owe Prince Edmund a thing. If anything, Edmund owed *him* for saving his life all those years ago. When Rhys had served both princes, he'd done so faithfully, without reservation or prejudice. He'd left Edmund for Llywelyn at the point he could no longer execute his duties with a pure heart.

With this new death of John le Strange, Rhys found himself in the very strange and unanticipated position of actually being able to help both king and prince again. Back in the Holy Land all those years ago, Rhys hadn't thought the activities of the Baphomets or the Templars, for that matter, were directed at either royal brother. Maybe back then they hadn't been. But if a Baphomet conspiracy had made its way all the way to Gwynedd, he was the logical person to root it out. And if it was someone using the Baphomets for his own despicable ends, there was no one more qualified in Gwynedd than he to discover that too.

Guy had led the way down the corridor, and now he opened the door to Edmund's quarters, such as they were, given that this was a castle under construction, and gestured them inside.

As Rhys stepped into the room, Edmund swung around from where he'd been looking out the window, open to the sea air as few of the windows in the castle had yet been filled with glass. With a flick of his hand, he dismissed two men who'd been conferring with him, and they left by another doorway.

For a long moment, the two men gazed at each other. And then Rhys remembered his manners and bowed. "My prince."

"Reese."

By the time Rhys straightened, Edmund was only three feet away, and he kept coming, ultimately grasping Rhys by the upper arms and looking him over thoroughly. "You look well, particularly for a dead man. Thinner than last I saw you."

Rhys's slighter build must have been pretty obvious for Edmund to have noticed. Two years ago, Rhys would have said he felt much the same as he had as a youth when he and Simon had gone on crusade. At the time, he'd been heavier set with thicker shoulders from a lifetime of warfare.

Cilmeri had changed all that. Rhys was almost slender now, compared to when he was in his prime, thanks to the long recuperation from his injuries. He had headaches when the weather changed, and his knees creaked. And this last year had put white streaks at his temples, with more white in his beard.

By contrast, the prince was shorter than Rhys, with fine Norman features and dark hair he kept cut above his ears. At thirty-nine, he was six years younger than the king and only a year older than Rhys himself. But he'd developed something of a paunch since Rhys had last seen him, masked to some degree by expertly crafted clothing.

"My lord." Rhys would have bowed again if Edmund hadn't still held his arms. "I never thought I would stand before you again. And I would say the same about you, except for the latter observation, of course."

It was a jest about Edmund's rounded belly, and perhaps a daring one, but it broke the ice, and Edmund actually grinned. "That is prettier talk from you than I remember." Then he waggled a finger at Rhys. "Except for casting aspersions on my weight." He glanced over at Simon. "It was always you who was the diplomat."

Simon bowed. "Do not misconstrue, my lord. The mind behind those pretty words remains the same."

Edmund met Rhys's eyes again. "You have hidden yourself away long enough, Reese. It is time you stepped back into the sun."

Rhys cleared his throat. "My lord—"

"Don't perjure yourself by telling me it was never your intent to deceive. Of course it was." The prince barked a laugh. "But no longer. You will give me your pledge before another moment passes." He finally let go of Rhys enough to gesture to the emblem on Rhys's chest. "You wouldn't be wearing that if it was a pledge you couldn't keep."

Rhys didn't allow himself to sigh or give any indication that his appearance here was under duress. From the moment he'd heard the king was coming to Caernarfon, he'd known he was being confronted with a choice. He could have ridden away then, but he didn't, and that meant he'd known this moment was possible—and had accepted it.

Still, until he'd walked into the room, he genuinely hadn't known if he was capable of going down on one knee before Prince Edmund, just the two of them, without a phalanx of other lords between them. In the great hall after King Edward had arrived, Rhys had sworn, along with the rest of Tudur's men, to follow him. When he'd done so, however, it had been as an anonymous knight, one of many who served Tudur. The king had accepted in similar fashion the fealty of a thousand men over the last year.

This was different. This was pledging his allegiance man to man, and Edmund would expect him to look into his eyes when he did it.

No lies, Rhys had said to Simon, but rarely in his life had he felt the desire to equivocate more than he did in this moment.

And yet, in the breath he took before he said, "Of course, my lord," he found the answer he needed. By offering himself to Edmund, he could avoid pledging directly to Edward, at least for the immediate future. And it was even possible that Simon had known exactly what he was doing when he dropped his tunic with Edmund's crest over the top of Rhys's head.

Although he'd been blunt with Simon earlier, he had still kept back some of what he felt. What Rhys still hadn't said out loud was that his feelings for Edward had gone beyond mere hatred to something that frightened even Rhys. Edmund, however, hadn't been at the ambush at Cilmeri. His disagreement with Llywelyn had been that of one lord to another, over power and land. Like Simon, Edmund was a younger brother who did only as his lord commanded.

Like Simon, Edmund could be forgiven.

24

Day Three

Rhys

"*I* pledge by my honor that I will be faithful to Edmund, Prince of England. I will never cause him harm and make my homage to him in good faith and without deceit."

The words were those of submission. But also ones Rhys could adhere to. He'd pledged them before, of course. Even with his resignation and service to Prince Llywelyn, from a certain point of view, he hadn't ever violated that particular vow.

Regardless, Edmund seemed to see the matter as resolved, a duty done, and now he could move on to other issues. As Rhys rose to his feet, the prince gestured toward the plank, which Simon still held in his hand. "What is this?"

Simon turned over the wooden board to show Edmund the incomplete hexfoil, while Rhys told him of its discovery, along with the important details of John's death. Edmund hadn't been at the castle long enough to know much about the other deaths beyond that they'd happened, and though little expression showed on the prince's face beyond a narrowing of the eyes, his aura grew colder the more Rhys talked.

Then Guy, who had been witness to the entire conversation, including Rhys's submission to the prince, stepped forward. "Has Rolf been informed of his brother's death?"

"I'm sorry to say he has not," Simon said.

Guy's lips pursed. "Pray he hasn't heard the rumor of it already!"

Rhys thought it unlikely, given that Rolf spoke no English, but said it was better he heard it from someone he trusted. Edmund agreed and made a gesture of dismissal.

"Best not to give him too much information," Rhys said to Guy's retreating back.

Guy waved a hand. "Leave it to me."

As an investigator, Rhys would have liked to see Rolf's face when he learned of his brother's death—not out of vindictiveness but to make sure that Rolf himself wasn't responsible for it. At long last, however, Rhys's royal obligations were finally taking precedence.

With Guy gone, Edmund took the board from Simon and studied the carving. "Clever of you, Reese, to get him from the room before we spoke of the Baphomet, while at the same time making him think it was his idea to leave."

"I assure you, I had no such intent."

Edmund eyed Rhys, his expression disbelieving, and then he switched his gaze to Simon. "You concur with Reese's findings?"

"Yes. And I must point out that when Reese says, 'we', he really means that he discovered all these things."

"Who do you suspect is behind these deaths?"

"We have no suspects, my lord." Rhys turned up both hands. "I'm sorry. I don't even know if all three were killed by the same man."

"Surely that's a given!" Edmund said. "The symbol should tell us that!"

"Everyone in Gwynedd knows by now about the incomplete hexfoil at Cole's murder scene," Rhys said. "John's murderer could be someone else entirely, someone trying to hide his tracks by copying the actions of the man who murdered Cole and Tomos."

"Do we know why John was at the inn?"

"I'm afraid not, my lord," Simon said. "We haven't had the opportunity to question anyone as to his movements."

The prince began to pace around the room. "John came to Carnarvon on my orders."

Rhys had long experience at reassurance. "The only man responsible for John's death is the man who stabbed him, my lord. Don't take any measure of guilt on yourself."

Edmund glanced at Rhys. "You've been here all along, hiding in plain sight." It was as if he couldn't resist another dig. The resentment wasn't going to go away any time soon, deservedly so. "What do you make of a Baphomet in Carnarvon?"

"My lord, again I'm sorry. But I have no idea."

Edmund harrumphed. "Honest as always."

"To a fault, one might even say," Simon said.

Then Edmund suddenly reversed course and came right up to Rhys, stopping only a foot away. He could have been angry, but his eyes were merely curious, which was almost worse. "And yet, you deceived everyone here for a year. I am concerned it came so easily to you. Maybe you aren't the man I once knew."

"I did not murder John, my lord, as much as I have reason to detest the Stranges." And maybe it was just as well Edmund was accusing him now. Better to have it out in the open than festering inside. "You are correct, of course, that I alone, among all the current residents of Gwynedd, have knowledge of the Baphomet."

Edmund's eyes narrowed. "Why come forth now if not to take charge of an investigation into murders you yourself committed?"

"After Cilmeri, I could have gone anywhere in the world, my lord. I chose to come home. You, the king, even the Baphomet came to *me*."

Edmund plucked at his lower lip with his forefinger and thumb as he studied Rhys. "Your pledge to me was true?"

That was a question of honor, and enough to prompt Rhys to finally protest, "My lord—"

But then Edmund waved a hand dismissively, cutting Rhys off before he could complete whatever he was going to say, which maybe even he didn't know. "The man I used to know would be dishonored by my asking. He would not have lied to me. And maybe I was wrong. Maybe hiding yourself here didn't come so easily to you after all."

Edmund was more right than he knew about that.

"I am not lying to you, my lord. I did not kill those men. I am the same man you knew. Older, of course."

"Wiser too, my lord," Simon interjected again, knowing as Rhys had that he needed to let Edmund's suspicions and anger run its course. "While it's true he hid himself from everyone, including me, he isn't hiding anymore."

"It was information I'd rather he had not withheld." Edmund's lips remained a thin line.

Simon coughed gently. "Reese remains my closest friend."

Rhys waited. Either Prince Edmund was going to accept his renewed service, or he was going to lock him in irons. In that moment, both outcomes had an even chance.

Until Edmund snorted laughter. "Come here, you imbecile." And for the first time since Edmund had knighted him all those years ago, the prince embraced him. "By the saints, I believe you. More to the point, I want to believe you, and I want you with me. The world wasn't the same after you left." He canted his head towards the door on the other side of the room. "Come and see."

So Rhys and Simon came and saw: a dozen men or more were waiting for the prince in the adjacent room, and they all stopped talking as the three of them entered. It was required that conversation cease at Prince Edmund's arrival, but that didn't mean all eyes didn't fall on Rhys, and he could feel their questions:

Who is that with the prince?

Why does he appear to be in such high favor?

What effect will him having the favor of the prince have on me?

Once Rhys turned around and they saw the crusader cross embroidered on the back of his surcoat, they would have their answers, since it was the same cross sewn into the back of Edmund's.

Rhys scoffed under his breath, understanding further why Simon had so casually given him his own surcoat.

Edmund put an end to their uncertainty by simply waving a hand in Rhys's direction. "You will have heard of Reese de la Croix, of course, from our time in the Holy Land where he saved my life. He has returned to my service this very day and has my countenance."

Nods and assenting murmurs came from every throat, though Rhys still felt their eyes. Some of them would know more, and all would be wondering where Rhys had been all this time. Most were great lords with extensive lands, with only a few, like Simon, rising in the prince's service on merit and knowing their entire station depended upon his goodwill. As a prince, Edmund could do as he liked, so nobody was going to question his abrupt introductions, but they would all be feeling Rhys had no business in their company.

One of them, a few years younger than Rhys, stepped forward, his hand out. "Humphrey de Bohun."

Rhys looked him in the eye and grasped his forearm. "My lord." Humphrey was one of the great lords of the March, the borderlands between what had been Wales and England. Since the end of the war, his estates in Wales had doubled, now stretching west from Brecon along the Usk almost to Llandovery. The River Irfon, in fact, where Llywelyn had died, acted as the border between Bohun's lands to the south and Mortimer lands to the north.

Edmund stabbed his fingers in the direction of the other men in the room worthy of being introduced. "Thomas de Clare, John Gifford of Llandovery, William Mortimer, Owen de la Pole, Richard FitzAlan, John de Warenne, Henry de Lacy."

Given that these men had all arrived with Edmund, none of them could be the murderer. But they could be the source of other threats, particularly the ones against the king Simon had mentioned. The secrets these Marcher lords kept, to themselves and with each other, were numerous and varied and any number of them could be plotting against the king. Marcher lords learned conspiracy in their cradles.

The introduction of one of the men in particular had caused a red mist to pass momentarily before Rhys's eyes. Oddly, it wasn't William Mortimer, cousin to Roger and Edmund, but rather Owen de la Pole, whom Rhys knew better by his Welsh name, Owain ap Gruffydd ap Gwenwynwyn, a man who'd conspired to assassinate Llywelyn many years earlier. Rhys had known Owain had continued in the king's favor, having sold out to the English long ago, but he hadn't thought he'd come face-to-face with him on his first day back in royal service. Owain was also married to a niece of Roger le Strange.

"Wine, gentlemen?" Bohun moved to a side table laden with food and drink and gestured with the goblet he held.

"Thank you." Rhys suddenly found himself in a position to do what he'd been doing the whole of this last year: befriending former enemies, never mind they were Marcher lords instead of guardsmen at the gate.

"Reese! It's been too long." An elbow into Rhys's ribs had him turning suddenly and almost sloshing his newly poured drink.

Rhys found himself looking into the face of Peter Stebbins, whom, like everyone else, he hadn't seen in years. He served Henry de Lacy, who was all at once the Earl of Lincoln and Guy's brother. Rhys smiled and took his forearm in greeting.

Peter winced.

Simon noticed too. "Is something wrong, Peter?"

Peter let go of Rhys's arm. "It's nothing."

"It doesn't seem like nothing," Rhys said.

"A bramble scratch." Peter flicked out his fingers dismissively. "It is no matter."

"I'm no healer, but even a scratch can be deadly," Rhys said. "Has someone looked at it?"

Peter scoffed again. "No."

Simon made a *come here* motion with his fingers. "Let me see it."

With a put-upon sigh, Peter unbuckled the bracer covering his right arm to reveal three narrow, bloody scratches along his inner forearm. The center one was approximately five inches long, with the skin around it red and discharging yellow pus.

It looked terrible. "Brambles can surely be treacherous," Rhys said in a flat voice.

As much as it would have been convenient for Rhys to have found John's killer already, John hadn't sharpened his nails to points, and he and Peter would have had to have been wrestling or somehow contorted around each other to cause these wounds. The scratches but were clearly punctures from thorns, not made by fingernails, and looked days old.

"We have a good healer here, trained by one of the monks at Llanfaes," Rhys said. "After the meeting, you should see him."

Peter nodded his thanks.

Then Rhys felt Simon's hand on his elbow, urging him away from the table towards the back wall. As if moved by unspoken agreement, the great men had begun to gather around the map on the main table.

"I'm off to fetch the king. Don't go anywhere."

"I won't."

Simon guffawed and then left through a side door, leaving Rhys alone.

His friend had gone to tell the king everyone was present for the meeting, since he always appeared last. That so many great lords had come to Caernarfon while it was still under construction spoke volumes about King Edward's view of its place in his plan to control Wales. It didn't matter that the town was on the edge of the earth. Caernarfon was to be the new administrative center of the entire principality.

Not Conwy.

Not Rhuddlan.

Caernarfon, here at the heart of what had been Gwynedd. It was also the one piece of Wales the king was keeping for himself and not designating to one of his followers.

Caernarfon Castle wasn't meant only to be a symbol of kingly power to the people of Wales. It was also signaling to Edward's Norman vassals that they would do well to remember what happens to men who refuse to bend the knee when commanded to do so: they and their descendants would be wiped from the face of the earth.

Then the door opened, and the king entered. To a man, everyone bowed, and when Rhys's head came up, the king had stopped in front of him and was smiling directly into his face.

"Reese." He looked him up and down. "It's good to have you back where you belong."

25

Day Three

Catrin

"Are you really saying you stood before both Prince Edmund and King Edward, and you're not in chains?"

Catrin knew she was glaring at Rhys, but she was a little irate that all her concern for him had been for nothing—not that it hadn't been anyway, because if he *had* been in chains, there wouldn't have been anything she could do about it. It was easier to be angry than admit how relieved she was. That would be tantamount to admitting how much she had grown to care about him in only a few days.

So her hands were on her hips as she stood in the middle of the stables, currently located outside the castle proper, to which Simon and Rhys had retreated after Rhys's ordeal in the castle. It was getting late in yet another day, and they were still without answers or suspects.

"I did. All is apparently well."

"Prince Edmund embraced him, in point of fact." Simon sat on a stool. The front legs were off the ground, and he was tipped back against the wall. "The king already knew he was here, and he greeted Rhys with a smile. He was genuinely pleased to find him yet again in Edmund's service."

"I got off easy, I know."

Catrin felt foolish now for ever suspecting Rhys had been involved in Llywelyn's death. If he had been, the king and prince would both have known he was alive, and they would have feted him, not made him fear being torn limb from limb. The name of the man who actually *had* betrayed Llywelyn was a mystery that remained unsolved.

Rhys turned to Simon. "Events fell out the way they did, and I responded to them the way I did, because it seemed necessary at the time. Even with that, I need to tell you how sorry I am that I let you think I was dead. It was unfair of me and dishonored our long friendship."

All of a sudden, Catrin felt she was intruding, but for Simon and Rhys, it was as if only they were present.

The front legs of Simon's stool came down hard on the ground. "I could make a jest. I could pretend I wasn't hurt. But that would be a lie. I was hurt."

"You are my closest friend in life."

"And you are mine, as I told Prince Edmund," Simon said. "I forgave you the moment I saw you, though I couldn't admit it until you asked."

"Thank you." Rhys bent his head. "I have missed you."

"I only hope you in turn can forgive me."

Rhys's head came up at that. "For what?"

Simon was looking at him intently. "You spoke very frankly to me earlier today, and I am not blind to what losing the war is doing to your people, Rhys. I played my part in it at the time, and it may be that one day we end up on opposite sides in a war again. It would not be my choice."

The two men exchanged a long look. Catrin didn't understand entirely what they were silently communicating to each other, but in the end, Rhys stuck out his arm to Simon, and Simon took it without hesitation. A sense of wellbeing settled over her, and from the way Simon and Rhys eased back into their seats, it came over them too.

"But not today," Rhys said.

"No." Simon relaxed again against the wall. "Today we get to investigate murder."

"Murders," Catrin said. "The residents of the castle can talk about little else."

"Better than talking about *him*," Simon jerked a thumb in Rhys's direction.

Rhys acknowledged his interjection with a nod. "Which is the reason we are here. We needed a place to think." He'd returned to the overturned bucket on which he'd been sitting, and again put his feet up on a wheelbarrow.

Catrin looked from Rhys to Simon. "Why do I think you two have done this before, been *here* before?"

"Not so much here, in this barn, of course. But in a place like this?" Simon gazed around the stables. "Many times."

"This was in the Holy Land?" Catrin said.

"And after," Rhys said, "for a time, before I returned to Wales."

"Lady Catrin, you should go back to the castle," Simon said. "With three men dead, you need to leave this to us. It is more dangerous than ever for you to be involved."

"I know that, actually. But I came for two reasons: the first is to tell Rhys that the queen would very much like to see him, at his convenience; and two, to tell you that, except for whoever killed him at that inn, I think I was the last person to see John alive."

That got the kind of reaction for which she'd been secretly hoping, in that Rhys was on his feet in an instant and approaching her. "How is that?"

"Remember why I left you this morning?"

"You'd been summoned by the queen."

She tipped her head to look up at him, and he backed off slightly. "That was a lie, as it turns out. It was John le Strange who summoned me, in the name of the queen."

Rhys didn't show very much emotion most of the time, but at her news, his hands clenched briefly into fists. "Why?"

"To warn me against spending time with you."

Rhys blinked, and Simon said, "Really?"

She glanced over at him. "You find it so surprising that John would show interest in me?"

Simon let out a laugh. "Not at all. Only that he would take it upon himself to speak to you that way, on so short an acquaintance."

"I suppose it doesn't matter now what he thought or did," she said.

"Maybe," Simon said. "But I will tell you, as I told Rhys, for your own protection before we go any further, that John le Strange was Prince Edmund's spymaster."

Catrin drew in a breath. She hadn't known that. She hadn't even guessed.

Simon was looking grim. "Who else knows you spoke to him?"

"Adeline, another lady-in-waiting, was there moments after, asking if he was Rolf. She has her eye on Rolf."

"I know Adeline." Simon's jaw clenched. "If she tells anyone else you spoke to him this morning, you could become a target for the killer, who might know John well enough to worry he confided in you."

Catrin couldn't help arguing. "I can't really be in danger, can I? I know nothing."

"You've been helping Rhys, haven't you? Is there a soul who doesn't know that too? And who was it that stood in front of the mob—was it only last night?"

"Catrin," Rhys said forcefully. "I agree there's something to be said for keeping her where I can see her. If the murderer fears she knows something that could implicate him, she may not be safe on her own, even in the castle."

Simon grunted. "Maybe especially in the castle. No place is safe, it seems."

"Right now, everyone is a suspect," Rhys continued, "which is why Simon and I were just discussing the idea of returning to the inn to question the barman again and anyone who may have been there earlier in the day. Someone will have seen something."

Simon frowned. "Too bad Rolf is indistinguishable from John except for the badges they wear. It's always been impossible for me to tell them apart."

"Rolf sneers more than John, if that's even possible." Then Rhys put up a hand. "Not to speak ill of the dead."

Catrin made a gesture to gain their attention. "When I speak to them, I always look for a little feature that makes them different from one another—a scratch on the back of a hand, for example, or a bug bite on the neck, like today. When I spoke to John, he scratched one repeatedly, and it was quite red. I almost mentioned to him that he should have it looked at. It's something anyone would notice and a good way to tell them apart if someone at the inn saw the brothers, separately or together."

Both Simon and Rhys were looking at her with identical quizzical expressions on their faces.

"Are you sure about the bite?" Rhys asked.

"Yes."

"Are you sure you were actually speaking to John?" Simon said thoughtfully.

"He wore the blue chevron." She paused. "He behaved like John."

Simon and Rhys gave each other yet another long look, and then Rhys said, "I don't remember the dead man having an ugly bite on his neck."

"We must look for it immediately," Simon said. "They *were* twins. They could have switched identities yesterday morning."

"And if they did, what does it signify?" Catrin thought back to Rolf's strange behavior at the funeral. He had looked like Rolf. He had sneered like Rolf, but his interest in her had been that of John. As had been John's interest in her this morning. If the brothers had switched identities at any point in the last two days, it had been for reasons that remained hidden. Both Stranges had been in the great hall when Gruffydd had arrived to tell them about the rabble of townspeople threatening the village.

"If it's John left alive, did he kill his brother and assume his identity for his inheritance?" Simon said.

"According to the guards, Rolf never left the castle. We checked that. Only one twin passed through any gate."

"And you said John had just arrived the night Cole's body was found," Catrin said. "That twin didn't kill Cole and Tomos, though admittedly Rolf—or the man we viewed as Rolf—was here already."

Simon scratched the back of his head. "I don't know why I never thought about them switching chevrons."

"Nor I, but it seems obvious that they might," Rhys said.

"Both have been in and out of the king's circle this last year since I've been in the queen's service," Catrin said, "but only recently has John expressed interest in me."

"So was it Rolf or John at the funeral?" Rhys glowered a bit. "He didn't have an ugly bite on his neck then, but that means nothing because he could have been bitten crossing the water back to the castle."

"In either case," Catrin said, "if the man I spoke to as John is currently presenting himself as Rolf, it makes me think I shouldn't accompany you to inspect the body but instead keep an eye on whichever twin is still alive. If we're sure he didn't kill his brother, he will be the one man in the whole of the castle with whom I can be safe."

"Do you *want* to do that?" Rhys looked at her in surprise.

She spread her hands wide. "Are you asking if spending the evening in his company is something to look forward to? Of course not. But if the killer meant to murder John, not Rolf, and John is the one still alive, wouldn't it be best to make sure the killer doesn't try again?"

"Indeed," Simon said. "All effort must be put to making him think he succeeded."

26

Day Three
Catrin

Rhys and Simon weren't gone very long, a matter of an hour at most, and when they returned to the castle, they found Catrin in the great hall, where she'd been lurking. Truth be told, more than watching John/Rolf, she'd been making an inventory of the diners to see who held his knife in his left hand when he stabbed his vegetables. There were more than a few, and she could draw no conclusions.

The surviving twin sat at one of the long tables near the head of the hall, his head in his hands. It hadn't been very hard to keep an eye on him because he hadn't moved in that hour except to lift his cup from the table to his mouth. She didn't know for certain how long he'd been drinking steadily, but it appeared he had begun at least from the moment Guy told him his brother was dead.

Earlier, the king himself had come down from the high table to express his condolences. Others had come up to him at various times, including Guy, who'd broken the news to him in the first place.

This second time, Guy had pressed John/Rolf hard about his whereabouts while his brother was dying, but he appeared to have come to the same conclusions as Simon and Rhys: unless John/Rolf had found a secret way out of the castle, or an effective disguise, they had to look elsewhere for the murderer.

And then there was the matter of the incomplete hexfoil, the presence of which at this latest murder scene did not seem to be common knowledge amongst the residents of the castle, even if it must have spread throughout the town already.

"The dead twin's neck is bite-free," Rhys said as he slid onto the bench next to Catrin. "How about you?"

"You can see for yourself this Strange has it. He's definitely the man I spoke to this morning. I still think he's John."

Simon had found a spot to stand against the wall, not yet ready to sit, and his arms were folded across his chest. "The lateness of the hour means that little is going to be accomplished outside the castle until tomorrow."

"What do you need to do that you haven't?" Catrin asked.

Simon ticked the items off his fingers. "Discover where the mason laid his head at night, find the missing possessions of the victims, though Guy has sworn to do that himself starting tomorrow, and return to the inn for further questions."

Rhys put out a hand to his friend. "At least we could speak to the surviving twin. Should we do it here in the hall?"

"My quarters would be better."

"I'll bring him." Catrin stood. "He'll come with me." Without further ado, she made her way to where John/Rolf was sitting and settled herself on the bench beside him, though with her legs towards the room instead of underneath the table.

She nudged him. "John."

He was a good enough mummer that he didn't rise to the bait, but he didn't look up from his drink either. "I'm Rolf, as you well know."

"I'm sorry, Rolf, for your loss. Would you come with me? I would like to talk to you in private."

That was an unusual enough request, even if he was Rolf, that he actually turned his head and showed interest. "Where?"

She rose to her feet. "Just come."

He stood, refilled his drink, and followed her out of the hall, still carrying the cup. Every eye in the room was on them, but that couldn't be helped. Simon and Rhys had already departed, which was good because she didn't want to put John/Rolf more on his guard than he already was, if he was really John. Calling him *John* should have put him on alert—but then, he *was* drunk.

They crossed the bailey, and though John/Rolf hesitated when she opened the door to the guardroom, he followed her inside. "I've already been questioned by Guy. I had nothing to do with my brother's death."

"We know that."

The guardroom itself was empty, indicating Simon had ordered everyone away moments before. She led John/Rolf through it and then gestured for him to precede her into Simon's quarters.

Now John/Rolf finally did balk, frowning at the sight of the two men waiting for him. "What do *you* two want?"

Simon was sitting behind his table, and Rhys was leaned against the side wall in a relaxed stance, his arms folded and his ankles crossed. If he'd been eating an apple, he would have resembled John when Catrin had seen him that morning. Thankfully, the two men otherwise looked nothing alike.

"Please, sit down, Rolf. Reese and I were the ones to care for your brother in death, and I thought you might want to hear about it." Simon put out a placating hand, gesturing across the table to a chair.

"We thought, as well, that you might prefer not to talk in the hall." Rhys had brought another chair for Catrin, which he moved to hold for her. "Catrin was kind enough to assist us."

John/Rolf looked around the room, but then sighed, set down his cup, and sat in the chair opposite Simon as he'd been bid. For a moment he didn't speak, and then he said. "Did he suffer?"

The question was not one Catrin would have thought a soldier such as John/Rolf would have asked. It made him more human and approachable. Of course, he'd just lost his brother, had too much to drink, and his guard was down. She had little experience questioning suspects or victims in an investigation, but she had plenty of experience with drunk men. Sometimes drink made men angry. Other times it made them despondent. Likely John/Rolf had been despondent before he'd started drinking. Drink made few men happy.

But it always made them uninhibited.

Catrin could see in the men's faces that John/Rolf's dead brother *had* suffered as he was dying, so again it was she who answered, putting a gentle hand on his arm as she did so. "I'm sorry to tell you that he was stabbed three times, just like the others."

Even deep into his cups, John/Rolf recoiled. "What does my brother's death have to do with those—those—*others?*"

"Something, clearly," Simon said. "An incomplete hexfoil was carved on the door next to where he died."

John/Rolf's mouth genuinely fell open. "He wouldn't have been involved in anything like that!" He could have been overly protesting, but his surprise looked genuine to Catrin.

Then he collapsed forward, his forehead in his right hand and his elbow resting on the table. With his left hand, he scratched his neck. The bite was truly inflamed now. If he scratched it much more, it could suppurate.

Rhys and Simon simply watched, completely silent. After a moment, John/Rolf arrested his motion and looked up. "What?"

Simon canted his head. "That bite on your neck, Rolf, or shall I say, *John*, is distinctive. Catrin noticed it when you spoke to her this morning."

He was ready to be irate. "I don't know what—"

"I almost mentioned to you then that you should see the healer for a salve, since it was so red." Catrin spoke gently. "You were John, then."

"What we want to hear from you is *why* you switched identities with your brother, and which brother you actually are," Simon said. "Our guess, as I said, is that you are John, and it is Rolf who is dead."

"From how easily you are currently pretending to be Rolf, we suspect you and Rolf switched identities often," Rhys said.

Yesterday's John/Rolf would have sneered at Rhys just for speaking in his presence, but today he was subdued by his brother's death—and newly discovered in fraud. Even with that, he kept his head bent and didn't answer. They settled in to wait him out. Even as a novice investigator, Catrin knew enough not to fill the silence.

Finally, he looked up. "You're right. I'm John. My brother and I switched identities often, from a very young age. I can't ever remember a week where I wasn't Rolf for at least a few hours, except for the times we were apart on campaign. I was the better leader, but he was the better fighter. Sometimes we switched places just so I could give a speech to the men.

"When we were younger, we always could campaign together. It is only in recent years that we have spent weeks at a time apart. Our father is in direct service to King Edward, but it fell out that Rolf and I both served Edmund, so we could continue to wear the same colors."

"Why did you switch identities today?" Simon's voice was even and calm, despite the magnitude of this revelation. It was what they'd expected, though on a grander scale than Catrin herself had imagined.

"I didn't know we were doing it today until I happened to glance into the bailey to see Rolf leaving the castle wearing the blue chevron. It was odd. He wasn't in mail armor but in gear more like you wear." John was looking at Rhys. "*I* was currently wearing my blue chevron, so I quickly switched it out." He reached into the purse at his waist and pulled out the blue chevron of John. It was really two chevrons, with a thin band linking them together. Pinned to his shoulder, the badge would show front and back. Catrin had always assumed it was sewed permanently.

Simon glanced at John's badge and then back into his face. "Do you know what Rolf was doing at that inn?"

"I questioned my manservant as soon as I returned to our room, and he said Rolf opened a message intended for me. It was from one of my—" he glanced quickly at Catrin.

"She knows you spy for Edmund," Simon said. "You can trust her."

John ducked his head, not looking at Catrin anymore. "One of my people wanted to meet me in that inn. Rolf helps me in my work, in large part because he can't help it, since we are easily mistaken for one another."

"So it was usual for him to read messages addressed to you?"

"And vice versa."

The trust the two brothers had in each other was humbling, thus the magnitude of John's loss. "Your manservant knows you switch identities?"

"Of course. He couldn't serve us and not know. Vincent has been with us practically since we were born. He could always tell us apart. Even if he hadn't helped Rolf dress and switch his chevron, he would have known I was John." He bit his lip nervously. "Please don't tell the prince. I will do it myself."

"Oh, we don't want anyone to tell the prince or king, not yet," Simon said.

John gaped at him. "What? Why not?"

"If the killer intended for you to die, we want him to think he succeeded," Rhys said. "At least for now."

"What does that mean?" John said, and there was a bit of an aghast tone to his voice, as if he'd already guessed what Rhys was thinking.

"In case we decide to set a trap with you as bait," Simon said.

John's eyes narrowed. "I would gladly participate. Anything to catch my brother's killer."

"Who sent the message?" Catrin asked.

"I don't know. Rolf held it to a candle and did not tell Vincent what it said."

The obvious next question formed on Catrin's lips, though she glanced at Rhys before she asked it. He raised an eyebrow and nodded. She didn't know if he was reading her mind or realized, as she did, that John responded better to her questions than to his or Simon's.

"My lord, how many people could it have been from?"

John looked at her for a heartbeat, confusion in his face, and then he laughed. "How many spies do I have, you mean? I consider everyone a possible informant."

"Yes, but how many can write?"

"Oh." He nodded. "I see. Many fewer have that ability, but you must see my problem: I could have an informant who cannot read but knows that I can and asked someone to write the message for me."

"Who delivered this message?" Catrin said.

"A guard at the King's Gate, but it was a girl from the town who brought it to him. And before you ask, he wouldn't know the girl again. It could be anyone. It could have been you."

"I can read."

John actually laughed. "Of course you can."

Rhys grinned too. "Her father was Prince Llywelyn's steward, required to have the ability to read and write. He taught his sons, so any one of them could take his place upon his death, and he included Catrin because it was easier than leaving her out. With her, that's usually the way of it."

"Odd of the killer to expose himself by sending a note," Simon said thoughtfully.

"Unless the one who asked him to come to the inn isn't the one who killed him and genuinely wanted to meet with John," Rhys said.

"How many knew about your particular service to Prince Edmund?" Catrin asked.

They all looked at John, who shrugged. In the last quarter of an hour, he'd sobered considerably. "More than you might think."

Rhys nodded. "And as we realized quite some time ago, all it takes is one."

27

Day Four

Rhys

To say that tensions in Caernarfon were running high was to woefully understate the case. Guards on the town walls had been doubled, and the identity of anyone going in or out of the castle was being checked and double-checked. Somehow, Rhys had lost half the day again and was no closer to finding the killer than he'd been two days ago. Or four days ago. And the Baphomet conspiracy? He was completely in the dark as to how it fit in to any of this, if it did at all.

As Rhys entered the town through the east gate, having spent the morning in fruitless pursuit of answers outside the castle, Simon appeared at his shoulder as if he'd been watching for him. Perhaps he had.

"We haven't yet found where Tomos the mason was staying," Simon said, without preamble.

Rhys almost snapped a quick response back at him but managed to moderate his tone at the last moment. Still, his answer came out sharper than he intended. "You don't have to tell me. Where do you think I've been all morning? But so far, inquiries have produced no results." He sighed. "I feel as if I am being stonewalled by my own people."

"That is irksome."

Rhys tsked. "Especially as my entire use here is to find answers amongst the Welsh where Normans fear to tread. But I am leaguing with the devil, to their eyes."

"Better the devil you know—"

"—than the one you don't? Normally I would agree. Normally, they would too."

"Do you think nobody will talk because they're afraid?" Simon asked. "After the other night, they can't want to put themselves forward."

"Likely."

Simon looked hard at Rhys. "You genuinely don't know either, do you?"

"I do not. And yes, part of me doesn't want to know, because then Guy might accuse one of them of murder, arbitrarily, just as he did with Aron. I would prefer to focus on finding the real killer."

"Which brings you back into the town ... why?"

"I meant to visit the inn again yesterday, but we got distracted by Rolf's body and that bite. I need to more fully question the bartender."

"I will come with you."

Rhys narrowed his eyes at his friend. "Are you my minder, Simon?"

Simon chewed on his tongue for a moment, before nodding sharply. "You can't be surprised that not everybody trusts you, especially now." He laughed. "I think they are less likely to trust you now that they know who you really are. All I've heard this morning is *the crouchback* this and *the crouchback* that."

"I'm surprised," Rhys said, and genuinely was.

"My arrival has elevated your station far above what anyone thought you were. Some are embarrassed; some feel threatened; all are curious."

Rhys gestured down the street. "Come on then. No time like the present."

A wind had started blowing in the night, bringing rain for the first time that week. It wasn't raining at that very moment, but as this was Wales, it undoubtedly would within the next few hours. During the spring, most days included some rain, which is what had made the last few days so unusual.

The streets were moderately full of people for the middle of the week. Tomorrow was Friday, market day, where farmers from miles around came into town to sell their wares and buy what they couldn't make for themselves. Many were Welsh, since much of the countryside was still farmed by his people.

At Conwy and Denbigh, English farmers had been given Welsh land to farm, but quite literally *no* Englishman had wanted to settle this far west. So far, the merchants in the town consisted of innkeepers, craftspeople, and traders who sold their wares primarily to the people building the castle and the Welsh people outside, though among the Welsh, coinage was extremely limited.

Market day was always a treat for the English amongst them—though the Welsh were a different story. A representative of each family was required to attend, and if he didn't, the family would be fined. It tended to put a damper on the joviality of the day.

Rhys was curious to see who would come tomorrow. It would depend on which the people feared more: the killer or the king's officers.

Puddles had formed in the streets, which had not yet been graveled or cobbled as they were in Conwy. The king liked things neat, Rhys would give him that. Raindrops began to fall, and even though they had a short walk to the inn, Rhys tugged his cloak closer around himself and pulled up his hood. It wasn't that he feared getting wet but rather that he had no squire to dry and oil his leather gear, so either he'd have to do it himself tonight or start teaching one of Gruffydd's grandsons to do it for him. The latter sounded like a much more sensible project. If and when Rhys acquired a new mail shirt, he would need a squire to polish the links so they didn't rust.

Since they were into the afternoon and it had started to rain, the inn was full, which was exactly what Rhys had wanted to be there for. More than twenty people drank and ate in the common room, with men outnumbering women four to one, but there were a number of women in the room, several accompanying their husbands for a drink by the fire. One had three men hovering around her and was smiling coquettishly at each one in turn. As Rhys entered, her eyes turned for a moment to him, and she winked.

It stopped him in his tracks, far more than the way the room had briefly hushed at their entrance. Having lived and served in

Gwynedd for the past year, Rhys himself was recognized by many, and now that he was accompanied by Simon, they were both nodded to respectfully. Then the woman looked away, and conversations began where they'd left off. Rhys and Simon were dressed in royal gear, in an English town. The populace didn't fear soldiers, and everybody hadn't suddenly started talking loudly in Welsh, which would have happened if Rhys had worn his tunic into an inn in Gwynedd back when Prince Llywelyn had ruled the region.

Inside the tavern, everyone was speaking English. Most of the noblemen at the castle would not speak it, which is why they needed Rhys and another reason he and Simon were best suited to conduct this investigation. For his part, Simon had learned French from his family, English in the cradle from his nanny, and then, apparently, Welsh in self-defense.

The two men went to the bar.

"My lords." Tom the barman swept a cloth across the already polished surface. "What can I do for you?"

"One mead, one ale, and you can answer some questions, if you will." Rhys was being polite, and Tom should know it. Refusing to answer questions put by the king's officers was not really an option.

Tom blinked, finally recognizing them from the day before. "Apologies, my lords. It will just be a moment." Once he came back with their drinks, he said, "On the house."

Simon dropped a small coin on the bar. "We pay for what we drink."

Tom slid the coin into his hand. "This is again about the man who died? As I told you yesterday, my lords, I barely spoke to him. I don't know what more I can say."

Simon tipped his head to indicate Rhys. "The investigation has progressed since then. Can someone else pour drinks while we adjourn to the back?"

Tom didn't quite manage to swallow down his sigh, but he signaled to one of the servers, a young man half his age, who then slid behind the bar to take his place.

"This way." Tom led them down the corridor. The back door had been propped open to allow easy passage from the common room to the kitchen, located in the yard. Sensibly, out of fear of fire, the kitchen had its own building, accessed by a covered walkway, rather than being part of the main structure.

Tom gestured them into a curtained off pantry, full of stacked cheeses and other food items ready to be served. As if he and Rhys had discussed how to proceed in advance, which they hadn't, Simon faded against the back wall. He knew what was coming next, having seen it before, though not for some time.

Rhys was out of practice, but he looked into Tom's eyes anyway and said, "Please take a deep breath and let it out slowly."

Tom was wary, and his expression reluctant.

"It's possible you remember more than you think," Rhys said. "I'd like you to close your eyes and listen to my voice as I talk you through the events of yesterday."

"I don't know what you think I'm going to remember," Tom said, but he did as Rhys asked, accustomed to obeying a knight.

"Take another deep breath and let it out."

Tom obeyed. As for Rhys, he could almost smell the dust and heat of the crowded streets of Acre, and in his own head hear the voice of his Saracen tutor, instructing him on how to get better answers from witnesses.

"You are standing behind the bar when John le Strange enters—"

"I didn't know who he was at the time, and I wasn't standing behind the bar. One of the regulars had spilled his drink. While Bob cleaned it up, I delivered another to the patron personally. Oh—" Tom opened his eyes. "I hadn't remembered that."

Rhys made a soothing motion with his hand. "Close your eyes again, take another breath in and out, and remember what you saw."

Tom was warming to the exercise now, taking two deep breaths and visibly relaxing, before speaking again. "He blew into the inn like the west wind, as if he was in a hurry. He went straight to the bar. He wasn't in mail, but I remember noting the fine weave of his cloak, so I knew he was a nobleman, and when he took out his purse, I saw it was heavy with coins. I asked what he wanted, and he ordered ale, and paid—too much, really. He could have had four drinks for that amount, but he told me to keep it. I remember now—I asked if he was all right, because his forehead was beaded with sweat. He told me he just needed the drink, which he drained without taking a breath. I refilled the cup, and he took it to a table. I helped another customer, and by the time I again looked to where he was sitting, he was gone."

"To the latrine? He would have had to walk down the corridor to get there."

"He might have, though I didn't see him. But as I said, I was busy."

"He overpaid," Rhys said. "That didn't make you wonder?"

"If he came back for more, I would have served him, but the room was full. Rumor had it Prince Edmund was coming to town, and people wanted to talk about it."

"Did you see anyone else who was remarkable enter the inn?"

"You, my lord," he said bluntly to Rhys. "Nobody else." He still had his eyes closed, but now his brow furrowed. "Coroner Guy had stopped by shortly beforehand, looking for Rosie."

"Rosie?"

"She's one of our barmaids. She wasn't here then, so I asked to take a message. He shook his head and left."

Out of the corner of Rhys's eye, he saw Simon drop his arms and straighten against the wall.

"You're sure it was Guy?"

"Of course. He comes here often."

"And Rosie?"

"She was talking with some men when you came in. I can point her out to you if you like."

"We would be grateful." Rhys studied Tom, but when no more information was forthcoming, he decided the barman had had enough. He put a hand on his shoulder. "Thank you. You've been most helpful. If you think of anything else that might be useful, come find me or Simon at the castle."

"I will." Tom opened his eyes and blinked, looking around as if surprised to find himself in the pantry, and his expression became one of embarrassment.

Rhys tipped his head towards the doorway. "You can get back to work."

He ducked his head. "Thank you, my lord."

As he left, Simon shook his head. "I'd forgotten what that was like. I was almost ready to reveal my darkest secrets to everyone within shouting distance if only you'd asked."

Rhys scoffed. "People want to remember, just like they want to tell the truth. You simply have to get past the barriers they put up preventing it."

28

Day Four
Rhys

"Where to next?" Simon asked as he and Rhys left the inn and stood in the street. "Track down Rosie? Though I don't see how she would be important. It was Guy who wanted her, not Rolf."

Rosie had turned out to be the woman who'd winked at Rhys, but she'd left before they'd come out of the pantry.

"What better source of information about the goings-on in Caernarfon could there be than a barmaid?" Rhys said. "They see and hear more than any man. Maybe that's who Rolf was meeting."

"And there she is—because you are the luckiest man I know." Simon pointed towards a side alley, out of which the woman in question was just coming, heading for her place of employment.

Rhys would have disputed that assessment on pretty much every front, but in this instance, Rosie's return was fortuitous. "Excuse me!" He spoke in English, thinking that language might be best.

Rosie stopped and didn't retreat or run away. Taking the lead again, Rhys approached. "We just want to ask you some questions. John le Strange was looking for you."

"You mean Guy fitz Lacy, don't you?" Simon said from behind him.

Rhys could have meant that, but he was throwing out a guess on a hunch. Fortunately, she either didn't hear Simon or took Rhys at his word because she said, "He was supposed to meet me at the start of my shift. I was on my way to the inn when I saw all the commotion. The people outside told me he died in the latrine." She shivered.

"Why were you late?" Rhys said.

"I was early. Our arrangement had been for me to send him a note as to the day, but the time and place was always the same, when the bell tolled for mid-afternoon. He never liked to arrive before I did. I don't know what was different this time."

The difference was Rolf came to meet you, not John. But Rhys didn't say what he was thinking out loud. "Did you know him well?"

Her eyes narrowed, and her attitude wasn't quite as open as before. "I did. I'd come to Carnarvon ahead of him, and Alice employed me based on his recommendation. But we hadn't had a chance to talk beyond a few exchanged words the first night he arrived."

Which explained why Rhys had encountered him entering the castle from the town through the King's Gate. "Go on."

"We agreed to wait a few days before speaking. I was to send a message when I would be free to talk about whatever rumors I could dredge up. By now, I had a list of them, from a warning he should keep an eye on the southeast corner of the castle because the stonemasons had bungled some of the mortar to asking him to tell Coroner Lacy to leave me alone."

"Guy was bothering you?"

"I think he knows what I do for Lord Strange. He didn't like that I poked my nose where he thought it didn't belong, and that John and I were—" she paused, hesitating.

"More than friends?" Rhys said gently.

Rosie nodded, and her mouth turned down, but she didn't weep. "Where Lord Strange went, I went. Somehow Guy found out."

"What was your relationship with Guy?"

"I didn't have one, other than trying to avoid him."

"That could be motive for murder right there," Simon said in an undertone, for Rhys's ears alone, "but it would be a reason for John to murder Guy not the other way around."

Simon's phrasing had Rhys looking at him sharply. "You suspect Guy?"

Simon stared at him. "What? No, of course not. It was a figure of speech."

Rhys didn't know about that. His friend had insight at times, even if, as a Norman, he ruthlessly suppressed it when it bobbed to the surface. "Her information does beg the question as to why John didn't mention Rosie when we questioned him."

"We'll have to ask him," Simon said.

Rhys turned back to Rosie. "What do you know of his brother Rolf?"

"They were close, I know that much, and John looked up to him. Rolf didn't approve of me. He even went so far as to warn John off. John refused to put me aside. I think it was the one time he went against his brother's wishes."

"When was this?"

"A few months ago."

"Did you see them together often?"

"No. After that, John kept me away from Rolf, and it isn't as if we would ever move in the same circles." As she answered, Rosie looked away, towards the inn, a thoughtful expression on her face.

"Do you have an idea about who killed John and why?"

"Other than Guy?" She looked back to Rhys and made a deprecating gesture with one hand. "I heard you say his name."

"Would Guy have been jealous enough of your relationship with John to murder him?"

She made a moue of disagreement. "No. He wouldn't risk anything for me. He is a striver."

"All Normans strive."

"But he would stab his best friend in the back to gain a social advantage. That would be the only reason he'd go after John, and really, Guy is about to become Sheriff of Denbigh, so he and John were not rivals."

"Except for your affections."

"Honestly, Guy wasn't picky, and he didn't care if a woman returned his interest or not. He'd have his way with her anyway. If you have a woman up at that castle, I'd keep her well out of his path."

Rhys didn't like hearing that, not that he was surprised, and his next question came out more than a little grimly. "You know him that well?"

"I've been around, as has he."

"My lord!" One of the younger men of the garrison huffed up. It appeared he'd sprinted all the way from the castle, because he stood before them with his hands resting on his knees, breathing hard. Rhys had never had so many instances of being chased down in his life. It almost made him start to think he was important.

He put a hand on the guard's shoulder. "Take a breath. What is it?"

"Coroner Guy has found the murderer!"

Simon actually laughed. "You could have led with that, young man. Who is it?"

"A farmer from the outlying area. The clothes and gear from the first two men who died were found hidden in a corner of his barn. He also had that symbol carved on the wall in front of an unholy altar!" Even breathless, the man's voice conveyed the horror and deliciousness of the discovery.

"An unholy altar, eh?" Simon's lips curved in a wry smile.

But Rhys had turned grave. "He's a Welshman?"

"Of course."

"His name?" Rhys's heart was in his throat.

The guard, who'd straightened by now, made a dismissive motion with his hand. "Davey? Something like that."

"Dafi." Rhys unthinkingly corrected his pronunciation. "He has been brought to the castle?"

"They are coming now, my lord."

"We will come too," Simon said.

The guard ran off to return to his post, and Rhys turned to Rosie. "This isn't over—" He hesitated. It was hard not to tell her John was alive. "Just don't leave town."

As she went into the tavern, Simon and Rhys started up the street, their pace considerably faster than when they'd come down it.

"Who is he?" Simon meant the man Guy was accusing of murder.

"Old Dafi, we call him. He's crotchety and cantankerous. He lives up the river and keeps more goats than sheep, which you should understand by now is viewed as very strange behavior indeed."

"Could he have killed these men?"

"Physically he's capable. He's worked a farm all of his life. He's an older man but still strong."

"But why would he?"

"He wouldn't. For starters, I know him. He hates people. Given that, he never would have entered the town, even if the guards had let him in."

"Hatred is a powerful motivator. It could be enough."

"Of course Dafi hates Normans. But so does every Welshman in Gwynedd. It isn't enough. And what would he know about the Baphomet, living his whole life as he has herding sheep and goats up and down the mountain?"

"The Baphomet aside, while Strange was the only Norman killed, all three dead men were associated with the king. Cole was English but working for a Clare, and Tomos was working on the castle. To a fanatic, those two could be viewed as traitors, and that's why they were targeted."

"I suppose." But Rhys didn't believe it. "More likely, the real murderer planted the evidence to distract us from himself."

"As I recall, you suspected that was going to happen from the start." Simon rubbed his chin thoughtfully.

Once inside the castle, Rhys could see by the clear relief in the faces of everyone around them that news of Dafi's capture had spread. People who never smiled were smiling—though their smiles turned to growls and narrowed eyes as Dafi was paraded through the Queen's Gate and into the bailey, heading for the prison cell Aron had occupied.

Guy led the company, smirking all the while. Simon and Rhys stepped aside to let the marching soldiers pass, and Rhys caught sight of Dafi's face. It was bruised and bloodied, with one eye swollen shut.

Simon then said to Rhys in an undertone, "You are thinking this Davey has been set up to take the fall for the real killer?"

"It's what I would do if I had just killed three people, one of them the son of a favorite of the king."

"Not as much a favorite anymore, though, is he?" Simon spoke somewhat musingly, almost absently, his eyes still on the marching soldiers.

Rhys turned his head to look at him. "Isn't he? I thought Roger le Strange could do no wrong."

"In wartime, yes. He was the mind behind Llywelyn's death, not to mention the one who wrote the letter to King Edward telling him of it—and he knew all about it because he'd been there that day."

Simon paused at the stricken look on Rhys's face. "You didn't know?"

Rhys shook his head.

"You may have noted that while Roger is a baron of some note in England, his reward hasn't been land in Wales, like the Lacys, but to become justiciar of all forest lands south of the River Trent, a lucrative position to be sure, but more like being a sheriff than a lord."

Rhys nodded, wondering if the slight contributed to the sneer permanently affixed to John's face—and on Rolf's when he was alive.

Simon continued, "While Roger's strong arm at Castell y Bere was exactly what King Edward thought the region needed last year, the king now views his measures as too harsh."

"That's hard to believe," Rhys said, under his breath, prompting a sharp look from Simon.

"Don't say that. Don't even think it."

Rhys bobbed his head. "Apologies. I will keep my peace. But this investigation? It isn't over."

Now the captive was gone, the workers went back to their tasks. An hour remained of daylight, and many were starting to put away their things. Tomos, if he'd been among them, would have been thinking about where he was going to lay his head that night.

Then Guy appeared in front of them, the grin on his face stretching from ear to ear. Earlier, he'd been wearing his helmet, but now he carried it under his arm and had pushed back his coif. "So, it's over."

"So it seems, my lord," Simon said before Rhys could say anything. "Congratulations are in order."

"Thank you." Guy turned his head to look towards the prison tower. As he did so, part of his neck, which had up until then remained hidden under his armor, was revealed, showing two deep scratches.

Rhys put a fist to his lips, thought about whether or not he should say anything, and then did anyway, even if Simon wouldn't have approved. "You've hurt your neck, my lord. Earlier today I was speaking to Peter Stebbins about scratches from a bramble on his arm. The healer can help you too."

Guy's head swung back to Rhys, and his hand went to his neck. "These? They're nothing. A whore's nails, that's all." He returned to smirking.

Rhys allowed his eyes to drop to the ground. "Of course. My apologies."

By the time he looked up, Guy was heading to the great hall.

Simon put a hand on Rhys's arm. "Watch your step with Guy. He is illegitimate, but his brother loves him. If the king had to choose between believing a Lacy and believing you, it wouldn't even be a choice. I can protect you only so far."

"But you saw the scratches—"

"I did."

They shared a moment of silent understanding, before Rhys said, "I will say nothing to cast doubt on Dafi's guilt until we can prove he's innocent." Rather than making him uneasy, Simon's warning had calmed Rhys's mind and sharpened his focus. "With no murder to investigate and no reason to have anything further to do with Guy at all, I will be free to look into whatever I want by myself."

"That may be, but I can't accompany you without drawing attention to what you are doing, so you'll have nobody to watch your back. You must be careful."

Rhys pressed his lips together, thinking. Then his mouth twitched. "That's all right. I'll take Catrin. After Rosie's warning, I certainly can't leave her unattended in the castle with Guy roaming the halls."

Simon didn't look reassured, but now Rhys grinned openly as he gestured to the prison tower. "Besides which, all is well, don't you know? Guy caught the killer!"

29

Day Four
Catrin

"You're sure?"

"Do you want to come or not?"

"Of course I want to come!" Catrin swept around the room, first picking up her cloak to hand it to Rhys and then tying her purse to her belt. "I'm just surprised you're asking."

"The investigation is over. Everyone can go back to normal. Nobody need pay attention to either of us at all." He helped her adjust her cloak around her shoulders.

Catrin gave him a side-eyed look. "Which is, of course, why we are leaving the castle at sunset to revisit the scene of the crime in the dark."

"Well ... not exactly the scene of the crime."

They'd been speaking in Welsh, progressing down the corridor and out into the bailey. From the easy smiles turned in their direction by everyone they passed, the mood had definitely lightened.

"What does that mean?" Catrin asked.

"We have a stop first. It might take a while." He had a horse waiting, held near the Queen's Gate by a stable boy. Rhys mounted, and then the boy boosted Catrin up behind him.

Catrin cinched her arms around Rhys's waist, deciding not to press him. She *was* glad to be included and, in truth, she didn't much care where they were going. It was embarrassing, really, how quickly she'd come to prefer Rhys's company to anyone else's.

But before they could actually leave the castle, John le Strange hastened through the quiet building works, calling to them to stop before they could vanish through the gate. Once Rhys reined in, John halted by his left boot. Laughter could be heard emanating from the great hall, since the main door was open. Within the bailey, it was quiet, and he kept his voice so low Catrin had to lean forward to hear him.

"You're still investigating, aren't you?"

Rhys evaded boldly. "We're going for a ride."

"You won't tell me the truth, and I understand why. We both know this poor fellow didn't kill my brother. It's absurd to think it. He was never seen in the town, for starters. He certainly was never let in any gate."

That had been Catrin and Rhys's conclusion. Because John had been honest, she decided it was safe to ask, "How do you know?"

"You aren't the only one who can ask questions."

Catrin felt Rhys shift in the saddle within the circle of her arms. She didn't like John. She certainly didn't want to be courted by him. But there was something raw about him tonight that aroused her empathy.

Rhys took in a breath. "We have to be somewhere else, but I promise we will talk tomorrow morning, first thing."

John still looked pensive, but he stepped back and replied with a straightforward, "Thank you." It was an amazing transformation in a single day.

Catrin had a sudden thought. "Without a protector, Dafi might not live through the night. Since it was your brother he supposedly killed—"

John's expression cleared. "Leave it to me. Who better to protect him?"

Rhys and Catrin rode out of the castle with the sun setting behind them, a clear moment in an otherwise overcast and rainy day. Catrin found herself breathing deeply.

"It's too constraining isn't it? The castle, I mean." Rhys shook his head. "These Normans and their stone walls ..."

"Llywelyn didn't need them because he was one of us," Catrin said. "Only a foreign conqueror needs to protect himself from the people he rules."

"We can never go back," Rhys said softly. "We can only go forward."

"That's what we're doing." Catrin tightened her arms around his waist and pressed her cheek into his spine, feeling the warmth of him.

A quarter of an hour later, they were trotting down the lane through the village to Gruffydd's house. It was the only house with light inside. After they dismounted and tied the horse, they entered to find it packed to the rafters with villagers.

At their entrance, the babble of talk stopped like the dousing of a candle. At the sight of everyone looking at her, Catrin forced herself to breathe easy. Then, to her surprise, Rhys took her hand and threaded his way towards where Gruffydd stood in the center of the room. Upon reaching him, Rhys seated Catrin on a suddenly vacated stool a few feet from where he and Gruffydd had chosen to stand.

"Thank you for coming." Rhys turned in a slow circle, taking in the faces of everyone present.

And it really was *everyone*, from six-month old babes to ancient grannies. Catrin sat with her hands clenched in her lap, not meeting anyone's eyes. She understood the great trust Rhys and his people were placing in her to allow her at this meeting. If she hadn't helped save the village, it might never have been possible at all. She also now understood why, after they'd dismounted, Rhys had removed his surcoat with Edmund's crest. He wasn't here today as an officer of the king but as one of them.

"You know why I'm here. Guy fitz Lacy has arrested Dafi. *Our* Dafi. Even if he rubbed every single person in this room the wrong way at one time or another, we can't let him hang for a crime he didn't commit. He didn't murder any of those men. Which means someone else did. It's time you told me what you know about it, so I can find the real killer, and a Welshman isn't blamed yet again for a crime he didn't commit."

A red-headed older man raised a hand. "How do we know Dafi didn't kill them, even this noblemen found in the latrine?"

"How many of you are allowed free passage into town enough to encounter a Norman at an inn and kill him? How many of you even speak English or French?"

Gruffydd grunted. "Not even Dai speaks English. In fact, you're the only one I know who speaks all three languages."

"And I didn't do it."

There was a stirring around the room at Rhys's flat denial, prompting Catrin's head to come up. She found so many eyes on her, she realized they needed her to speak too. So she rose to her feet and approached Rhys's side. "I have been away a long time. Some of you may remember me tagging after Rhys and my brother Hywel, pigtails ratty with twigs, trying to keep up with them."

Silence enveloped the room as they waited for her to continue. The moment was pivotal for her—not only with these people, but with Rhys—and she knew she had to speak from the heart.

"I was married away from here when I was only sixteen years old. My father did what he thought was best for Gwynedd in giving me to Robert. I serve the queen now. We all serve the queen now. But I remain as Welsh as you are. At sixteen, I had no say in what happened to me. I do now. Let me help you as Rhys does."

She found Rhys's hand wrapping around hers again. "Let *us* help," he said. "We have a day, maybe two at most, to save Dafi's life. If we can't exonerate him, and he is found guilty of murdering Lord Strange, then this entire village will be punished. It will be not only Dafi, but you as well, who pay the price for these deaths."

A stirring swept through the audience like a breeze through the leaves. She couldn't fault them for their self-interest. She and

Rhys were taking a risk in being so open with them. It might be that one of them was tempted to inform the authorities about where their true loyalties lay. John le Strange hadn't been here long enough to set up a network of spies, but she knew for a fact that King Edward already had informers in several locales in Wales. It was a Welshman who'd betrayed Prince Llywelyn, and another who'd betrayed his brother Dafydd, there at the end, and ensured his capture.

But even if someone here today chose to forsake his people, in this they would gain nothing. Rhys was right that they would suffer along with the rest. If they didn't, the whole village would know who'd betrayed them.

Gruffydd cleared his throat. "What exactly do you want to know?"

"Where did Tomos sleep at night?" Rhys said immediately.

The question fell into dead silence, which nobody filled for a long moment.

Rhys spread his hands wide. "I know you know. Why is it so hard to say?"

"Because we are ashamed to admit we shunned him," Sian, Gruffydd's wife, said finally. "He was working on the castle. In the end, he was the *only* Welshman working on the castle."

"He refused to help a fellow *combrogi* out." This came from a black-haired younger man with a baby asleep on his shoulder. "I know how to work stone, but he didn't put in a good word for me. My family barely has enough to eat."

Heads nodded all around.

Catrin wanted to say something, and she glanced at Rhys, who tipped his head encouragingly.

"Perhaps he was trying to protect you," she said, and then because the man started to frown, hurried on, "He was the only Welsh stonemason at the castle. Conwy has more, but fewer and fewer have been hired because of fear of sabotage. Tomos knew that if something went wrong, it was a Welshman who'd be blamed." She gestured to the baby. "You have a family to care for. Tomos had nobody anymore."

Then she put out a supplicating hand, not wanting him to think she was chastising him or any one of them. "This is a new world you live in. But I have lived in it for twenty years. Normans want to be obeyed, and they are quick to anger if they are not. The king has a strong sense of justice, but in his mind, justice is best served when there is order, and he would rather punish the wrong man for murder as an example to everyone of what happens when they defy him, and let the real culprit go free, than punish nobody at all. If a wall falls down, the important thing is that everybody works harder to ensure it doesn't happen again. Same with murder. Tomos may have known that."

It was a long speech, and she didn't know if her explanation was making sense to them, but it followed along the lines of what she'd heard from Aron when she'd visited him in his cell. Before the Welsh were conquered, they'd maintained an elaborate system of laws and courts that relied on lawyers, juries, and adjudicators. The system fined culprits (rather than killing or maiming them) according to the severity of the crime. Two months ago, Edward had codified English law as it applied to Wales, but what those laws were, and how they applied to these villagers, remained, for the most part, a mystery to them.

"What Catrin is telling you is true—and especially after Guy hanged two of your number last autumn," Rhys said.

Oddly, the instant he spoke, his back stiffened, and he gripped her hand more tightly. Though his words, in and of themselves, were supportive and innocuous, something had dramatically changed in him.

Furthermore, his tension didn't ease even after Gruffydd, head hanging, finally answered Rhys's question: "Most nights, Tomos could be found sleeping in the barn where we found Cole."

After the meeting, rather than returning to the scene of the crime, which apparently hadn't ever been Rhys's intent anyway, he deposited Catrin back at the castle (somewhat against her will), to allow her to sing the queen to sleep.

But before he left her, she caught his hand. "What happened to you at the end of the meeting?"

"You mean when Gruffydd finally told us the truth?"

She shook her head. "Something changed in you after you spoke of Guy hanging the two Welshmen, and you've been silent ever since."

He didn't pretend not to understand. "I'm almost afraid to speak of it."

She moved a step closer and looked up at him, waiting.

"We had a series of accidents that prompted the removal of all Welsh workers from the castle save Tomos—and I didn't know about him at the time. Two Welshmen were hanged. One volunteered, like Aron. He was near death anyway and chose to stand for his people. The second was a man Guy picked out himself, someone he found rooting around the old palace."

Catrin's breath caught in her throat. "Like Cole?"

Rhys wet his lips. "Maybe."

30

Day Four

Rhys

Rhys had guessed Tomos had something to do with the barn, if only because the deaths of the two men occurred in a similar time frame. The reason nobody had told him made perfect sense as well. Refusing shelter to a fellow Welshman, especially in this new age they were living in, wasn't just in poor taste, it was a sin. It made no difference that they'd justified their behavior by telling themselves Tomos wasn't worthy.

Compounding their indiscretion was the way they'd kept the truth from Rhys himself, also a guest among them, not to mention someone they knew to be actively working to care for and protect them.

When Rhys had searched the barn for clues, he'd seen the blanket in the loft but had assumed he'd found the love nest of the pair who'd discovered Cole's body. They'd sworn they sounded the alarm before anything had happened between them, but he'd assumed they'd said that because they didn't want to confess the truth in front of their fathers. How much effort might he have saved had he believed them? The question before him now was how and why Tomos ended up dead, not in the barn with Cole, since he'd found no blood there, but in the millpond.

And Rhys's next task, after leaving Catrin, was to speak to Dafi.

"He won't tell us anything," Simon said, by way of a greeting, as Rhys stepped through the guardroom door. It was nearing midnight, but Simon was still awake and apparently unsurprised to see Rhys. "Not that we could understand him if he did. All I've heard from him is *mochyn*. Don't think I don't know what that means! Perhaps you'll have better luck."

Rhys waited until Simon and John had disappeared up the stairs and then entered the cell.

Dafi was leaned up against the wall with his legs bent at the knees. Their presence had deterred any further beatings, and someone had actually seen to the poor man's wounds, though he peered at Rhys now through an eye still swollen closed.

"Come to gloat?"

Rhys crouched in front of him. "Now why would you think I'd do that?"

Dafi tried to sneer, though it obviously hurt his mouth, which had a cut in the corner, and then he gave up, raising and dropping a hand helplessly. "Ach. I know you. I know what you've done for us—"

Rhys made a slashing motion with his hand.

Dafi nodded. "Right. I didn't kill those men."

"I know you didn't. Any thoughts as to who did?"

"None."

"Did you see anyone around your place in the last few days? Someone had to have planted the evidence and built, as the messenger gleefully told me, an 'unholy altar' in your barn."

"You know how it is. I slept these last nights in a croft up the mountain with my herd. I came back down only because it's market day tomorrow, and if I don't attend, I'll be fined."

Then Dafi's expression turned rueful. "That poor Tomos lad. He lost his way there for a time, but he was doing better these last weeks."

"You knew him?"

"He bunked with me some nights. I let him stay even when I was out."

"Just tonight the villagers told me he slept in the barn where we found the dead Englishman, Cole."

"He slept there when he got out of the castle late. I didn't expect him any night, much less that one, so I didn't know he was missing until I heard he was dead. He showed up when he felt like it, and we rubbed along well enough. He brought food when he could, helped out when he could." Now Dafi's upper lip lifted again. "Those snooty folks down in the village couldn't give him a *good day* because he worked for them Normans. The man was just trying to make his way in the world the only way he knew how. Like we all are." He gestured to Rhys, indicating the surcoat he wore. Rhys had taken it off before entering Gruffydd's home, but donned it again upon entering the castle. "Like you are."

"That's what I told them tonight. I feel remiss in not looking out for him. I didn't even know a Welshman was working on the castle." He frowned. "How did I not know?"

"He spoke English like a native. He looked English. No reason for you to think anything else, and it took us a while to trust you."

Rhys tsked. "They didn't trust me with their little secret until tonight."

"I sent you on your way right quick when you came to see me a year ago. No reason for you to come back."

Rhys accepted that was the only apology he was going to get, and he wondered how many other of his countrymen, like Catrin, had been suspicious of how he'd survived Cilmeri when everyone else had died. He had to assume at this point that Gruffydd had initially taken him in to protect the village. After all, Rhys was working for the king just as much as Tomos had been. The difference was that Rhys was a crusader and a minor nobleman, whom some of them had known from birth. They couldn't turn him away, and Gruffydd must have thought it better to keep Rhys where he could see him.

Rhys rose to his feet and stood looking down at Dafi, his hands on his hips. "I'm going to get you out of this."

"Don't you worry about me, lad. I've had a long life. This is a small matter."

"That may well be, but this isn't just about you."

Dafi grunted. "I have no love for those down in the village, but I don't want to see them punished for something none of us did, just to keep our new masters happy." He gave Rhys a wry smile. "You better work quick, though. I don't think I'll be given much time. That coroner is set on a hanging."

31

Day Five

Catrin

The next day, Catrin was kept busy with the needs of an increasingly irritable queen, to the point that she hadn't been able to speak to Rhys for more than a few exchanged greetings in passing as he went about his business and she hers. She hadn't even had time to look in on the market fair—though the second time she saw Rhys, he bowed over her hand and left in it a new green ribbon for her hair he'd somehow found time to acquire for her.

She was sent back to the kitchen three times throughout the morning for food, not only for the queen but for the other ladies. Nearing noon, she was eventually dismissed and thus given the freedom of movement to seek out Rhys and Simon, running them to earth in Simon's domain within the guard tower.

They were sitting around Simon's table talking to John, amazingly enough. Outwardly he remained Rolf, but since Catrin knew the truth, she was finding it very difficult to call him that. Fortunately *Lord Strange* was all that was required in public.

Last night, after singing Queen Eleanor to sleep, Catrin had passed through the great hall to find Adeline moving sympathetically towards him. It had actually made Catrin feel bad for John that he had to respond to Adeline as Rolf rather than himself.

Dutifully, the first thing Simon said was, "How is our queen?"

"Irritated her confinement has begun."

"Some would have thought it should have started sooner," Rhys said.

"The priest who mentioned it nearly had his ears boxed." Catrin laughed. "She told him she didn't have time for that nonsense and, as she was the Queen of England, with the full support of the king, there was nothing he could do but leave. Now, the baby's arrival really *is* imminent, and she wants to survive the birth. So she stays put."

"Leaving you to wander about?" This Rhys said to her in Welsh.

She suddenly found herself grinning at him and replied in French. "Actually, I think I have a plan."

All three men perked up.

"We were just discussing the shortness of time left," Simon said. "The only reason Guy hasn't hanged Dafi already is because the queen has not yet birthed the child, and the king views a gruesome death so close to her time as unseemly."

"It's a superstition I won't argue with in this instance," Rhys said.

"But we are closer! You know we are." Catrin slid onto the bench set against the wall, putting her side by side with Rhys and across from Simon and John. Rhys squeezed her hand for a moment, which she took to mean he hadn't yet told John about their suspicions of Guy. Fortunately, that didn't change what she'd come to tell them.

"Let's talk about what we know rather than what we don't: first, the murderer is someone who is able to travel freely between the countryside and the town. That's a truly limited number of men. Second, he knew Rolf—excuse me, John—well enough to lure him to the inn—"

"Rosie wrote the note," Simon interjected. "The killer may have had no idea where he was going until he arrived."

"Right. Sorry." Catrin bobbed her head, undeterred. "Regardless, the murderer either followed the man he thought was John from the castle to the inn or he saw him at the inn and followed him to the latrine. What I'm trying to say is that the three murdered men either have something in common we haven't yet discovered, or we are looking at the murders all wrong, and they have nothing in common. And that's the point."

The three men gazed at her, and it was Rhys who finally had the wherewithal to say, "I don't understand. You think the three men were killed at random? Why?"

"That isn't quite it." She shook her head. "What if two of them were killed to cover up the murder of the third? Have we found a Baphomet connection anywhere beyond the symbols carved on or near the bodies? We have no Templars here and nobody who has ever been involved in the Templars except you few crusaders. What if the incomplete hexfoil is simply a ploy to distract us from the reason *one* of these men was murdered?"

"All right," Simon said. "Which one?"

Catrin gave Rhys a side-eyed look, and he gave her a tiny nod, telling her to continue. "We have recently learned that both Cole and Tomos have a connection to that barn. What if Tomos saw the murderer hiding Cole's body in the barn and was caught too? The murderer would have had no choice but to kill him as well. Only then, faced with two dead men, did the murderer strip the bodies and carve the unfinished hexfoils."

"But why kill Cole?" John asked.

Catrin again glanced at Rhys, who lifted one shoulder, and this time it was he who answered. "He saw something he shouldn't have."

"What about my brother?"

"Your brother was dressed as you at the time," Catrin said.

"My guess? Same as Cole, you know something or saw something that the murderer thought was going to get him caught," Rhys said. "Possibly you said something you viewed as innocuous, but which his guilty conscience perverted."

John's posture became fixed and a befuddled look entered his eyes, an expression she'd never seen in him before. "I wish I could think, but since Rolf's death, my mind is wandering in a fog."

All of them had lost someone close to them, and the truth of his words stilled them for a moment.

"Alternatively," Simon said, "if Catrin is right, he just didn't like you."

"Which brings me to my plan," Catrin said, pleased to have had the conversation come back around again. "We can lay a trap for him."

Rhys sat up straighter. "We talked about that earlier, using John as bait."

"This is a bit different."

"*Different* is usually your approach," Simon said to Rhys.

"Tell us," John said.

"This afternoon, before the funeral, we should start spreading the idea—actually, *I* should start spreading the idea—that—" suddenly Catrin was embarrassed, "—well, what I'm about to suggest is a total lie, actually."

"Perhaps in this instance we can be forgiven," Rhys said. "All good lies contain a kernel of truth, so what's this one about?"

She forged on, "What if I wonder out loud what happened to Cole's ring, given to him by Gilbert de Clare for his years of service? It wasn't among the possessions found in Dafi's house, which means Dafi must have hidden it. It's a real ruby and very valuable."

"That's a good idea," Simon said, "but what's to prevent any treasure hunter from going to Dafi's house to search for it?"

Catrin's face fell. "I didn't think of that."

Rhys patted her thigh, telling her not to worry. "Catrin needs to suggest instead that the ring must have fallen off Cole's finger at the place Cole was murdered, because both Dafi's house and the barn have been thoroughly searched. She says she's thinking about asking

Simon to put together a search party tomorrow to comb the area for where Cole was killed."

"But we know where he was killed," Catrin said.

"*We* do, but—" Rhys's face took on a pleased expression, "—I never told anyone else that you and I had found it."

Simon blinked. "You didn't tell me, certainly, and you should have. You didn't even speak of it to Guy?"

Rhys shook his head. "After we found Tomos's body, it suddenly became much less important."

"So where is it?" John asked.

A wary look entered Rhys's face. "I think I'm not going to say, particularly to you."

John's eyes started to narrow, but Simon put out a hand. "You should be grateful for that, since you're going to be drinking yourself into a stupor as the evening progresses, telling everyone within earshot what Catrin has concocted. That way, you can't give away the location by mistake."

John still didn't like it, but at Simon's reassuring nod, he acquiesced.

Rhys stood, prepared to leave. "All of you have to attend the funeral, but I don't. I will leave now to scout the place. I'll wait all night for the killer to come if I have to."

Catrin wrinkled her nose. "I wish I could go with you."

"That is one thing you can't do."

"What if the killer catches you like he did Tomos?" John said.

Rhys looked at him with amusement. "I will be quiet and clever and simply lie in wait. I'll let him search and find nothing and leave. Then I'll come back here and tell Simon who it is, and he can arrest him."

Simon shook his head. "That might not work if we don't have definitive proof and it's only your word against his. I'd rather catch him in the act of searching. I should be going with you."

Now it was Rhys's turn to shake his head. "Your absence from the funeral would only call attention to what we're doing. And really, the most important thing is to know the truth for certain."

Catrin herself nodded, feeling more confident about the plan now that they'd put their heads together about it. "And then we can work backwards from there."

32

Day Five

Rhys

Rhys shifted in the tree he'd climbed, trying to get comfortable. Near sunset, he'd walked around the whole palace complex again, and now he'd returned to his perch, acknowledging that thirty-eight was far too old to be climbing trees. But he wanted to be both safe and discreet, and taking up an eagle-eye position so he could see the entrance to the building where they'd found the large quantity of blood (presumed to be Cole's) seemed like the best approach.

He'd been waiting a while now, and with the moon rising in the sky, about a third full but shining brightly in the clear night, he was beginning to doubt anyone would come. Of course, if the murderer was as well-placed as Rhys thought and feared, then it would take some doing for him to get away.

He had a few alternate guesses as to who the killer might be, but still, when Guy fitz Lacy turned off the main road and entered the palace ruins, his heart sank into his boots. While Rhys had become nearly certain Guy was the killer, given all the information they had, it would have been easier if it were someone lower on the social hierarchy. Worse, Guy was in the exact position in which Prince Edmund had accused Rhys of being—in charge of the investigation into his own killings.

Rhys watched Guy tie his horse's reins to the old hitching post near the main gate and stroll with far too casual an air towards what had been Llywelyn's quarters. And as all this transpired, Rhys realized Simon had been right, as usual. Knowing Guy was the murderer and convincing anyone else of it were not equal results. Rhys hiding here and determining it didn't necessarily take him closer to convicting Guy of murder.

In one hand, Guy held a lantern turned down very low. In the other, he carried a shovel, which he rested on his shoulder. He wasn't exactly whistling, but his confidence was chilling. He had murdered three men, and nobody knew it. Any desire Rhys might have had to confront him dissipated. All he wanted now was for Guy to search the room, find nothing, and leave.

The coroner disappeared into Llywelyn's quarters as Rhys hoped he would and spent a quarter of an hour, about the length of time Rhys would have expected, searching for the ring. Rhys couldn't see what he was doing inside the room, but the lantern was brighter than it had been outside, and the light bobbed and weaved within the walls.

He wasn't at all sure what the shovel was for, but then grunting sounds carried through the still night air. Rhys feared he'd come upon some other poor stranger and was burying him in the dirt. But then, a moment later, Guy came out, carrying a satchel over one shoulder, the lantern again in one hand. He propped the shovel against a wall, went to his horse, heaved the bag onto his horse's back, and affixed it there with straps and ties. He then mounted and rode away. He didn't head back to the main road, but followed the palace wall east towards the church.

As soon as Guy was out of sight and sound, Rhys dropped down from his tree and followed, hurrying at first until he was at the palace gate and then moving more slowly once he was on the road again. Guy was walking his horse and apparently in no hurry, particularly once he turned onto a lane just before the entrance to the churchyard. With the lantern and the moonlight, he was easy to follow.

Guy rode along the lane for roughly a hundred yards and then dismounted directly north of the church, while Rhys tried to blend into the stones that formed the outer wall of the churchyard. Looking both directions, in what Rhys interpreted as a suspicious manner, Guy swung the satchel onto his right shoulder, pushed aside some thick bushes and brush, and disappeared.

Rhys stood where he was, as unmoving as possible, before it occurred to him that Guy would have to return by the same path. Rhys had entered those bushes a thousand times as a boy, so he knew where Guy had gone and that, once he returned, he would pass within a few feet of where Rhys was currently standing. So Rhys heaved himself over the church wall, a matter of a five-foot-high obstacle, with less grace than he would have liked, and dropped down to the other side.

From similar childhood ramblings, Rhys also knew the churchyard like the back of his hand. The main gate was behind him, facing the main road, and a second wooden gate was in front of him, located in one of the northern corners of the churchyard. It opened directly onto the lane on which Rhys had just been standing and was only a few yards from those bushes into which Guy had disappeared.

Rhys hastened forward so as to crouch behind the little gate, peering through the cracks in the slats and waiting for Guy to reemerge, which he did hardly ten breaths later. Guy readjusted the branches to hide his passage and, actively whistling now, went to his horse. He no longer carried the lantern or the satchel.

But then, before he could mount, Father Medwyn, the priest of St. Peblig's Church, entered the lane coming from the other direction, carrying a lantern of his own.

The priest stopped, evidently taken aback to see a man with a horse in the lane at this time of night. "Hello, my son," he said in French, and Rhys had a moment's pride that his priest was so educated. "What brings you to St. Peblig's?"

"My job," Guy said bluntly. He did not appear equally disturbed by Father Medwyn's presence.

Guy's back was to Rhys, so Rhys couldn't see his face, only Medwyn's. Guy's hand had gone to the hilt of the knife he wore at the small of his back, Saracen-style. For a time, Rhys had tried wearing a blade there, but the positioning prevented him from lying on his back comfortably, so he'd abandoned the technique.

"I'm Guy fitz Lacy, the coroner."

A sudden fury rose in Rhys's chest, and it had him sliding his sword from its sheath in preparation for launching himself at Guy if he gave any sign of threatening the priest.

Father Medwyn, meanwhile, appeared to have no notion of the danger he was in. "Is that a blade at your back? I've never seen one worn that way."

Guy pulled the dagger from its sheath and held it out. Though desperate to keep Medwyn safe, Rhys held his position, praying Medwyn's innocence would save him before Rhys had to. Rhys knew he was risking Medwyn's life by not showing himself, but he hoped even Guy would think twice and maybe a third time before murdering a man of the cloth.

"If the stories of the Crusades are true, that's how the great William Longspee wore his knife." Medwyn stepped closer, showing himself to be more curious and knowledgeable about weaponry than Rhys had ever suspected either.

"So I understand."

"Ah, that's right. Your family has a long association with him. I understand your brother married Longspee's granddaughter." Father Medwyn took the knife, turning it over in his hands. "

"He did." With remarkable gentleness, Guy took back the knife from Medwyn and resheathed it. "With practice, it's a faster draw, and I like to fight with the knife in my left hand and my sword in my right. Plus, it's serrated on one side, the more easily to cut through armor."

Then Guy bent his head. "Good day to you, Father. I'll be on my way."

"God bless you, son."

Though every nerve in Rhys's body was demanding he confront Guy right then and there, he let him go, back down the lane to the main road. It really was the smart thing to do, especially since the knife would have long since been washed clean of blood, and what Rhys wanted even more was to discover what had been inside that satchel.

By letting Guy leave, Rhys had a chance to find out.

"I am very curious to know why my favorite crouchback is hiding in the corner of my churchyard." The words came low in Rhys's ear, and he nearly jumped out of his skin at the sound.

One moment Father Medwyn had been standing in the lane, and the next he had slipped through the gate and come up behind Rhys, who'd been dithering as he watched Guy ride away.

As Rhys swung around, Father Medwyn stepped back and put up both hands. "I apologize, my son. I knew I was sneaking up on you, and I did it anyway."

"For a man who's spent his life in a church, you do have an uncanny ability to scare a man! I almost took the name of the Lord in vain!"

"But you didn't." Medwyn smiled gently. "That counts for more than you think."

Rhys's heart was pounding more than it had been when he'd been watching Guy exchange pleasantries with Father Medwyn. "Do you have any idea what bear you were just poking, Father?"

"A bear, eh?" Medwyn peered over the wall before turning back to Rhys. "What should I know about him that I do not?"

"He's a murderer." There was no point in lying to the priest, even if Rhys was inclined to do so. The man had long since earned the trust of Rhys and every other Welshman in Gwynedd.

The moonlight caught the widening of Medwyn's eyes. "Guy fitz Lacy? He killed those three men?"

"So I do believe, Father. I set a trap tonight, and he walked into it. I am even more convinced after listening to him tell you about the knife he wears. Each man's wounds were caused by a dagger wielded in the left hand and serrated on one side."

Medwyn settled back on his heels. "You always were one to see what others didn't."

Rhys gave a shake of his head. He didn't want to talk about himself. "Perhaps you would be so kind as to act as witness to what I'm about to do, and then much might be explained."

"Of course."

Rhys marveled at the total lack of hesitation. "Just like that?"

"Of course."

"Even if Guy returns?"

"Son—" Medwyn put a hand on Rhys's arm, "—I awoke an hour ago and felt the need to wander the churchyard. I saw Guy come up the lane. I saw you leap the wall and crouch by the fence."

Rhys's heart rose into his throat. "Why then did you confront him?"

"Evil does not scare me, my son, only ignorance of what passes amongst my flock."

Rhys's expression remained stricken.

"You feared for my life?"

"Yes."

"God has already spared me once tonight. Who am I to question where he next sets my feet?"

Rhys shook his head, awed by the man's confidence—which wasn't innocence at all, just certainty that he was where he was supposed to be.

But because he was glad of the witness and the company, Rhys returned to the gate and led the priest through it to where Guy had entered the bushes. The spot was northwest of the church and northeast of the palace, which took up the high point of the hill they were on, so the few yards they walked towards it led them gently upward.

The whole area was wooded and overgrown. To the north, the land sloped downwards and led to the River Cadnant five hundred feet away, upon the banks of which the Welsh village nestled, though it was too dark and tree-covered to see from here.

When they reached Guy's hiding place, Rhys parted the branches and went through them, holding aside one-half for Father Medwyn to follow, now with his lantern turned up as brightly as it would go. From there, the ground descended sharply, bringing them to the entrance of what appeared at first to be a dark cave. A few steps more and the priest held up the lantern, revealing the stone walls of a house-like structure. They were standing in an anteroom, and several steps led down even farther to a stone floor, beyond which lay an altar with long stone benches on either side.

Father Medwyn stopped on the bottom step. "Ah. I haven't been in here in many years."

"Nor I, Father. Though we came here often as children," he glanced amusedly at Medwyn, "never telling our parents or any adult that an abandoned Roman temple was our playground."

Medwyn crossed himself, but without haste or desperation, and then moved across the floor towards the altar. Near one of the benches, he rubbed the toe of his boot in the dirt that had accumulated over the stones. Rhys saw no small footprints, indicating the children in the village no longer came to play here.

Lowering the lantern, Medwyn revealed tiny square tiles, not unlike those found in the prince's palace on the hill, which had been built over the ruins of what had once been a Roman fort. The palace had taken advantage of the existing water system, which even after nearly a thousand years was still functioning, and the fact that the fort lay at the intersection of good roads.

While the palace had been blessed and purified centuries ago, this ruined temple had been left as it was and always had been.

"What would Guy want with this place?" Medwyn said.

"He had a satchel over his shoulder when he went in, and it was gone when he came out."

While Rhys had been speaking, Father Medwyn had rounded the altar, and now he stood looking down at what he'd found on the other side. "Ah."

Rhys moved to look too and smiled in satisfaction at the sight of the satchel tucked into a hollow in the stone behind the altar pedestal. He knelt to it, undid the straps, and pulled the opening wide.

The bag was full of gold and silver.

"One always hopes men do bad things because they think it is actually the right thing," Father Medwyn said.

"That does not seem to be the case in this instance."

Medwyn nodded sadly. "I'm afraid I find myself constantly disappointed. The sin of greed has led more men astray than any other."

33

Day Six
Catrin

R hys hadn't been assaulted or abducted. He wasn't dead. All of which was a huge relief to Catrin as she watched him enter the bailey of the castle at the very late hour of two in the morning, one day short of a full week since the deaths of Cole and Tomos.

The walls of Caernarfon Castle weren't quite finished, so she and Simon had been able to sit with their backs to the inner wall and watch for his coming down the eastern road with the view unimpeded by battlements. By now, she and Simon had grown enough used to each other that their shoulders rubbed without either feeling discomfited. Simon's legs were stretched out in front of him. Catrin had brought a pillow to sit on.

By the time Rhys was through the gatehouse, Catrin and Simon had walked (a little stiffly, truth be told) down from the heights.

"Did you see Guy fitz Lacy return a bit ago?" Rhys said in an undertone, not even objecting or surprised that Catrin and Simon were still awake, waiting for him. It was almost disappointing that he didn't bother to chastise her again.

"We did," Catrin said.

Simon embellished the answer. "We didn't see when he left, but he returned by the Queen's gate about an hour ago, and then left again by the King's Gate, presumably for his lodgings in the town."

"He was whistling," Catrin added.

"He would be." Rhys was carrying a heavy satchel on one shoulder. "I have something to show you."

They followed him unquestioningly into Simon's quarters. At this hour, the only men awake were those on duty outside, so the guardroom was empty. Rhys shut the outer door, and once they entered Simon's private office, shut that door too before humping the bag over to the table and setting it down with a *clunk*.

Simon put his hand on top of the satchel. "I presume you haven't brought me rocks to look at."

"Not rocks." Rhys gave a summary of his adventures in the night.

Simon still hadn't opened the satchel, and he kept his hand on top of it as he settled heavily in his chair. "I didn't want it to be Guy."

Rhys spread his hands wide. "I think it must have happened very much like Catrin said: he was hiding his stolen wealth in the remains of the palace—or adding to it—when Cole came upon him. In Guy's mind, he had no choice but to kill him. He chose to move the body rather than have it found in the palace itself, which he might have feared would somehow implicate him. He didn't want to risk drawing attention to his hiding place, nor to the pool of blood he left on the floor.

"Earlier, Catrin suggested that Tomos woke in the barn and saw Guy laying out Cole's body, so Guy had to kill him too. But Tomos wouldn't have had to encounter Guy in the barn itself, seeing as how both men apparently roamed Gwynedd in the night at will. If Tomos came upon Guy on the road, leading the horse with Cole thrown over its back, Tomos's immediate assumption might not have been that he had killed him. Guy is the coroner! Dead bodies are his business.

"Guy would also have been someone Tomos would have obeyed, if not trusted, as a matter of course. He would have gone with him to the millpond if Guy ordered him to come. And died there."

Catrin swallowed hard, envisioning the scene. "Two dead in a single night, and neither planned."

"If it is really Guy," Simon said, "what you've described doesn't explain the incomplete hexfoil."

"It does if Catrin is right about that too, that it was a misdirect. With two murders, both associated with incomplete hexfoils, we would be pursuing a Satanist, not a coroner who got greedy," Rhys said.

"How would he even know about the Baphomet?" Simon said.

"As I was reminded this very night, his brother's wife is the granddaughter of William Longspee," Rhys said simply.

Simon let out a puff of air. "I'd forgotten."

Catrin didn't want to appear ignorant, but she had to ask, "This is William Longspee, the crusader? But he died thirty years ago."

"Indeed," Simon gave her a small smile, "but his legend lives on. Certainly, we heard a hundred stories about him when we crusaded with the princes. Longspee was an inveterate storyteller, and I wouldn't be surprised to learn that half the stories he told about his adventures he himself made up. His son would have known them to tell to his own daughter."

"He died in the company of nearly three hundred Templars, betrayed, so the story goes, by one of their own," Rhys added.

Catrin finally understood. "A Baphomet."

Rhys spread his hands wide and repeated, "So the story goes."

Simon had finally opened the satchel, and Catrin looked in it with him. Guy had acquired bags of coins, containing both silver and gold, silver cups and candlesticks, brooches and rings. It was a treasure trove.

"Where do we think all this came from?" she asked.

"He could have stolen some of it from Llywelyn's palace. You and I saw the small treasure room in what used to be the prince's bedchamber," Rhys said. "There was nothing in it anymore, but Guy could have found it after Llywelyn's death. As a Lacy, he was trusted and would have come to Gwynedd immediately. Most certainly, he has been stealing from the king. As coroner, he would have collected fines and payments throughout the county."

"You could have taken the wealth yourself and left the country." Simon spoke casually, as if his words were of no matter.

- 296 -

Rhys, however, immediately turned on him, protest in every line of his body. "I wouldn't!" And then at the bemused expression on Simon's face, he barked a laugh. "That was a test, was it?"

Simon gave a little shake of his head. "Not for me, you understand?"

"Do I?" Rhys sounded angry still.

"What Simon is trying to say," Catrin said gently, "is that it was a test for *you*."

Rhys suddenly dropped himself onto the bench against the wall, his shoulders sagging, and gestured helplessly towards the satchel. "I did offer several silver pennies to the good Father Medwyn, who came with me into the temple. He refused them."

"As he would," Simon said.

"How do you know? You've never met him," Rhys said.

Simon looked at his friend with a wry smile. "I have now."

Catrin could have been jealous of the way the two of them communicated, even after so many years apart, but she decided she wouldn't be. "The Lacy name and Guy's brother's station should have ensured Guy's loyalty."

"Some men lose their minds when faced with this much wealth." Simon allowed a cascade of pennies to return to its leather bag. "This doesn't prove Guy killed anyone."

Rhys sighed. "I know it. That's why I didn't leap out and confront him myself."

"Wait." Catrin looked from one to the other. "Why doesn't it?"

"Guy stole from the king, Catrin," Rhys said. "He stored his wealth in the old palace, but that doesn't mean he killed Cole or the others."

"But he knew where Cole died! He wears the dagger! We just talked through what must have happened."

"We did," Simon said. "But perhaps his decision to go to the palace tonight was on the assumption that a search party would find his stash. He wanted to spirit it away before that could happen."

"It wasn't why." The words came out more petulantly than she liked.

"It also doesn't answer the question as to *why* he killed Rolf," Simon said, "if he did kill Rolf."

"He thought Rolf was John. I can think of a very good reason for Guy to have chosen him, and it wasn't because of Rosie." Rhys's eyes strayed to Catrin, and she caught her breath.

"You can't think it! It couldn't have had anything to do with *me!*"

But Simon's eyes had turned thoughtful, and he and Rhys exchanged what Catrin interpreted as an annoyingly condescending look. "Two birds with one stone," Simon said. "Kill a rival *and* distract us by murdering someone who had nothing to do with Cole and Tomos."

"There has to be another reason," Catrin insisted.

"We will try to find it," Simon said, "but it will require us to think of another trap for Guy. Everything we have against him at the moment remains circumstantial."

"We have his money," Rhys said. "We could lure him with that."

"We have John as well," Simon said, "but again, neither links to Tomos or Cole. I don't believe, even if he knows he hit the wrong mark, he will go after John again. He cares about money, not people."

"If we were still governed by our laws, in a day we could have a hundred men testifying in court as to how he came by this wealth," Catrin said. "They could tell the court how much they paid. Someone has to know the accounts Guy is presenting to the king are falsified."

"But this is England now, whether we like it or not," Rhys said gently. "Welsh law no longer applies. It's up to the king to decide who is guilty and who isn't, who lives and who dies, not a court."

"We do have a system of courts," Simon said mildly.

Rhys gave him a withering look. "And who presides over them in Wales? Anyone who speaks Welsh? Anyone who won't instantly favor the testimony of an Englishman or Norman over that of a Welshman?"

The bitterness in Rhys's tone was the same as which sliced through her too, but Catrin put a hand on Rhys's arm. "Rhys—"

Simon didn't react, but simply gazed at Rhys for a count of three before saying, as if Rhys hadn't spoken angrily, "For now, we will take what we have to the king—"

"*You* will take what we have to the king," Rhys said. "The less said about my role in its discovery the better."

Ignoring Rhys, Simon turned back to Catrin. "Guy will lose his position, but Rhys is right. The gold is evidence of theft, not of murder."

"But without proof Guy is the murderer, Dafi will be hanged for a crime he didn't commit, and the village punished!" Outrage rose again in Catrin's chest.

"I will ensure the latter, at least, doesn't happen," Simon said. "Without an alternative culprit, I don't know that I can save Dafi."

Catrin's hands clenched into fists. "We must."

Rhys put out a hand to her. "We will keep trying. Believe me, we will. I don't want Guy getting away with murder and an innocent man punished any more than you do. But you must realize that accusing a nobleman, even if he is a bastard, is fraught with peril. Likely, the king will believe Simon—and Father Medwyn when called upon—that Guy was in possession of this treasure, but even that could be explained away out of a misguided notion of keeping it safe until he could safely deliver it to the king. Also, Guy's brother is physically in Caernarfon. The king gave Henry de Lacy more land, power, and authority in Wales than any other magnate. He won't be taking kindly to accusations against Guy, particularly because the king made Guy coroner here at *Henry's* request."

Simon looked at Rhys. "We could set upon Guy the next time he leaves the castle and kill him ourselves. That churchyard has so many graves already, what's one more?"

"The thought is tempting." The look Rhys gave Simon sent chills down Catrin's spine. She saw the truth of it in their eyes. They could do it and never mind the consequences to themselves.

Simon took a long drink of ale and then carefully set down his cup. Catrin had been with him enough by now to recognize the action as a delaying tactic he used while he gathered his thoughts. "Ultimately, it was your man who was killed, Catrin. My apologies for not serving the murderer up on a platter."

She shook her head. "It isn't your fault. Guy's punishment aside, what most concerns me is that we don't know why Cole rode all this way alone. But that is something I will eventually know. As soon as the child is born and the queen able to travel, I will be heading south with her and the king. You already sent a messenger to Clare to inquire as to Cole's purpose. I'd just hoped to discover it before then so I wouldn't have to wait that long."

"You won't be staying here?" Simon was speaking to Catrin, but his eyes tracked to Rhys.

"I am indentured to the queen." She shrugged casually, masking her desire to cry. "Perhaps it's for the best. I am no longer a child, and it would be a mistake to think I could come home, and things would be the way they were. One never can really go back. Best not to try."

After Rhys escorted her to her quarters, Catrin stood alone in the corridor for a long while, thinking. Even if the king accepted the truth about Guy, he would want to avoid a scandal. Guy was leaving Caernarfon anyway to take up his position as sheriff of the town of Denbigh on behalf of his brother. Even if Simon told the king flat out he believed Guy killed three people, one a nobleman, there was no guarantee the king would find their evidence credible—or worth acting on. As Simon had correctly pointed out, it was all circumstantial. Plus, no king, and especially this king, liked to admit he'd made a mistake. Appointing Guy had been a big one.

Simon and Rhys were also right about the matter of Guy's brother. Henry de Lacy would protect Guy for no other reason than to save his own name and reputation.

With that, Catrin felt a kernel of an idea forming, combined with the certainty that she had only one path left open to her, as much as she hated to take it. She couldn't let the investigation end with the investigators themselves being hanged for murder, not if she had any say in the matter.

So she climbed the stairs to the queen's room and peered through the door that had been left ajar. Somehow, she was not surprised to find the queen sitting up in bed, papers scattered all around her. Queen Eleanor was a large landowner in her own right and, pregnancy aside, she had a business to run.

"Where have you been all night?"

"I apologize, my queen. I was seeing to—" Catrin broke off as no credible excuse came to her.

Eleanor made a sound of disbelief. "You were with that crouchback of yours. Don't bother to lie. Can you believe Margaret has come down with the chills? Now she and three of the other women are confined to the floor above, and I have only Jane to attend me." She gestured to a young woman asleep on a pallet beside the bed. "The poor thing can't seem to stay awake past midnight."

Catrin approached and curtseyed. "What can *I* do for you?"

"You can fetch me that goblet over there, and then you can tell me why you have returned to the castle at this late hour. And come to my room, no less. You want something from me, do you?"

Catrin could have ground her teeth at how perceptive the queen was, but since she did want something, she couldn't be that resentful. So she fetched the wine and then accepted Eleanor's command to sit on the edge of the bed.

"We know who murdered those three men, my lady, but we find ourselves unable to prove it."

And then Catrin told the queen everything.

34

Day Six

Rhys

Rhys woke with a start at a banging on the door behind him. Bleary-eyed from too little sleep, he peered through the arrow slit at the bright light of day outside before opening the door to be confronted with five of the king's guards.

"The king requests your presence," the leader said.

After Rhys had returned from escorting Catrin to the Eagle Tower, he and Simon remained behind, talking over their strategy—or lack of strategy, in this instance—for the morning. Rhys had acquired food in the kitchen at one point and had finally fallen asleep by the door, leaving Simon to adjust the wealth in the satchel so he could use it as a pillow. Neither dared leave it alone for a moment, knowing Simon would have to see the king about it first thing in the morning.

Morning had, apparently, come.

Simon threw the heavy satchel over his shoulder as Rhys had done the night before. Though the guards didn't actually tie Rhys's hands behind his back, there was a definite menace in the way they corralled and herded them in the middle of their escort. These were Simon's own men too, or had been for the last few days anyway, but he didn't question them or even ask their orders. They'd come from the king, clearly.

As they were escorted through the bailey, with the workday in full swing and all eyes on them, a feeling of doom settled on Rhys's shoulders. Catrin had warned him that it could be a mistake to go up against Henry de Lacy. He had a horrible feeling that not only had she been right, but Simon was about to suffer the consequences of Rhys's actions too. He began marshalling arguments in his head, working to explain to the king why everything that had gone on was *his* fault, not Simon's. They entered the long southern corridor inside the walls of the castle and were eventually ushered into the king's private chapel.

The king was its sole occupant.

The rarity of the audience took Rhys's breath away. Henry de Lacy wasn't present. Guy wasn't smirking behind the king's chair, or worse, on his knees beside him.

Instead, King Edward was sitting on a bench near one of the narrow windows, staring up at the cross on the altar, which at the moment was the only adornment in the room. Rhys and Simon stood together in the doorway, hesitating. Their guards had melted away, and the three of them were, to all appearances, alone.

"Tell me what happened." The king spoke without turning around. "All of it."

Rhys stared at the back of the king's head. He had removed his cap, and he was going bald at the pate, a change from the last time Rhys had seen him before his arrival in Caernarfon.

When neither Simon nor Rhys immediately responded, Edward stood and swung around. His eyes were hard and looking at Rhys. "Don't keep me waiting."

While initially Rhys had found favor with Prince Edmund and King Edward because he'd found a murderer who would have gone free, they kept him close in the aftermath because he told them the truth when few people ever did.

Rhys could evade and elide day and night to Guy. He'd done so for an entire year.

But he had never lied to anyone's face.

And he couldn't start with the king.

So he began, laying out step by step what he'd done and how he'd done it, while keeping Catrin out of it as much as he could and attempting to keep how he felt about these events in check. He spoke of Aron coming forward as a scapegoat, even though he hadn't found Cole's body. He explained to the king other information he'd withheld and why. He told him in full the kind of man Guy was.

Rhys knew he was taking a huge risk to speak the truth so clearly. His confession had the real danger of ensnaring Simon and Catrin in whatever punishment the king devised for him. But the more Rhys revealed of the investigation—along with the pain, humiliation, and anger at what he and his people had endured—the more his confidence grew and his spine straightened.

This was who he was, come what may, and it was best the king knew it before another hour passed.

Throughout, Simon stood stoically beside Rhys, looking straight ahead and not speaking. He didn't even adjust the satchel on his shoulder, which must have started hurting by now from the weight of the treasure inside.

When Rhys finished, the king nodded. "Catrin was lighter on the details than you, and where you tried to protect her involvement, she worked to protect yours, but the minutiae are immaterial at this point."

Rhys's mouth actually fell open, and Simon spoke for the first time, "What?"

"The man in custody has been released and sent home, on the word of one of Queen Eleanor's maids, who has sworn that, at the time of Rolf's murder, she was conferring with him about acquiring fresh eggs and milk for the queen's meals."

Rhys's astonishment was so complete his feet were frozen to the floor, and his jaw was practically on it.

King Edward laughed. "Come. We will dine." He walked towards them, and they parted to let him through the doorway.

Even Simon, who'd spent more years in the king's company than Rhys, had been rendered speechless. In Edward's personal quarters, a table had been laid for three, with silver plates and goblets, along with a breakfast of sausage, eggs, and bread on platters. Edward sat on one side of the table and gestured them to the chairs opposite.

Simon was the first to obey, and he set the satchel down with a clunk on the stones of the floor.

"I gather that's for me?" the king said dryly.

He'd been speaking ostensibly to Simon, but his eyes went to Rhys's face, so it was Rhys who had to answer. "Yes, my lord."

"I am disappointed." The king spoke heavily.

Rhys didn't know whether he should reply, but in the end repeated, "Yes, my lord," in as soft a tone as he could manage while still being heard. He was trying very hard not to think about anything at all, afraid to upend whatever was going on here that had them eating breakfast with the king.

Then, as Rhys slowly lowered himself to his chair, the king shifted, visibly putting aside the weight of his disappointment—in Rhys? In Guy?—and began loading food onto his plate. "You should know that Guy sailed with the tide, heading to Denbigh. We got word in the night of a rebellion brewing in his new jurisdiction that had to be seen to immediately and put down."

"Apologies for my ignorance, sire, but knowing what we just told you, and with you apparently believing us, you let him go?" Simon made no move towards the food so Rhys didn't either.

King Edward looked at Simon carefully. "No." He dragged the word out a bit. "That isn't what has happened. Not at all."

Rhys sat back in his chair, pure astonishment welling up inside him, as he suddenly realized what the king was telling them. "Who's captaining that ship?"

"A man loyal to the queen."

"And his orders are … what?"

The king stabbed at an onion. "Not something to speak of out loud, even in my private quarters." He made a broad gesture with his knife, almost flinging the onion off the tip. "The walls have ears." But then he said anyway, feigned sadness in his voice, "I fear Guy will never reach Denbigh."

Simon finally started spooning eggs onto his plate. "My lord, pardon me for saying so, but it isn't exactly justice."

"Isn't it?" Edward said mildly.

"It is justice," Rhys glanced at his friend, "just not the law." Then he looked back to the king. "Does Guy's brother know what lies in store for Guy on that ship?"

"He does not and will never know." The king spoke softly but firmly, in a tone Rhys recognized as one that brooked no argument.

Simon, for once, or maybe because he *was* the captain of the king's guard, was still ready to argue. "I still don't like it, my lord. It isn't the kind of solution that gives anyone closure and puts the minds of the citizens, Welsh or English, at ease. At the very least, what are we going to say about who killed Lord Strange?"

Edward ripped a piece of bread from the loaf and buttered it. "Before the boat sailed, Rolf le Strange's men dragged one of the sailors in chains through the hall and out the gate to the dock. It was all very public. You must have still been sleeping."

"Why are we saying he did it?" Rhys asked, genuinely curious as to the completeness of the story the king and queen—and Catrin, apparently—had concocted.

"He killed Cole and Tomos and decorated them with the unfinished hexfoil to distract the coroner from his real target, John le

- 309 -

Strange, who, as you may recall, arrived the night Cole's body was found. The sailor hated John because he'd imprisoned his father, who died while in captivity."

Rhys set down his knife. "That's actually believable, my lord."

Edward raised an eyebrow in his direction. "You think you are the only one with clever ideas?" Then he laughed. "But you can thank your Catrin for that one."

"What about our remaining twin?" Simon himself managed a sardonic laugh, for which Rhys was grateful because it meant he didn't have to answer the king.

"His name is Rolf henceforth. With my brother's spymaster dead, our enemies will think they have free reign, and my new spymaster will discover who they are." King Edward's eyes had been bright with amusement, but now a degree of calculation entered them. "Rolf le Strange, meanwhile, has become my new coroner of Carnarvonshire."

35

Day Twenty-five

Rhys

"He can't want me."

"Of course he wants you. You are Reese de la Croix, master of arms, defender of princes."

"Edward's men assassinated one of those princes I defended. And the other he had hanged, drawn, and quartered, and dragged through the streets of Shrewsbury."

"You are splitting hairs."

"Am I?" Rhys folded his arms across his chest but exposed himself as a coward by refusing to look into Simon's eyes.

"Before you fought for Lewellen or David, you fought for Edward and Edmund, both princes at the time, as you may recall."

Rhys managed a glance at his friend before returning his gaze to the Gwynedd landscape. He and Simon were standing above the Queen's Gate, which had become a favorite retreat. "Why me?"

"Why does it matter? You are the best at what you do. Isn't that enough?"

"I wasn't the best this time. It was Catrin who figured out how to trap Guy."

"You knew already it was he."

"I was lucky." But before Simon could reply, Rhys waved a hand, dismissing the comment. "I am not actually bitter. You are right that Guy fitz Lacy was never going to openly pay for those deaths."

"The king can, however, pay you." Now Simon put up a hand, this time to forestall Rhys's natural protest. "Know that he doesn't offer you money because you can be bought, but because you love your people. One commission from the king will provide you with enough wealth to keep a dozen families fed next winter. You could alleviate a great deal of suffering."

"A suffering he causes."

Simon was silent.

Rhys scoffed. "Are those the same coins Guy stole from the king in the first place? I would be like Judas with his thirty pieces of silver."

"How is working directly under me for the king different from what you're doing now? Don't you understand yet? *Everything* in this entire land comes from the king. There is no piece anywhere anymore you can carve out for yourself alone."

Rhys looked down at his feet. The money was the carrot. The king didn't have to offer it. Fundamentally, he didn't have to pay anything for Rhys's services if he didn't want to.

Which meant Rhys needed to know the nature of the stick too. "What if I were to refuse?"

Simon tapped his fingers on his thigh as he studied Rhys, who was finally able to meet his eyes. What he saw in his friend's face had Rhys shaking his head again.

"You can't say no," Simon said.

"I can always say no. I just might not like the consequences of doing so."

"Your brother-in-law would never work again, not on any castle the king commissions. He might find work among lesser lords, but who would want to defy the king in so small a matter?"

Rhys knew the answer: nobody.

"And that is before we talk about the next Norman to whom Catrin would soon find herself betrothed."

Rhys drew in a quick breath through his nose. "He wouldn't."

Simon's smile was mocking. "Of course, he would. You know he would. And she could not refuse the man to whom the king gave her. My guess? Rolf le Strange. We know he wants her. Why would the king favor you over his new coroner?"

Rhys clenched his hands into fists. In truth, he had been warring with himself all day, desperate to think how to prevent Catrin from leaving. He loved her. He always had. Whether that love could be something that could carry them into the future together he didn't yet know, but he very much wanted to find out. This last fortnight since the birth of the king's son had been the best of his life. He couldn't imagine how gloomy his world would become if he couldn't wake up every morning knowing he was going to see her.

Simon was offering the opportunity for him to stay close. He would be the king's new spymaster—and quaestor when needed—

masquerading as a member of his guard. That meant Rhys would always be at King Edward's side, charged with the safety of his person as well as that of the queen herself. And since the king and queen were never separated if they could help it, chances were, he would be spending a great deal of time with Catrin.

It would mean leaving Wales, however, sooner rather than later.

"Who better to protect your people, Rhys," Simon said softly, saying Rhys's name the Welsh way one more time. Maybe, in fact, for the last time. Each successive conversation cleared the air between them a little more. They were going to disagree—maybe often—but they loved each other, which meant they needed to find a way through those disagreements and out the other side. "Accept that you still have a future and a role to play."

Rhys let out a breath. Simon was right. From the moment the king learned Rhys was alive, he'd never had a choice. "So be it. But if I stay with him, I won't pretend not to hate everything he's done to Wales."

"He takes that as a given. But you don't lie, and you keep your word, once pledged. He knows you will fight to the death to protect him."

Rhys managed a real laugh, maybe the first one in a long time. "Rhys de la Croix, member of the king's guard." He shook his head.

Simon laughed too. "God help us all."

EPILOGUE

Day Thirty-six
Father Medwyn

The royal party had passed by the church on its way south, heading for Criccieth. The morning had started out fine, but now, in late afternoon, the clouds had rolled in, and fat raindrops speckled the stones of the porch.

Father Medwyn pushed open the church door and entered, instantly feeling the peace of his domain settle upon his shoulders like a mantle. He recited a psalm in a sing-song voice as he moved through the nave, navigating around the few benches placed there for the elderly in the parish, who couldn't stand during an entire service. He squared several of the benches and then bent to pick up a stray leaf that had blown in through the open door.

When he reached the alms box, he stopped. It had a strong lock on it, but the lid appeared to be popping up just a bit, as if the box was full. In the old days, the box had only ever been full after the prince had come to stay at his palace.

With fumbling fingers and his heart beating a little faster, he jammed his key into the lock and lifted the lid to reveal two bags and a silver cup that would be perfect for communion—something he'd noted when he'd seen it in the satchel Rhys and he had uncovered in the Roman temple.

Irked that Rhys had disobeyed him, fearful for his wellbeing, and uncertain what to do with the knowledge that his friend had stolen from the king, he lifted the cup and the bags out of the box. For a moment, he gaped at the wealth in his hands, and then he carried everything to the altar.

After setting the cup in the center of the linen altar cloth, he opened the bags one at a time and dumped out their contents. The first bag contained nothing but silver pennies, a hundred of them. The second contained an equal number of pennies, but also a note, once sealed with the Boydell crest but already broken open. Unfolding the letter, it was revealed to be written in Latin and signed by Simon Boydell himself.

"Father, forgive me, for I have sinned. Rhys wanted you to take some of what he found, but you wouldn't, for good reason. It is better for his heart that he does not steal, even from a king he hates. I am not so burdened by honor as he, so I leave you now with what you refused before. Help your people, Father, in Rhys's name."

That was the first paragraph. The second, added at the end in the same hand but not as legibly, implying haste, said, "It appears Rhys has left you a bag too. Know that it contains his entire wages for the last ten days. Spend it wisely, for it is not so much silver he's given you as his heart."

Then came a quote from the very psalm Medwyn himself had just been singing: "Let me hear Your loving kindness in the morning; For I trust in You; Teach me the way in which I should walk; For to You I lift up my soul."

A rush of air poured in through the door, lifting a lock of hair from Medwyn's forehead, and sending a shiver down his spine. Though he was not a superstitious man, he had learned over the years to trust even when he couldn't see. A new wind was blowing. Today it smelled strongly of rain. What it would bring to Wales, Medwyn didn't know and only time would tell. All the same, he couldn't help thinking the wind that had brought Rhys home to Gwynedd, even though it had swept him along like a hurricane, boded only good.

"Godspeed, my friends," he whispered to the air.

Then he locked the alms box and gathered up the wealth. He would use it, as Simon had asked, for the good of his people.

Historical Background

Crouchback is set in the medieval world of 1284 and is based on true events surrounding the death of the last native Welsh Prince of Wales, Llywelyn ap Gruffydd, who was ambushed at a place called Cilmeri in eastern Wales, late in the afternoon on December 11th, 1282.

From a contemporary chronicle:

And then Llywelyn ap Gruffydd left Dafydd, his brother, guarding Gwynedd; and he himself and his host went to gain possession of Powys and Buellt. And he gained possession as far as Llanganten. And thereupon he sent his men and his steward to receive the homage of the men of Brycheiniog, and the prince was left with but a few men with him. And then Edmund Mortimer and Gruffydd ap Gwenwynwyn, and with them the king's host, came upon them without warning; and then Llywelyn and his foremost men were slain on the day of Damasus the Pope, a fortnight to the day from Christmas day; and that was a Friday.

—*Brut y Tywysogyon*, Peniarth manuscript 20 (*The Chronicle of the Princes*)

The men who killed Llywelyn cut off his head and carried it to King Edward, who ordered it displayed on a pike in London. Legend says that the rest of Llywelyn's body was buried at an abbey north of Cilmeri.

Llywelyn's brother, Dafydd, who took up the mantle of leadership of the Welsh forces after Llywelyn's death, was captured a few months later and then hanged, drawn, and quartered and dragged through the streets of Shrewsbury, the first man of significance to experience that particular death. Gwenllian, Llywelyn's infant daughter and only child, was abducted from Llywelyn's palace at Aber and sent to a convent in England, where she remained a prisoner for the rest of her life.

At Llywelyn's death, Wales lost its independence and, after the birth of Edward II in Caernarfon in April 1284, King Edward declared him the new Prince of Wales, ensuring that the titular ruler of Wales from then on would be the son of the English king rather than a Welshman.

Unlike my *After Cilmeri* series, which is set in an alternate universe where Llywelyn lives, *Crouchback* is set in the real world, our world, where he does not.

All that sounds terribly depressing doesn't it? Why would anyone want to read a book (never mind write one!) with all that as the background?

One of my favorite writing quotes, the provenance of which I am uncertain, says to write a good book, the author needs to give her characters a very bad day and make it worse. In the world of medieval Wales, there was nothing 'worse' than the conquest of Wales by King Edward of England. For Catrin and Rhys, their world had, in a very significant way, come to an end. In writing this book, I found myself exploring how a person could have something so terrible happen and still *live*.

Which the people of Wales *did*. They endured and even prospered for over seven hundred years, speaking their language and living their lives as Welsh men and women.

I also wrote this book as an *80,000 word subtweet*, as my daughter says, to a question posed to me a few years ago: *if the Welsh had actually hated Edward or resented their colonization, why would they have enlisted in his military in droves and, more to the point, joined his personal guard?*

To my mind, the answer is obvious. Worldwide, military service in a conqueror's army provides stability and income to people who would otherwise have none, regardless of their feelings about their situation. That was clearly the case with medieval Wales, and I wanted to explore that question more fully.

On an even more personal note, my mother was dying of metastatic breast cancer as I wrote this book. In the weeks before she died, we made one last trip together to see family, and I finished the first draft of the book with her sleeping beside me on the plane home. She'd heard all about *Crouchback*, of course, and I was looking forward to reading it to her out loud in the following week. Instead, she died the next day.

Which brings me back to my question—*why write a book set in such a dark time?* The answer, for me, is because *Crouchback* isn't about grief, as it turns out, but about hope and perseverance, courage and love—and finding joy in the darkest moments of our lives.

Sarah Woodbury

August 2019

About the Author

With two historian parents, Sarah couldn't help but develop an interest in the past. She went on to get more than enough education herself (in anthropology) and began writing fiction when the stories in her head overflowed and demanded she let them out. While her ancestry is Welsh, she only visited Wales for the first time while in college. She has been in love with the country, language, and people ever since. She even convinced her husband to give all four of their children Welsh names.

She makes her home in Oregon.

www.sarahwoodbury.com

Printed in Great Britain
by Amazon

69484806R00196